Rising Wolf

by

Sarah E. Stevens

Calling the Moon, Book 3

Rising Wolf

Cover Art by *Debbie Taylor*

The Wild Rose Press, Inc.
PO Box 708
Adams Basin, NY 14410-0708
Visit us at www.thewildrosepress.com

Publishing History
First Mainstream Paranormal Edition, 2019
Print ISBN 978-1-5092-2769-3
Digital ISBN 978-1-5092-2770-9

Calling the Moon, Book 3
Published in the United States of America

The wraith jolted quickly toward us. It moved about fifteen feet in just a couple of seconds.

Behind me, I felt a surge of warmth as Newt called his fire. I hunkered down, prepared to lunge, and growled low in my throat. Purple light flickered in the corner of my eyes and then arced overhead as Newt lobbed his flames at the wraith. Its keens turned shrill and piercing as it hurtled through the air, closing the distance to reach Newt.

I leapt as the wraith came into range and slashed at one smoky pseudopod with my fangs. Even knowing we were on the same plane, I half expected my teeth to snap through the storm-like body, yet my jaws closed upon it, rubbery in my mouth. I bit down hard and pulled, like pulling on a jellyfish or a chewy bit of taffy. The wraith's body swelled and rolled in my mouth and grayness flooded my senses, colored the air around me, and choked me with amorphous regret and despair.

White-hot flames burst above my head, and I ducked, then rolled to the side. The wraith shrieked, a formless sound drowned out by the roar of flames that grew taller, brighter. Fire consumed the wraith as it jerked and stretched, melted into a bubbling mess of char and bruise-colored taffy, then disappeared into nothing.

Newt's flames snuffed out.

Dedication

For Carmen,
Without you, none of these books would exist.
Brain waves and love always

Chapter One

"Julie, are you ready?" Eliza poked her head in the kitchen door just as I zipped my blue puffy jacket and tugged Carson's hat lower to cover his ears.

I don't know why I bothered, since we'd be wolves in a moment and our clothes would disappear into whatever magical limbo swallowed Werewolf belongings. We wouldn't need them to keep us warm, even in the chilly April night air.

"As ready as I'll ever be," I said. Which might not be terribly ready. I pushed my dark curls behind my ears as my stomach jangled with nerves. I wasn't sure what it was like for someone born a Were, but for me—a dark moon wolf suddenly turned furry after a bite from my Were pup son—nothing about being a Werewolf came naturally. Born Weres always transformed by the age of eighteen, so perhaps I was just too old to learn new tricks smoothly. Or perhaps some dark moons always struggled as much as I did. Or perhaps my difficulties rose out of my contradictory feelings about being a Werewolf in the first place.

Regardless. A Werewolf I was.

Carson squirmed in my arms. Fourteen months old and walking even in his human form, he loved to toddle around the house and resisted being held. Plus, he sensed the moon rising.

"Let's go," I said to Eliza and gave her a firm nod.

We slipped out the back door. I handed Carson to Eliza and faced the rising moon, which I felt even now as a faint pull on my skin. I visualized the moonlight sinking through me and calling out my wolf. I closed my eyes, which Eliza said was ridiculous and totally unnecessary, but then she wasn't a dark moon. My brows tensed before I took a deep breath, forcing the stress out of my muscles. There. Yes. I pulled on the darkness around me, pulled with my mind as I'd gather strands of wool or cobwebs with my hands, and felt it mass around me. Slow, still too slow, but maybe smoother than last night? I relaxed and felt the moon call me from myself, pull on my core like a hand reaching inside a glove, grasping, then suddenly tugging me inverted and into my wolf.

I shook myself, feeling the new form settle until natural: four legs, tail, muzzle. The world exploded into a tapestry of scents. My thick undercoat protected me from the cold, the longer guard hairs sent a constant stream of information about the breeze and movements around me. When I opened my eyes, the night was no longer dark, and I saw Eliza grinning at me while Carson stretched his arms in my direction.

"Okay then, pup," Eliza said. As soon as she set Carson on the ground, he shifted into wolf form between one eye blink and the next, then pounced on my neck with yips of joy.

I allowed him to push me over, and we wrestled in the grass. Carson mock-growled with puppy fierceness. My bark echoed in the cool night air, and my hind claws dug into the dirt as I flipped Carson onto the ground and tussled with him. A moment later, Eliza joined in with a pounce, and the three of us tangled in

2

the yard, then rose to play tag in the tree line.

Eliza raised a howl. Carson sat on his haunches and joined her. I caught the scent of some pronghorn antelope a second later and joined their chorus, then bounded into the tall grasses after Eliza and our prey. The three of us chased the antelope—just for sport, not for the hunt. We crashed through underbrush and groves of cottonwoods, raced across fields, and harried the herd from all sides. I loved the way the antelope bounded away from us with their tails flashing white in the night. Finally, Eliza dropped to her belly and rolled to one side, her long tongue lolling in a smile that called off the chase. We scuffled and rolled in the grass for a moment, then Carson and I trotted down the bank of the Bighorn River to get a drink.

Eliza loped into a grove of trees, probably to follow a rabbit trail. After lapping up my fill, I sat in the springy grass and watched my pup—my son—splash in the shallows. Carson growled and worried at a stick, then flung it into the river where it bobbed in the moonlight. Carson yipped, his sharp cry echoing across the water.

Then he leaped.

I bolted to my feet.

Carson landed in the water with a splash and the current grabbed him immediately, dragging him toward the middle of the broad river. His small legs paddled like mad to keep his head above water. His nose quested for the stick—the stupid stick he'd thrown.

I stood at the edge of the river, the April water icy on my paws. I howled into the night, and Carson let out a whine. The water pulled him away from me.

Frantic, I ran down the bank to keep him in sight. I

barked sharply, *Swim, Carson!* I splashed into the shallows, braced myself to jump in. How could I reach him in time? A whine rose in my throat.

Eliza rushed past me in a blur of buff-colored fur, nearly knocking me over as she leaped straight into the river. She bobbed under the water and surfaced again. She arrowed through the river with her nose on point, slicing through the fast-moving water toward Carson. I tried to keep pace with them on shore, my feet scrabbling and slipping on wet rocks until I climbed onto the bank. I whined with frantic worry.

Eliza reached Carson and grabbed him by the scruff of the neck. She shook him hard, until he floated limp and let her tow him to land. The current slammed into them, but she fought it and held Carson's head above the water. She made slow, steady progress across the river. My limbs and lungs ached in sympathy.

I met them on the bank and shifted to human form. Eliza dragged Carson the last few feet and dropped him where he lay panting in the mud. I fell to my knees beside my son and gathered him to me, hugging his wet, cold fur and trying to project warmth into him.

"Thank God," I said. "Carson, sweetie, are you okay?"

Eliza changed form and stood in her sodden clothes. She pulled her wet hair out of her eyes and wrung her ponytail.

"Thank you, Eliza," I said. "Thank you. I've never...I didn't know if I could..."

"No problem," said Eliza. "We better make sure you can swim, though. It *should* come naturally to you in wolf form."

Shame rushed through me. Eliza saved my son

while I did nothing. I was a Were now, but I felt just as useless as I had when human. I fought back angry tears that threatened to spill down my cheeks and focused on Carson.

"Carson, change back. Come on, shift now."

Carson scrabbled against my chest with his little claws and pushed his nose into my armpit. I hugged him tighter to reassure him. "Carson?"

I guess he didn't want to change forms, though, because he stayed furry. Eliza probably could have gotten him to shift with a sharp growl or two, but I didn't want to ask her for any more help. Maybe he was warmer as a pup, anyway. I stroked his fur until he pulled away and shook, spraying droplets of ice water all over me. I didn't care.

"Are you all right?" I asked Eliza. "Thanks again."

"I'm fine. Water's cold, but I'll dry quickly. I'm going to shift back to fur and run off the chill."

"Okay," I said.

She dropped into her wolf and prodded Carson with her nose before they both took off at a run. They played as if my son hadn't just almost drowned in the middle of the Bighorn River while I did nothing but watch and whine.

I sat on the bank and shivered in the dark. Eliza and Carson romped through the trees in a game of tag. I thought about changing into my wolf and joining them. I'd be warmer. I knew sulking by myself certainly helped nothing. But I didn't *want* to be a wolf right now. I wanted to be myself.

Eliza would say my wolf *was* myself and I needed to stop resisting.

Sometimes, I felt like it would be easy to lose

myself in my wolf. The Weres had been really helpful since Carson bit me and I moved to Greybull. But other times, I hated everything about the pack. During our fight against the Salamanders this past fall, I saw Werewolves at their worst, obsessed with power, control, and domination. Possessive. The pack Council viewed Carson as their property. The strongest Were, an asset to all Werewolves, a tool in the struggle for paranormal dominance. They weren't sure how to best use him—or how to control his wild powers—but they believed he was theirs to use as they pleased. Me? The mother who used to be human? I worried I mattered little to them in the end. Even to Eliza, my friend, my confidante, my partner in crime. In the moment of testing, even Eliza chose pack over truth. Over decency. Over friendship. She lied to me about Newt being gravely injured, tried to trick me into giving up Carson to whatever fate the Council had decided. To her, allegiance to the pack and obedience to pack hierarchy mattered most.

I took a deep breath and held it for four beats. I just wanted to maintain my humanity, even if I weren't fully human any longer. And I wanted to raise Carson to do the right thing, not just what the pack wanted. I couldn't truly trust Eliza.

Still, over the last six months, Eliza taught me, consoled me, helped me with Carson, and stood by my side as I learned about this new world. Tonight proved, yet again, that I still needed help and Eliza was the expert.

I appreciated her, of course. I wouldn't have survived the last six months as a Were without her. But I resented the hell out of her. Not only a more experienced Were, as a full moon Werewolf, she'd also always be more powerful. She made me feel inadequate without even trying. Now that I'd been bitten, I had the powers of a half-moon Were. My abilities were significant. I could call darkness regardless of moon phase. Eventually, I'd be able to shift during at least half the days of the month, even though right now I only managed it the seven days of the fullest moon. Last month during the full moon, Eliza tried to teach me to draw water from the ground near the creek in the backyard of the old farmhouse where Carson and I lived. Didn't work. Even the effort felt like running a marathon, but Eliza assured me practice would help and I'd grow into the power. Meanwhile, she and Carson pulled a veritable spring out of the ground with hardly any effort.

Tonight, I couldn't even jump into a river and swim—something every other wolf and dog in the world did without thought.

Carson darted out of the grasses, tackled me, and knocked me sprawling on the ground. He started licking my face and pawing at my shoulders until I laughed and pushed aside my grumpy thoughts.

"Okay, Carson. I'll come play," I said, then set him down, where he pranced and pounced. I looked up at the moon, hanging full in the sky and sending black shadows across the ground. I pulled on mother moon and became a wolf.

I howled—sounding all my frustration, loneliness, and fear until I felt clearer. Then, Carson by my side, we ran after Eliza.

****

Weak daylight glowed from the east-facing kitchen

windows as I joined Eliza at the table.

"Asleep?" she asked.

"Yeah. You'd think all the running would wear him out, but I always struggle to get him to bed when the moon is full." I stifled a yawn and stretched out the ache in my arms and legs. Running in wolf form exhilarated me, but left me with sore muscles. "I hope he sleeps late. Do you want some coffee? Or are you going home to bed?"

"Coffee sounds good."

I rose to make a pot. With my back turned, I said, "By the way, thanks again for rescuing Carson. That was scary."

"No problem. You don't have to keep thanking me."

"I should have jumped in after him. My instinct would have taken over."

"We'll have to spend some time in the water once the weather warms up. Make sure you can swim," Eliza said.

"Did someone have to teach you how to swim? As a wolf, I mean."

"Not exactly. But I started changing form a lot younger and I was never a dark moon."

"Right," I said.

"Seriously, Julie, you can't expect too much from yourself."

"All wolves and dogs can swim."

"So, maybe when you try, you'll find it's easier than you thought." Eliza crossed the kitchen to get a couple of mugs.

I shifted my feet to keep my back to her. I was sure she could read my emotional state—my shame, my anger—but Were etiquette kept her from mentioning it.

Sunlight strengthened outside, and I heard the birds rouse. Even with the still-chilly weather, they sensed spring coming. Their chirping songs held anticipation as they called back and forth. Probably flirting. Thinking about mating for the season.

As if she read my thoughts, Eliza broke the silence to ask, "Have you heard from Tony lately?"

Great. A question even worse than our discussion of what a pathetic wolf I was.

"Yeah. I guess," I said. "We texted for a while yesterday. He's up in Saskatchewan chasing a lead."

"Important work," said Eliza.

"Sure. Yes."

Tony. After he disappeared into his wolf for five years, most everyone gave up on him returning to human form. His ability to become human again after such a long time led to this new work—he sought out other Weres who'd gone wolf and worked with them to regain their human selves. I agreed with Eliza. The work *was* important. In the last five and a half months, he led two other Weres back to their forms, back to their packs, their family, their friends. He'd convinced a third to regain his human shape two times, but then the Were changed back to wolf and fled for good. Tony beat himself up about that one—maybe he pushed too hard and the guy wasn't ready, maybe there was something else Tony needed to say or do. When Tony brought a teenager named Miranda back to her parents after two years, I watched their reunion. I cried along with half the pack who witnessed their first meeting.

I shouldn't feel deserted.

Yet, in the moments before I turned Were, I

thought maybe Tony and I would end up together. Certainly, I'd been drawn to him since the first time I saw him in human form: dark hair that wanted to fall in his face, amber eyes warm as honey and wild as his wolf. The smell of him. The feel of his strength rolling over me when his power rose, even when I was a dark moon.

When I kissed him the first time, he utterly rebuffed me—changed form and fled into the night. But then, during our last fight with the Salamanders, *he* kissed *me*. Not a chaste kiss. The kiss shot down to my core, possessed me entirely, made me want to meld my body with his. And he held my hand during our final standoff. I thought…I don't know what I thought, exactly. But I never thought he'd find some reason to leave me only a week into my new life as a Were.

"Earth to Julie," said Eliza.

"What? I'm right here."

"Yeah, but the look on your face says you're miles away. In Saskatchewan?"

I shrugged. "Maybe."

"You could ask him to come visit for a while, you know."

"No. I mean he obviously doesn't want to be here. No one makes him run around the wilderness finding lost Weres. Yeah, the Council approves and everyone's amazed at what he's accomplished. Fantastic idea. No one has ever done this kind of rescue before, not in a sustained or focused way. Perfect for him."

Eliza gave me a long look. "Maybe he wants to give you space."

"Sure. Maybe. Space."

I finished my coffee and stared into the cup.

"Anyway, I don't need Tony. You've taught me lots about being a Were," I said and forced a smile. "Remember the first time I tried to change?"

Eliza grinned. "How could I forget? I kept telling you to relax and just let go. You clenched every muscle in your body and scrunched up your face until you were as wrinkled as a Shar-pei. Never saw anyone fight the change as much as you did."

"I didn't fight it. I really tried!"

"That's my whole point. When you try too hard, you get in your own way. Your wolf is always with you, right there." Eliza jabbed at me with her finger. "You just need to allow yourself to open and let the moon call your wolf out from where you keep her trapped."

I opened my mouth to claim my wolf wasn't trapped but shut it again and shrugged. I *did* think of my wolf as something other than myself. Some alien thing forced into me.

"You are your wolf, and your wolf is you," Eliza said. "Once you really understand and accept that, you'll be able to control your powers."

"Yes. I am my wolf, and my wolf is me. You've said that about a billion times."

Anger rose within me, and I pushed the feeling down with a deep breath. My wolf wasn't the only thing trapped. My entire life had spiraled out of control. The first few months, everything was so confusing. I was grateful when the Werewolves of my new pack stepped up, found a place in Greybull for me and Carson to live, arranged work for me, and taught me how to be a Were. Now, much of the time, I thought I might claw my own skin off if I had to be around the pack for another day. Even though I was part of the pack now.

"I think I need a vacation," I said, changing the subject away from Tony and my trapped wolf. "To get away. Maybe I'll go visit Newt. I need to leave Greybull for a while."

"Leave Greybull? You're hardly better than a pup, Julie, regardless of your age. You take whole minutes to change form, you still don't always act naturally in your wolf, and the only other thing you can do is call darkness." After seeing the angry look on my face, Eliza quickly added, "You're improving. Truly. No one would expect more of you after only six months. But I don't know if Lily will let you go."

"*Lily Rose* is not in charge of my life," I snapped.

Eliza narrowed her eyes at me and got up to pour more coffee into her cobalt blue mug. After she sat back down at the table, she continued. "Julie. Pack life isn't second nature for you. I get it. But Lily is the pack Full and anything that concerns the well-being of our pack members *is* her responsibility. I know this transition has been hard for you, but you need to stop fighting your wolf and you need to stop fighting your pack."

I rose from the table and paced the length of the kitchen, my heels striking hard on the tile floor. I turned to Eliza and strove to keep my voice calm, but even I heard the bitter edge in my tone. "Maybe I'm not truly part of this pack."

Eliza shot out of her chair. "*What?*"

"Maybe that's what I need to find out. I need some…space. Time to myself. All of this"—I gestured widely to indicate the entire last six months—"has been

12

overwhelming. I'm still trying to process everything and to understand what being a Were means for me. I know it sounds like a contradiction, but time away from the pack might help me value it more. I think that's what I need."

"Carson is Mac's son and blood of our pack. You belong here."

"Do I?"

Eliza ran her hands through her hair in visible frustration. "Julie Hall. The pack has taken you in, helped you in every way possible, and now you stand here in the kitchen Lily helped you buy and tell me you don't feel like part of the pack?"

"God, Eliza, I just don't know!" My voice rose until I worried Carson would wake. I stopped and took several deep breaths to calm down before I said something unforgivable.

"I am grateful," I said, finally. "I know how much the pack has given me. I'm just—I'm restless."

"Restless, I understand. Now you sound like your wolf."

"I need space."

"That makes sense, too. But please, Julie. Everyone understands your change has been a huge life transformation, but I guarantee you don't want Lily to think you don't understand the basic meaning of pack. You and Carson *are* pack, like it or not."

"Yeah. I know."

And I did know, mostly. Maybe. But I didn't understand the pack's motivation. Did they just want to claim Carson, the strongest Werewolf anyone could remember? Was this about control and dominance, a desire to rise to further prominence on the national level? Or did they actually care about our well-being?

Eliza moved across the kitchen to me. "You've come a long way in six months, Julie. I imagine it's hard to get used to all of this. Changing from human to Were—it's a whole different world. How is your family doing these days? Still hurt you chose to move to Wyoming?"

"Hurt's not the right word. Confused. From the outside, it makes no sense for me to suddenly move to Greybull—this small town in the middle of nothing. I'm not some rancher type. I never longed for open spaces and sparse population. They just know I moved closer to Carson's grandparents right after I met them. I know my parents wish we'd would move closer to them instead. They'd like to be the grandparents on the ground, helping me with Carson. They feel rejected."

I fell silent, feeling the weight of my sadness about the growing distance from my parents. An only child, I'd always been close to them, but now this huge gulf stretched between us. They were human, and I was Were. My mom was a dark moon wolf; I'd discovered that much and even made contact with second cousins in a pack near Cleveland. But I could never tell my parents about my new life, never help them understand.

Carson and I were on our own with only the pack supporting us. And I needed to do everything in my power to make sure Carson grew into his full potential as a person.

Chapter Two

I sat in my parked car for the space of several minutes. Outside the town hall, flags fluttered in the wind, the U.S. flag flying above Wyoming's state flag—blue with red and white trim, sporting a bison front and center. Why the hell did I live in a state represented by a bison? A green pickup truck rumbled down the street past my parking spot, and my gaze followed it around the corner. The sky was pale blue with just a hint of spring to come, the bright sun providing a promise of warmth not fulfilled by April in Wyoming.

Okay. Here I sat, procrastinating, and Lily would start our conversation already annoyed I was late.

I swung the car door open, glad I left Carson with his grandparents and didn't have to occupy a one-year-old in the mayor's office. As I walked to the building, I ran through scripts in my head. I would stay calm and present rational arguments about my need to get away.

The bell on the door chimed my arrival, and the bored-looking clerk in the reception area looked up.

"Hi," I said. "Julie Hall, here to see Mayor Lily Rose."

The clerk nodded and gestured his hand at an empty seat. "I'll let her know you're here."

I glanced at the clock, 10:03. Three minutes late, damn it. As if in payment for my inability to be on time,

Lily made me wait an additional ten minutes before the clerk's phone rang, he picked up, then nodded at me.

"She's ready for you now, you can go back."

"Thanks."

I smoothed my hands over my jeans and walked past the desk, down the right hand corridor toward the office of our mayor and pack Full, Lily Rose.

I knocked lightly on the door frame before stepping into the room. Lily sat behind her desk and motioned for me to take a seat across from her. Not a great sign. The other two times I'd been in her office, we sat at the table near the windows. As soon as I sank into the chair, I felt the power differential in the room.

"Julie."

"Hi, Lily. Thanks for letting me come in and talk to you. I'm sure you're busy."

Lily straightened the small stack of papers on her otherwise tidy desk. She flashed me her million-dollar smile, the one I figured won beauty pageants back in the day. When I first met Lily, I hadn't understood how much power she concealed in her petite frame with the immaculately groomed hair, nails, and makeup, and the ready-for-a-photo-shoot outfits. Now, as a Were, I felt the power radiating off her and straightened my shoulders in response.

"Not a problem. I always make time for my pack."

Her pack.

"Yes, well. I'd like to formally thank you for everything the pack has done for me over the last six months. Quite a transition for me, and for Carson, and, uh, I appreciate it."

Lily's eyes narrowed, showing a further slice of her shimmery taupe eyeshadow.

"Also, I want to let you know I'm planning a vacation. Carson and I will go visit my friend Newt for about a week. Maybe two."

Lily looked at me for a moment before nodding.

"Fine," she said.

"Fine?" I echoed.

"Of course. You're not a prisoner here, Julie. I understand your need to get away. You've had a lot of upheaval in the last six months." She leaned forward slightly in her chair, placing both hands on the cherry wood of the desk in front of her. "Newt's your Salamander friend, yes?"

I nodded. "Newt Sanders. He lives in Colorado now."

"You'll leave Carson here with his grandparents to ensure his safety."

"What?" I shook my head to clear it. "Wait a minute. No. Carson's coming with me. Why would I leave him here?"

"We need to keep him safe."

"He's safer with me."

Lily's perfectly shaped eyebrows rose. "Safer with you, an untrained Were, than with his grandparents and surrounded by the pack?"

"Well. No. But—I mean—this shouldn't be a dangerous trip. I'm just going to visit a friend."

"Julie Hall. Taking the most powerful Werewolf we know—a one-year-old Were pup unable to defend himself—away from his pack with only one untrained Were to guard him involves a certain amount of danger."

I started to speak, then closed my mouth as her words sank in. Our experiences with the Salamanders last fall proved some people saw Carson's strength as a threat. And the mafia in Las Vegas tried to gain control over Carson for their own purposes. She was right. Carson needed protection until he was old enough to protect himself.

Lily nodded as if she knew my thoughts. I reminded myself Weres were *not* telepathic. Lily just had an eerie ability to read people.

"Carson will stay here with the MacGregors. You trust them, and he's comfortable with his grandparents. The entire pack is here to surround and protect him."

"I still think he'll be safer with me."

"Julie, you couldn't even protect him from drowning the other night," said Lily Rose.

"What?" I leapt to my feet.

"You heard me."

Every muscle in my body screamed with tension as I fought my urge to storm out of the room and slam the door in her face.

I stood shaking in front of Lily's desk. "Does she report every little thing to you? Is she *my* friend or is she *your* spy?"

Lily Rose leaned back in her chair.

"Sit down," she commanded.

I sat.

"I'm only going to say this once, Julie. Everything that happens in this pack is my business."

She waited until I nodded.

"Carson is one of our most-valued pack members and I won't let anyone harm him. You've had a rough transition here—dark moons always do, no shame there." Lily Rose added the last as she correctly interpreted the anger crossing my face. "A vacation would do you good. When you return, you'll be ready to fully integrate into pack life. The MacGregors can watch Carson."

The pack could keep Carson safer than I could. She was right. I couldn't even swim. I fought my wolf at every turn. I couldn't teach him anything about being a Were.

Carson didn't need me. I'd miss Carson, but he'd be okay.

Did I want to get away that much? I'd never been apart from Carson, not for more than a workday. But I trusted the MacGregors with my life, with Carson's life. I could go for just one week. Carson and I could video chat. Just thinking about being away from Carson gave me a panicked feeling. And yet. A week on my own? Taking care of only myself? No diaper changes and middle-of-the-night wakings and naps to schedule? No temper tantrums? No screaming in the car seat?

Maybe I could do it. Just for a week.

"That might work," I said. "Carson can stay here with his grandparents, safely surrounded by pack. I can take a shorter trip. I need to travel, to move. This restless feeling—it's almost like an itch. I just need to go. To do something. Then I'll come back and settle into my new life. Things will be better."

Lily broke into a smile. "That's the most Were you've ever sounded."

I tried to smile back. Was she right? Had I changed to become more like a Were? That was a good thing, right? I needed to accept my Were powers, my Were identity. I still…I still felt like myself. Didn't I?

****

"Sheila, have I changed a lot?"

"Jules? How about a hello?" Sheila's voice sounded amused, though she should be used to me blurting out strange questions as soon as she answered the phone.

"Hello. Have I changed a lot?"

"Well, let's see," she drawled. "In the last year or so, you've become a mom and a Werewolf. You've fought off both the mafia and a rogue group of Salamanders trying to kill us all with their fire powers. You used to live in the small town of Jacksonville, Oregon, and we went to the music festival for fun. Now you live in Greybull, Wyoming, and I can only assume you go to rodeos or hunt rattlesnakes. Yes, Jules, I think it's safe to say you've changed."

"No. I mean me. As a person."

"What's this about?" Sheila dropped her joking tone.

"Since becoming a Werewolf, has my whole personality shifted? Have I become less human? Do I seem ruled by my senses, like a beast? Do I seem like a completely different species? *Am* I a completely different species?" I sat in the car, still outside the town hall, held the phone to my ear, and stared past the windshield at nothing.

"Julie. You're still you. You will always be yourself. You're not a beast. I'm not even sure why Werewolves don't consider themselves human. They are human—after all, they breed with humans. They just have some special genes and powers. Witches are humans, too. We don't consider ourselves some completely different species. That's just Werewolves, well, being Werewolves. Focusing on being special and better than the rest of us. They are human, whether they like it or not, and you're human, too."

"Okay." I hated that my voice sounded choked up and I cleared my throat. "Thanks. Never mind, I'm fine."

"You're obviously not fine. What's up?"

"Carson nearly drowned the other night, and Eliza had to rescue him," I said.

"Wait. What? What does that have to do with any of the rest of this?"

"I don't know. I don't want to lose myself in the pack, so I'm doing a crappy job at being a Werewolf. I can't even swim. But I think I'm doing a crappy job at being myself, too," I said. "I want to leave Greybull for a while. I need to get away. Lily Rose says Carson's safer here with the pack and I should go alone. She's probably right."

"Okay. That's a lot to parse. First, Carson would never be better off without you, but I think he *would* be okay if you took a vacation alone and gave yourself space to regroup. Second, you're not doing a crappy job at being yourself. You're still Julie Hall. You're going through a lot, and you need to be gentler on yourself right now."

I relayed the rest of my conversation with Lily Rose, and asked, "Do you think I'm crazy to take a trip to visit Newt without Carson?"

"I think you need the break. He's fourteen months now, right? He'll be just fine without you for a week."

"Are you sure?"

"Positive. I actually agree with Lily."

"Oh. Okay."

Sheila sighed. "Jules, I don't mean you can't keep him safe. He's not better off with the pack. I just mean that it's okay to take a trip by yourself."

My body flushed with relief at her words. "Thank you. Okay. I'm doing this."

****

" 'Sup, dog?" Newt's voice exuded cheer and brought a smile to my face.

"Oh my God, stop it with that dog stuff, lizard man," I said, causing him to snort with laughter. "I'm calling to ask if you'd like a surprise visitor. I need to get out of Greybull for a while—just take a break from things here—and I thought Estes Park, Colorado, sounded like the perfect vacation destination."

"Really? I'd love that, Jules!" Newt said. "You know you're welcome anytime, and this is perfect. Fire season doesn't start until May, so we're still in training right now. I'm not officially on duty for a few more weeks, and I shouldn't have to travel."

"How's training going?"

"Fantastic. I feel so lucky, Jules. I can't even express it. This is what I'm meant to do."

I smiled at the fervor in his voice, usually so light-hearted.

"I'm glad, Newt. I didn't even know there was such a thing as a hotshot, but you're right—it seems perfect for you. Newt Sanders, the Alpine Hotshot."

"Just a temp this year. But give me time. One day, I'll be a supt."

He pronounced the word "soup," but I'd picked up enough hotshot lingo in the last few months to know he meant the superintendent, head of the crew. The Alpine Interagency Hotshot Crew operated out of Rocky Mountain National Park and was one of two elite fire management teams run by the National Park Service.

22

Newt joined the crew over the winter in a seasonal position and spent the last few months engaged in physical training, ready for the field work of the fire season.

"Are you sure I won't interfere with your schedule?"

"You could always join in, Jules. You haven't lived until you've hiked ten miles carrying sixty pounds of fire-fighting gear."

"I'll pass," I said. "Do you ever get annoyed with all the equipment? Seems like your paranormal powers would be enough."

"And give up the opportunity to carry my own Pulaski?"

"Your own what?"

"Combo of an axe and an adze. We use them to chop wood, dig fire lines. Things like that. Anyway, some of the gear's necessary even for me. Flares, rations, water, fire shelter, first aid kit. Things like that."

"Well, you'll have to tell me more about it when I get there," I said, switching gears before he got too technical on me. I didn't even know what an adze was. Nor did I think I needed to, if I hadn't encountered one yet in my life.

We discussed dates for a few minutes and decided the sooner, the better. After wildfire season started, Newt and the Alpine Hotshot team could be called out to travel to national parklands anywhere in the country. As we chatted, I pulled up flights on my laptop, found a last-minute deal, and booked a seat for two weeks later.

Chapter Three

Saying goodbye to Carson left me in tears, and my one-year-old unaffected. I told myself his lack of concern was good, since I didn't want to traumatize him. He had no concept of a week, after all, and I knew he would miss me. Nevertheless, I felt slightly miffed at his complete lack of interest as Grandma Erin held him in the doorway and cooed, "Say goodbye, Carson. Bye-bye, Mama. Talk to Mama later."

Carson's fist, which he busily stuffed in his own mouth and coated with drool, interested him more than goodbyes. So, I hovered between sadness and a feeling of freedom as Eliza drove me to the nearest airport in Cody, Wyoming.

The journey took two planes and a stop in Salt Lake City, but finally the wheels touched down in Denver. After grabbing my carry-on, I waited impatiently to get off the plane and practically ran through the airport to the pick-up area.

"Jules!" Newt saw me as soon as I burst through the doors. He stood outside his little white hatchback and waved to get my attention.

I dropped my carry-on bag on the ground near his feet and leaned in close for a hug. Newt wrapped his arms around me. He felt like a furnace, warmth radiating into the otherwise dreary day. He squeezed me extra tight for a moment, then held me at arm's length and looked at me. His blue eyes crinkled at the corners with his smile.

"You all right then, Jules? Wolves haven't gotten you too down, have they? It's great to see you."

"Everything's fine, I guess. Just needed to get away from all of it. I'm glad to see you, too," I said.

Newt moved away to stow my bag in the back of the car, and the day got colder, like the sun was covered by a cloud. I took a half step toward him.

What the hell, Julie? I shook my head to clear it and hopped into the passenger seat.

Newt's freckles caught the light as he pulled the car into traffic. He glanced at me, and I read concern in his face. "The Weres can be a bit much. You and Eliza okay?"

"Yeah. Better than we were, anyway."

Newt nodded, our shared thoughts about Eliza and her betrayal last fall sitting between us with a nearly tangible presence.

"And Carson?"

"Walking, teething, throwing the biggest tantrums you've ever seen, and romping as a wolf whenever he can. And throwing lots of food. Last month I made couscous—huge mistake. I found it all over the house for a week. No clue how it got all the way up in his bedroom and into the bin of blocks."

Newt laughed. "Bet you're glad to get away for a while." His statement held the smallest bit of question.

"I am. Mostly," I said. "I texted the MacGregors as soon as the plane touched down, and Erin said he's just fine."

"How's Sheila? And Tim?"

"Great. Still going strong. I think this is the longest

relationship Sheila's ever had. Tim's in Germany right now for some Council business."

"And how's Tony?"

I shot Newt a quick look, but his gaze remained fixed on the road and his expression pleasantly neutral.

"He's doing well. Up in Saskatchewan last I heard."

"Not been around too much, then?"

"No. He's busy finding Weres who've gone wolf."

"Important work."

Damn it. Would people stop saying that?

"Yes, important work," I said, through gritted teeth, and shifted in my seat. "But let's talk about your work. Tell me all about the Hotshots."

Newt grinned, and the sunlight seemed brighter. We passed the rest of the drive in companionable chatter, punctuated by my exclamations over the scenery.

****

Serving as the gateway to Rocky Mountain National Park and base of operations for the Alpine Hotshots, Estes Park was nestled in a valley surrounded by pine tree-dotted hills and snow-capped mountains. The scenery reminded me of Southern Oregon and brought a pang of nostalgia for my former town. Greybull was much, much different, and I didn't know if I'd ever feel like it was truly my place.

Newt's apartment immediately seemed like home. Rather than cramped, his small place felt snug and comfortable. His orange tabby cat, Mr. Sprinkles, disappeared under the couch with a hiss at my arrival, but I knelt down and coaxed him out enough to sniff my fingers. After the cat and I established a potentially amicable future even though I smelled like wolf, I wandered around the living room. He grouped his books by genre, rather than author—once a librarian, always a librarian, so I noticed such things—and the front of the shelves held a collection of small objects. I ran my fingers across cut geodes, a small frog carved out of dark wood, three seashells, and a large sugar pinecone before I stopped to examine his framed pictures.

"Is this your sister Sally? Your twin?" I asked, as Newt came in from the galley kitchen holding two glasses of white wine.

"Yup." He crossed to stand next to me and handed me a glass.

"She's short."

Newt laughed. "Yup. Just over five foot and she hates it."

The photo captured Newt and his sister at the beach, his arm across her shoulders, the wind whipping her chin-length hair into her eyes. Sally had nearly as many freckles as Newt, and her hair tended more toward ginger than Newt's strawberry blond tones. I judged the picture to be a few years old because Newt looked younger and lankier with his sister a more solid presence at his side.

Actually.

I looked at Newt closely, better able to study him now that we were out of the car.

"I think you've bulked up since I saw you at Christmas," I said.

"Probably. That's what happens when you hike with all that gear. On off days, I run and lift weights. Need to be in top shape once we're out in the field."

Top shape. Yeah, he appeared in top shape. My face flushed.

Suddenly awkward, I nodded and averted my gaze back to the pictures to change the subject. I felt like I'd lost all my social skills in Wyoming—Newt was my friend and here I was, acting all weird.

"Who's this?" I said, pointing at another picture of his sister hugging a woman with dark brown hair and mirrored sunglasses.

"Sally and her girlfriend Fiona. They've been together about a year and a half. I like her."

"Is she a Salamander?"

"Nope, but she knows about us. Sally told her."

Wow. I digested that fact. Werewolves were extremely secretive about their existence. I knew a married couple in Greybull where the husband didn't even know his wife was a Were.

"Are Salamanders more laid back about letting humans in? Or is your family particularly open?"

"Probably both," Newt said.

"Are these your parents?" I said, pointing to the next picture.

"Yeah."

I studied them in silence for a moment, noting Newt's resemblance to his dad. "Tell me about them."

Newt shrugged. "Not sure what to say. I had a really happy childhood—ridiculously happy, actually. They were funny. Goofy. Well, you'd have guessed that from our names. Newt and Sally, the twin Salamanders." He paused for a moment. "We were twenty-two when they died. Drunk driver. Head on collision."

"How awful."

"Yeah. So much for paranormal powers. Negated by some guy's bottle of vodka."

"God, I'm sorry, Newt." I looked up at him. Did he want a hug? Should I...?

"Thanks. Almost four years ago. Seems like forever and seems like yesterday." Newt cleared his throat, then shrugged and broke into his characteristic grin. "Enough of all that, Jules. How about we cook some dinner?"

****

The next four days passed in a pleasant haze of hiking, visiting every coffee shop in Estes Park, eating excellent Mexican food and Newt's even better cooking, binge-watching a new-to-me television series, and laughing together so hard my stomach muscles legitimately hurt. All that punctuated with regular text updates from the MacGregors and Eliza, plus video-chatting with Carson twice a day. I'd forgotten how easy I felt around Newt and how his spirit brought fun to the simplest things in life.

I needed this break from the pack. Taking a vacation away from Greybull was one of the best decisions I'd made.

Until the phone rang.

"Hey, Eliza, what's up?"

"Julie," Eliza said. Some note in her voice started my heart racing and I sat upright from where I'd been lounging on Newt's couch. "Don't panic."

"What's wrong? What the hell do you mean, 'Don't panic'?"

Newt appeared in the kitchen doorway, whole body alert, listening with wide blue eyes that seemed to shine from within.

"Carson's missing. The whole pack is searching for him, and I'm sure we'll find a lead soon. He couldn't have gotten too far, and everyone is looking for him. We had the police put out an Amber Alert, so even the humans are looking for him."

"He's missing?" I gazed wildly at Newt, shaking my head in disbelief.

Mouth set in a firm line, Newt pulled out his own phone and started thumbing his screen quickly while he crossed the room to me.

"Carson stayed with Liam at the MacGregor's house, while Erin and Ian went to the grocery store. They came home about two o'clock to find Liam sound asleep with his head on the kitchen table—they had a hard time even waking him up. Carson was gone. He'd been in his high chair eating lunch."

"Gone," I repeated. My ears started to ring with my rapid heartbeat. I remembered this panic pouring through my body, the numbness in my fingertips, the urge to scream. My baby in danger. I fought to stay calm.

"Yes, but we're looking for him," Eliza said. "Everyone is out."

"Were there any scents? Do you know who was at the house?"

A moment of silence, then she said, "That's the weird part, Julie. There were no scents at all. No sign of anyone at the house."

"But..." I started, then stopped. How could the Weres find no signs?

"Tell Eliza we'll be there in seven hours," said Newt. He held up his phone and shook his head. "No quicker flights out today, so we're driving. Call her back from the car. We need to get on the road."

We both packed quickly. Newt texted his cat sitter, and we were on the road within ten minutes, which wasn't fast enough to calm me. I called Eliza back, then spoke to both Erin and Liam, who sounded like they blamed themselves for whatever had happened, and also checked in with Lily Rose. The Full updated me in her most no-nonsense tone, which helped me compartmentalize the freaked-out-mom part of me and settle into business mode. I found the willpower *not* to immediately remind her how "safe" she said Carson would be surrounded by pack. First, find Carson. Then, yell at my pack Full.

No one had much information. Carson disappeared sometime between 12:30 and 2:00 today. I was furious Eliza had waited until 4:00 to call me—long enough that they'd put out an Amber Alert, for Pete's sake— even if she wanted to know as much as possible before calling. No scent of strange Weres or even pack members at the scene, only Liam, Erin, Ian, Eliza, and Ian's friend Aaron Sanchez. And, yes, especially given our track record with friends of Ian, Lily assured me they'd thoroughly checked Aaron's whereabouts at the time and, no, he couldn't have been involved. Liam didn't remember anything helpful. He fed Carson a lunch of sliced cheese, puffed rice, and pears, then Erin and Ian shook him awake. No memory of falling asleep, no memory of any visitors. He still felt groggy and weak.

I'd been on the receiving end of called oblivion, a Were power. I remembered the overwhelming sleepiness, the desire to lie down on the grass. How normal it felt to want to nap in the middle of a life-and-death fight. I hadn't felt the way Liam described—one minute he functioned normally, the next minute, someone woke him. I didn't think the kidnapper was a Were. Newt said Salamanders had no ability to make someone fall asleep or lose consciousness.

What, then? Who? A Witch?

After gathering the limited information, I called Sheila and managed not to fall apart while talking to her. From my description, she wasn't sure if it could have been witchcraft, but she said she'd know more from the scene. Sharing my alarm, she promised to find the quickest flight and meet us in Greybull. She said she'd call Tim, but neither of us knew if he could come in time. I wished he were here. I needed my whole team. I needed everyone I trusted.

Which left Tony.

We drove for three hours before I decided.

"I'm going to text Tony," I said.

Newt nodded, not taking his gaze off the road. "Thought you might."

"Better to text than to call."

"Okay."

"That way if he's in wolf form, he can just read the text later, instead of listening to a voicemail. No one likes voicemail. Texting is more convenient."

Newt shot me a glance. "Makes sense, Jules. Text him. Sounds like a plan."

"Unless you think it's better to call?"

Newt said, "I have absolutely no opinion. You could text or call, whichever you want."

"But you do think I should contact him, right?"

"Julie? What are you really worried about?"

"Sorry. Yeah. I'm being stupid. Okay. I'm going to

text him now." I scowled down at my phone for several minutes before typing the text.

Carson's missing. No real information. He was with the MacGregors, something made Liam fall asleep, and then Carson was gone. Newt and I are driving to Greybull now. Everyone's hunting.

After I hit send, I stared at my phone, waiting for the "delivered" to change to "read" and show me Tony was there, holding his phone as I held mine, connected to me by this thread. After five minutes, I gave up and pocketed my phone. He must be in wolf form. Who knew when he'd get my message?

****

Forty-five minutes later, my phone rang and my stomach jumped when I saw Tony's picture flash on the screen. Damn it. I'd taken the photo last fall, right after I turned into a Were, just before I moved to Greybull. His dark hair contrasted with the utter blue sky of September in southern Oregon. His image smiled at me, his amber eyes seemingly fixed on mine as I jabbed my finger at the answer icon.

"Hi," I said.

"Have they thoroughly checked the area? Any signs of foreign Weres? Do you think you can trust the MacGregors and the rest of the pack?"

I frowned. "I trust them not to kidnap Carson. He lives in Greybull as part of their pack. They already have him right where they want him."

"Where have you been and why was Carson alone?"

"Damn it, Tony. Carson wasn't alone. He stayed with his grandparents and the rest of his pack. I came to Colorado to visit Newt, to get away for a bit. To think."

After a pause so short I might have imagined it, Tony asked, "How is Newt?"

"He's great. He's driving right now. We're halfway back to Greybull."

"And...how are you?"

A swirling mass of emotions rose up in me, impossible to parse. "I'm fine. I mean. I'm not fine. I'm freaking out. I'm holding it together. I don't know. Why is Carson always a target? How can I keep him safe?"

Newt reached over and grabbed my free hand, holding it tightly in his own with his gaze steadfast on the road. I took a deep breath and squeezed his fingers, feeling his Salamander warmth envelop my hand, cold from stress.

"To answer your other questions," I said. "The pack is on watch and spread through the area. They even alerted the humans, so the police are searching. No scent at the scene. None at all."

"But a Were called oblivion on Liam?"

"They don't think so. Too sudden. He remembers nothing."

"A Pneumaphage," Tony said.

"What?" I swung to Newt in a panic. "Newt, what's a Pneumaphage?"

"Crap, I guess it could be a Pneumaphage," said Newt. "Get off the phone and call Lily."

I didn't even say goodbye to Tony; I just hung up and dialed the Full. While the phone rang, Newt explained. Pneumaphages sucked the life force out of people to perform magic. Unlike Witches, they had no hereditary gift or intrinsic abilities. Instead, they drew upon ritual spells powered by other people's power and life force.

"Why, why, *why* has no one mentioned Pneumaphages to me before?" I tried not to yell.

Just then, Lily Rose picked up her phone.

"Lily here. We don't have an update, Julie."

"Tony says it could be a Pneumaphage," I said, before she could continue.

She took a beat to digest my words. "Possibly. That's a good idea, though we didn't see any evidence of a ritual and I'm not sure how he could have spelled Liam. We'll look into it. Where are you now?"

I told Lily we were still three hours away, made sure she didn't have additional news, and hung up the phone. My stomach churned. Carson had been missing for over eight hours. Where was he? Was someone taking care of him? Was he scared? Hungry? No matter how many times I blinked, I couldn't stop tears from leaking down my face. I turned to look out the window and watched the car lights as we passed. Newt drove at the upper limit of safety.

****

"No one told you about Pneumaphages because they're really uncommon," said Newt, jolting me out of the trance I'd slipped into while watching the miles flick past.

"How uncommon?"

"Not sure, but I've never encountered one. To my knowledge."

I wiped the back of my hands against my eyes. "Why does Tony say it sounds like a Pneumaphage?"

Newt frowned for a moment before answering. "I think because of Liam's description of being awake and feeling normal, then losing consciousness so suddenly.

Could have been a Pneumaphage drawing energy from him, though I'm not sure how he'd perform the ritual without Liam noticing."

"But what would a Pneumaphage want with Carson?" I asked. The million-dollar question. I took a slow, deep breath to quell the rising nausea in my gut.

Newt just shook his head. "Did you try Tony again? Maybe he knows more about Pneumaphages than we do."

"I can." I followed the words with action, but the phone rang and rang, just as it had the last four times. I ended the call. "Nothing."

I closed my eyes, seeing Tony against my eyelids, his huge black form racing through the night toward Greybull. That's what he was doing, no question in my mind. Somewhere in the darkness, he ran. I imagined Sheila overhead, tapping her fingers on the armrest of a plane and urging it to fly faster. She might know about Pneumaphages, but I couldn't reach her in the air. Our car sped past mile markers.

I needed all my allies together. Now.

Chapter Four

We pulled into the MacGregor's driveway close to midnight and I jumped out of the car before Newt turned off the engine. Nearly every light in the house was on. As soon as I started toward the door, a Were ghosted out of the shadows toward me.

"Eliza," I said. The buff-colored wolf wreathed herself in shadows and stepped forward in human form.

She moved in my direction, arms extended, but I shook my head and stopped with my hands up. No hugs. Not from Eliza, not right now. I felt too fragile to maintain all the boundaries I needed with her.

"Any news? Anything at all?"

"No," she said. "We would have called immediately. We have pack stationed at every road out of town, all the highways. Others scouring the countryside. No trace yet. Nothing."

"How is that even possible?" My voice rose to a near yell. "We're Werewolves. We scent everything. Hell, I can tell you that Liam and Erin are inside and Ian left in that direction," I pointed, "about two hours ago. Six pack members have been here today. I can still smell Carson."

My throat closed in a spasm that I turned into a cough. "What could interfere with our senses like this?"

Newt closed the few feet between us to stand right behind me. I felt him at my back and leaned into him.

He placed both hands on my shoulders.

"Magic," said Eliza.

I focused on the comforting weight and warmth of Newt's hands. "Magic," I repeated. "I'm sick of goddamned magic."

"I know," said Eliza.

Erin opened the front door. "Julie?" she said, before faltering. Her voice sounded thick with tears, causing an answering lump to rise in my own throat.

I hurried up the walk, up the steps, and fell into her arms. Longing for my own mom swam through me—I wanted her to swoop in, to make everything right like she used to when I was ten and life held nothing worse than not being invited to Jenny Baiocco's slumber party. But nothing could make this right. My Carson. Erin and I hugged and cried and hugged some more. After a few moments, I realized Liam stood in the hall to the living room. His arms crossed in front of his chest, he smelled like sweat, stale tears, and stress. The combined scents of wild grief. I unwrapped an arm from Erin and held out my hand for him to hold.

"I'm sorry, Julie. So sorry." He cleared his throat. "I was supposed to protect him and I let him...I let him...be taken."

"I know, Liam. I don't blame you." I cleared my throat. "Can we talk about this over a cup of tea? Now that we're here, I don't know what to do next."

"Of course," said Erin, drying her eyes on a tissue she pulled from her pocket. I just rubbed my sleeve across my face.

We settled into the living room, Erin and I holding mugs of tea, Newt opting for a bottle of pale ale, Liam and Eliza with empty hands. The MacGregors explained Ian and other pack members were canvassing the area in wolf form. Neither Erin nor Liam could change form at this time of the moon, so they'd spent several hours fruitlessly driving around before they returned home to wait for me.

Even though we'd arrived in the middle of the night, half an hour later, a knock sounded on the front door, immediately followed by Lily Rose walking in. As soon as I saw her, anger swelled past my grief and fear—the anger I'd managed to swallow on the phone. I stood.

"Julie," she said, nodding at our group. "Glad you made it back safely. The whole pack is still searching the area."

My body flushed with rage and my fists clenched so hard my nails bit into my palms.

"You said he would be safe," I said through gritted teeth. "You said I should leave him. You said the pack would protect him."

Lily's perfectly-arched eyebrows raised, even as her voice dropped to a deadly calm. "Carson *is* safer with his pack. I guarantee you if someone could kidnap him while he was under our protection, you couldn't have saved him."

"Your protection? What protection? As far as I can tell, you did nothing to protect him and you're doing nothing to find him now! How can an entire pack of Werewolves be unable to find one toddler?"

Lily's Were energy rose like a strong wave against me and I felt Newt move to hover by my side. Liam, Erin, and Eliza froze as the very air in the room crackled with power. I ignored the hairs rising on my arms and took a step toward Lily until we faced each other toe to toe. I looked down at her.

"Julie," she said, maintaining her even tone of authority, "I understand how upset you are—upset beyond rational thought. When you calm down, you'll realize the pack would never want harm to come to our strongest Were."

"Your 'strongest Were'? Is that all you care about?"

"Julie—"

"Carson isn't just the 'strongest Were.' He's Carson. He's a person, like any other person, and he matters just because he's Carson! He would matter even if he were *just human*." I spat the last two words.

Beside me now, Newt emanated a flash of heat and I realized he'd prepared in case of violence. No violence. There would be no violence. I took one deep breath after the other, forced my jaw to relax. After I got under control, I took a small step away from Lily. When I looked at Eliza and the MacGregors, all three of them froze like animals caught in a searchlight. Eliza stood next to the coffee table, her eyes huge and dark. The MacGregors sat straight-backed on the sofa and looked like they wished to flee the room. The charge in the atmosphere dissipated slowly as I met their gazes one by one. I reached out a hand and Newt grabbed it, as I knew he would. His skin felt hot against mine.

When I turned back to Lily Rose, my pack Full, my voice matched her mild, inexpressive tone. "Never mind. I know you don't understand. You can't. Newt? I want to go home. To my house."

He squeezed my hand before nodding. "Let's go."

"Eliza?" I asked. I held my breath for a moment as my gaze met hers, before she looked wildly at Lily.

"Eliza." Lily Rose's voice held a note of growl and Eliza's spine straightened even further, until she looked like a rigid automaton.

"Right," I said, nausea spiking in my gut. "Forget I asked."

I turned on my heel, and Newt and I walked out of the room, toward the hall, the front door, and Newt's car. My neck prickled the entire way, but no one uttered another word.

Chapter Five

My house stood quiet and way too empty without Carson. How could this happen? How could Carson be in danger again? I turned on every light in the hall, the family room, the kitchen, while Newt stood and watched. I drew all the curtains closed to shut out the world, wishing the cheerful lamps warmed my insides. Two-thirty in the morning and sleep felt like a distant land I might never visit again.

"Do you want a fire?" Newt asked, gesturing to the fireplace.

"Maybe. Yeah," I said.

He raised his hand, palm up and fingers cupped. Flames unfurled in the hearth, blossoming from the air and dancing behind the screen. No firewood, but Newt didn't need it; the fire obeyed his call without fuel. I crossed the room to sit on the rocking chair in front of the hearth. The radiant warmth couldn't permeate my core. Newt perched on the nearest edge of the sofa.

"Want to talk about it?" he asked.

"God, Newt. I don't even know what to say. My baby is lost—kidnapped—taken. And all the Weres think about is his power. Nothing else matters. Not people. Not friendship. He's 'the strongest Were,' and that's all they care about."

"At this point, I'll take all the help we can get, no matter what their motive."

"I know." Tears flooded my eyes and I blinked furiously to hold them back. "Newt, how are we going to find him? When the mafia kidnapped him, at least we knew who to blame, how to get him back."

"We'll track him, Jules. We'll bring him home."

I nodded, more in hope than agreement.

"Sheila should be here in a few hours, right?" Newt said. "We should try to get some sleep. Tomorrow may be a long day and we need all our wits and abilities around us. Any idea when Tony will arrive?"

"No. Where the hell is Saskatchewan, anyway?"

"North."

"That much, I knew."

Newt cracked a smile, but I didn't have the energy to return it.

"You need a hug?" he asked.

At my nod, he folded his arms around me and I sank against his shoulder. I rested there for several moments, trying to push away the whole world. What would I do without Newt? Eyes closed, I breathed in the smell of him—a faint scent of ozone and lit matches. I wanted to curl up with him and fall asleep. I wanted...

I sat up suddenly and jerked away from Newt. My friend Newt who'd never given me any indication of anything more. What was I thinking?

"I guess I'm pretty tired," I said.

I fetched towels, put a sheet and blankets on the couch, showed Newt the bathroom, and made sure he'd be okay for the night. I stood in Carson's empty bedroom for a long moment and breathed in his scent with my eyes closed. I climbed into my own bed with a pair of my baby's footie pajamas hugged to my chest.

Tomorrow Sheila would be here. And maybe Tony.

****

Sheila arrived in a rental car around nine o'clock, after several airplanes, a red-eye flight, and a drive. After I offset my scant few hours of sleep with large amounts of caffeine, Newt and I sat bleary-eyed in the kitchen when the sound of her car alerted me. I hadn't heard from the pack since last night's confrontation with Lily.

Sheila stood at the front step with her small purple rolling bag. Her blonde hair cascaded down the back of her black leather coat, hip-length and cinched at the waist. A fuzzy white scarf snuggled around her throat, matching the gloves on her hands, and her jeans glided over high-heeled boots. That was Sheila. Even after hectic all-night plane rides and with a worried frown on her face, she dazzled.

"Jules, Newt!" She swept me into a quick hug before handing Newt her coat and pulling off her gloves. My gaze caught on her right hand.

"Bit swollen from the flight, but I'm all right, Jules. Stop looking like that."

"Sorry."

"And stop apologizing. For anything related to my hand, the burns, the Salamanders, the mafia…shall I go on? Carson is the only person that matters right now."

"Sorry. I mean, okay." I tried to smile at Sheila.

"Any news?" Sheila asked.

"Nothing," I said. "Absolutely nothing. I don't understand how he disappeared without any signs to follow." I swallowed hard and blinked the tears from my eyes.

Newt asked, "Are you healing well, Sheila? Those

were bad burns."

She held up her right hand, palm facing me, then bent her fingers to make a fist, stretched them wide like a starfish, and relaxed her hand. The skin covering her hand was red and visibly thickened. Scar tissue stood out in shiny ribbons until it disappeared into her lightweight sweater.

"Very good range of motion and mobility for just over six months out, according to the occupational therapist. We're working on hand strength now. She was *not* pleased I'd be gone for a while and miss our sessions, by the way, so I promised to be religious about my exercises. The OT thinks her therapy's been particularly effective. I think we owe as much credit to the cream Tessa White taught me to make."

Head of a coven in Salem, Oregon, Tessa White had rushed to Portland when the helicopter transported Sheila to the burn unit last fall. Tessa couldn't witchcraft the injuries away, but her help kept Sheila's hand functional, to my deep gratitude. I would not apologize again—Sheila sounded adamant—but I struggled with guilt that she'd been so gravely injured while fighting my fight. First the mafia, then Salamanders targeted me and my baby. Each time, my friends leaped into danger to protect us. Who would pay the cost this time?

"Looks good, considering," said Newt, studying Sheila's hand with a much more clinical gaze than I could manage.

"Sheila, I know you must be exhausted, but can you scry for Carson? Or do you need to rest first?" I asked.

"I don't need rest. And I brought supplies. Let me

set up."

We filed into the kitchen. Sheila unzipped her roller bag and pulled out a silver sugar bowl I knew came from her grandmother's set, a lilac candle, a smooth gray rock, and a half-full bottle of mineral water. As she arranged the items, I ran upstairs to get one of Carson's pacifiers, definitely the items most connected to my toddler. We watched silently while Sheila studied the pacifier, turning it back and forth in her fingers. She set the pacifier right in front of her, poured water into the bowl, and dropped the pebble in with a plop and a clink as it hit the silver bottom. I found myself holding my breath as she lit the candle and blew softly across the water. The movement of air rippled the water and caused the reflection of the flame to dance. Sheila stared at the surface intently.

Ten seconds. Thirty seconds. One minute. Two.

I glanced at Newt, who moved his shoulders in a slight shrug and gave me a wink. I hadn't seen Sheila scry this long before. I shifted my weight back and forth on my feet, careful not to make noise but unable to stand still.

After what seemed like forever—but only four minutes according to the kitchen clock—the candle flared toward the ceiling and abruptly guttered. Sheila sat back with a sigh.

"What did you see? Why did that take so long? Is Carson okay?" I asked.

"He's okay. I watched as long as I could, hoping for more information. Didn't get much. He looks fine, Julie—maybe a bit pale. He's asleep in a crib. Light wood, probably pine. Sheets with little bears all over them. Green walls. That's all I got."

"Asleep?" I looked at the clock. Nine-thirty. "He's never asleep at this hour."

Sheila shook her head. "Well, he's asleep. Maybe he was up late? I mean...they must have been traveling."

"But traveling where?"

I knew no one had the answer.

Sheila promised to scry again in about an hour. Before then, she wanted to try a new spell. On her plane trip, she'd pored over two of her family's spellbooks—she'd grabbed four journals from her house in the hopes they would be useful. Right now, she wanted a spell to reveal traces of past magic in the vicinity. Of course, that meant we had to venture back to the MacGregor's house, but I could handle the awkwardness if it meant locating Carson. Perhaps she could find proof we were up against a Pneumaphage. Or something else. She pulled out a small notebook and ran down the list of ingredients for us: ice cubes, cedar chips, matches, a clay plate or shallow dish. I rummaged in the cabinet and brought out a pottery plate glazed with shades of blue and green, which Sheila approved. Ice cubes and matches likewise presented no problem. For cedar chips, we'd have to go to the pet store.

I texted Erin: *Sheila's here, coming to your house to look for traces of magic.* I couldn't find the words to express any of the emotions swirling inside me. Erin replied with an okay, which gave me no clue about how we'd be received or who would be there. I knew the MacGregors loved Carson, their grandson, their only link to their son Mac. But I also knew they'd been conditioned to obey the pack Full.

Eliza's car wasn't parked at the MacGregors, to my

47

immediate relief. Flanked by Newt and Sheila, I walked up to the front door, squared my shoulders, and knocked. Erin opened the door immediately—most likely warned of our arrival by her Were senses and waiting in the hall.

"Good morning," she said, after the silence between us became uncomfortable. Dark circles lined her eyes and she looked pallid with strands of her gray-streaked hair escaping her trademark braid.

"Hi," I said. "You remember Sheila?"

"Yes, we met last time she visited. Nice to see you again."

The two of them exchanged a few words and my nerves settled. If we could manage formal pleasantries, hopefully, the rest of this would be all right. I saw no trace of Liam or Ian, and Erin confirmed they'd joined today's search teams.

I tried to feel grateful the pack worked so hard to find Carson, but I just felt empty.

Erin led us back into the kitchen, the epicenter of whatever happened to Carson and the natural place for Sheila to check for traces of magic. Sunlight streamed in from the kitchen's east-facing windows, filling the space with a cheerful glow in absolute contrast to our moods.

As Sheila entered the room behind me, she let out a sudden gasp and strode across the floor to stare out the window above the kitchen sink. She spun to face the rest of us, then pointed.

"Do you see that? Is that a...that's a wraith." Sheila's voice shook with urgency. "Look!"

"What? Where is it?" Newt said, as we all crowded closer.

"It's right there." Sheila pointed. Her hand tracked something. I looked, scanned the grass, the chicken coop, the yard barn, the line of trees at the edge of the property.

"Are you sure it's a wraith?" Newt said.

"What else could it be? Don't you see it?" Sheila gestured wildly. "It's hovering near the chickens. Can't you see it?" She swung to face us, with her eyes wide and panicky. "Werewolves can't see wraiths? Salamanders? Can you smell it?"

"What's a wraith, Sheila?" I asked.

Sheila seemed jolted by my question. "Wraiths are—" She looked around at Newt and Erin for help but then continued. "Wraiths are incorporeal creatures. No one else can see them?"

"But what are they? What do they do, Sheila?"

"They're like ticks. Like spirit ticks. They latch onto people and suck out their life force," said Sheila.

"Wait," I said. "Like a Pneumaphage?"

"Wraiths don't use the life energy for spells. They feed on it and grow."

Newt studied the backyard with a grim look on his freckled face, as if he could will himself into seeing the wraith.

"Are wraiths common?" I asked.

"No, they're not," Erin said. "I need to call Lily."

"Sheila?" I tensed my stomach muscles to stop my voice from quavering. "Did the wraith kill Carson?"

"No! No." Sheila grabbed my hands and squeezed. "That's not how it works, Jules. Wraiths can kill, but they…Well, they drain the life force and leave the body. Wraiths prey on helpless people, mostly the elderly and babies—you know SIDS? Jules, nine times out of ten, SIDS is really a wraith, attracted to a baby's strong life force. But it couldn't have made Carson disappear."

"SIDS is wraiths devouring babies?" I asked.

"Yes, most of the time. Small wraiths can't usually kill a full-grown adult—not all at once, anyway—but they are attracted by new life." Sheila correctly interpreted the look on my face and hastily continued, "Don't worry, Jules. I protected Carson. Remember that mobile I gave you? I spelled it."

"You put a spell on his mobile? To keep away wraiths?"

"To keep away all malevolent spirit creatures, actually. Yep, sure did." Sheila mock-preened. "Pretty lucky to have a best friend like me, aren't you, Jules?"

"If only the crib protected him from this." I gestured around the kitchen, not even sure what "this" was.

"Wait. What about Liam?" Newt asked. "If the wraith drains someone's life force, would they fall asleep? Become unconscious?"

"Maybe." Sheila stared out the window. I followed her gaze and searched in vain.

"If the wraith made Liam fall unconscious, what happened to Carson?" I asked.

Sheila said, "I don't know. But as it absorbs energy, the wraith will continue to get stronger. We need to stop it now, while it's small."

"Is it small?" asked Newt.

Sheila seemed to deflate. "You really don't see it? None of you can see it?" She paced, stealing quick glances at the window with each turn, then smoothed back her hair. I averted my eyes from her scarred hand.

"Okay. I need chamomile, crushed pearls, and non-iodized salt. Water as a base. And the pearls can't be freshwater. I need real, saltwater pearls. Any color. Do you know someone with pearls?"

Erin stepped back into the kitchen from the hall, cell phone in hand. "Full says she's sending Eliza—"

"No," I said.

"—and Ian."

"Not Eliza. We don't need her help. Ian can come."

" 'Ian can come'?" Erin's voice rose. "You're giving our pack Full orders now?"

Sheila's voice cut through the rising tension. "We don't have time to argue. We need to kill this wraith, so I need to make focus serum so everyone can see it and we can fight it. Also, I need to cast the recall spell to see past magic in this area. After that, I need to scry again and see if we can figure out where Carson is."

"You're right," I said. "Sorry. Damn it. What can we do to help?"

"I need pearls, chamomile, non-iodized salt, and very cold water."

"I have a strand of pearls that were my mother's," said Erin.

"Not freshwater, but saltwater?"

"Yes."

Sheila fixed her gaze on Erin. "I need to smash them. Crush them into powder. They'll be completely destroyed."

Erin shrugged. "They're just pearls. I'd sacrifice anything we own to save Carson."

I felt embarrassed heat rush to my face and some of my anger deflated at the sincerity in her voice.

After we gathered the materials, Sheila gave crisp

51

directions. Newt took the pearls to the garage, where he would put them on a towel and smash them to powder with a mallet. I grabbed the MacGregor's mortar and pestle, and opened chamomile tea bags to grind the leaves into dust, along with a handful of non-iodized kosher salt. While we prepared ingredients to deal with the wraith, Sheila set up for the recall spell.

She placed the shallow pottery dish on the kitchen table and heaped cedar chips in a ring, like I'd do with mashed potatoes. In the center where gravy would go, she placed three perfectly-formed ice cubes raided from Erin's freezer. She sat there for a moment with her eyes closed, apparently collecting herself and her magical energies, and I ground the pestle slower and slower, watching her. I loved Sheila's witchcraft. Her spells seemed utterly different than the type of "magic" I accessed as a Werewolf. As a witch, she called on the four elements—fire, water, air, and earth—with precision dictated by the purpose of her spell. Every spell I'd seen so far called for a different set of ingredients. Sheila's spellbooks, passed down through her family line, were crammed full of handwritten lists and instructions. I'd spent some of my free time over the last few months helping her organize the spells into a database so she could cross-reference ingredients and group spells into categories. I guessed the recall spell fell into the general category of seeing or scrying spells, which all contained some form of water as a central reflective ingredient.

Newt came in from the garage carrying a bunched-up towel containing, I assumed, the powder from the smashed pearls. I motioned him to silence and tilted my head toward Sheila. He leaned on the counter next to me. I shifted slightly to lean against him, felt my shoulders relax because of his nearness. I glanced up at him.

I wondered when Tony would arrive.

Sheila opened her eyes and took three deep breaths. Then she picked up the kitchen matches and lit one, waiting until the flame grew strong. She touched the match to the cedar chips in four exact places, at twelve, three, six, and nine o'clock from her position. The wood chips ignited immediately, and the flame circled to form a uniform ring around the plate. The orange tongues licked upward in unison and I saw the ice cubes change state, melting in an instant into a smooth liquid surface. Almost at the same moment, the flames guttered completely, leaving a ring of dark ash, which floated across the water. Sheila stared at the now black puddle.

After about a minute, she blew hard across the surface, so hard a bit of water sloshed over the other side of the dish. She sat back and looked at me, her mouth set in a grim line.

"What? What did you see?" I asked, when she didn't speak immediately.

"Dark magic. Pneumaphagy."

"Explain." Newt put his arm around me as if he sensed my heart rate spike at her words, while his gaze remained fixed on Sheila's face.

"You have to understand, the recall spell doesn't give me a clear picture or a movie, not like when I scry. I can see the types of spells cast and some of the effects—more like the shadow cast by the magic than seeing the magic itself. So, here's what I can tell you. There was one spellcaster. He used a living source in this room to power his magic. Probably Liam and that's why he fell unconscious. It's strange because usually draining a source for energy is a lengthy and involved ritual—something the Pneumaphage does ahead of time, then stores the energy for later spell use."

"The Pneumaphage drained an unwilling subject as an immediate power source *without* a ritual?" Newt's voice held horror.

"You've never heard of that either? This is something new? But why would anyone ever be a willing power source? Can't that kill you?" I said. My fists clenched so hard I felt my pulse throbbing in my fingers.

"Your energy regenerates after a while. Unless you give too much. The Pneumaphage cast two spells. Some sort of veiling spell. That's probably why the Weres—you—can't find any scents. And a summoning spell."

"Summoning?" I echoed.

Sheila stood up and took two steps toward us, toward the kitchen window. "I think he summoned the wraith."

"Wait," I said, registering. "You keep saying 'he.' Are you sure it's a man?"

"Yes, not all Pneumaphages are, of course, but the signatures here are clear."

"Hashtag not all Pneumaphages," said Newt, and I faked a smile to reward his effort to defuse the tension.

"Okay," I said, unable to figure out what came next. I pulled away from Newt and stood in the middle of the kitchen, tugging at my curls while I thought.

Erin came into the kitchen after finishing her calls to various pack members. Sheila quickly updated her, and she texted Lily the new information. I fought down my spike of anger at the pack's involvement. We needed them, I told myself, needed them to find Carson. Regardless of their motives. If they wanted to use Carson, as "the strongest Were," then I could use them to get him back before deciding what the future held. I couldn't trust any of them, though. Not for what mattered.

"When does Tim get back from Berlin?" I asked Sheila.

She shook her head in rue. "He's not scheduled back until Saturday."

Today was Tuesday. Saturday seemed immeasurably far away. Surely this would be over by then. I'd have Carson in my arms, we'd be together, life would be normal.

I pulled out my phone and checked to see if I missed any texts. Maybe from Tony. None. And none from Eliza, not that I knew what I wanted her to say.

"Are all the ingredients ready for the focus serum?" asked Sheila.

"Yes," I said. "What exactly will this one do?"

"Allow you to perceive and affect incorporeal creatures, so we can kill the wraith."

Newt's eyebrows raised. "After it's prepared, we can use the serum anytime?"

"Yes, it keeps its potency for exactly a month. It lasts until the same moon phase when it was created."

Sheila took the crushed pearls, the chamomile leaves and salt, and the water, placing the ingredients in measured amounts into a small bowl. She stepped outside momentarily and came in with a handful of dirt, which she added to the mixture.

"Give me just a moment," she said, sitting at the

table with the bowl in front of her. Forehead creased with concentration, she used her index finger and stirred the blend four times clockwise, then up down through the center, four times counterclockwise, then up, then clockwise again. She repeated her pattern multiple times with some small variations, then removed her finger from the bowl and sat back.

"That should do it," she said.

"Where was the fire?" I asked, able to identify the other elements in her ingredients.

"My life spark."

"Is that the same as what a Pneumaphage does? Using life force?"

Erin and Newt turned to me with horrified looks on their faces.

"Yes, Julie Hall," said Sheila, quirking an eyebrow. "All this time, I've been dabbling in life magic without telling you. Thanks for noticing."

"Sorry."

She laughed and rolled her shoulders in a stretch. "My spells don't drain my actual life force. I just use my spirit to call to the fire element."

Just then, Eliza and Ian walked into the house.

Chapter Six

Ian—over six foot tall and lanky, newly turned eighteen, and usually full of late teen emotional reserve—fell onto my much-shorter shoulders and into my arms like he was my own little brother. I held him while he shook, but he managed to stave off actual tears. His shaggy, dark hair tickled my nose, but I ignored the urge to sneeze and just held him tighter for a few minutes until he finally straightened. He cleared his throat awkwardly and flipped his head until his bangs partially covered his eyes, then shoved his hands in his pockets and leaned against the counter. Erin took a few steps toward him in a maternal way and stopped herself, as his hunched shoulders clearly showed he needed a moment to pull himself together.

I glanced across the room to see Eliza, the picture of grace even while motionless, somehow embodying the impression of a dancer paused between movements, about to leap into another song. Her fawn-colored ponytail hung straight and sleek down her back. Her eyes looked dark and unreadable. I nodded at her stiffly, not finding any words. She tilted her head in return, giving me a closed-lip expression that might pass as a smile under other circumstances. Like if we were casual business acquaintances in an unwelcome project meeting.

"Good. Welcome, Ian, Eliza," said Sheila, breaking

the tableau. "We could use all the help we can get. Time to take out that wraith, so we can move on to the real work of finding Carson."

Her words spurred us all to movement, and we gathered around the kitchen table with quiet murmurings and gentle touches. Erin placed her hand on Ian's arm. Newt jostled me with his shoulder and gave me a small wink of reassurance when I turned to him.

"Eliza, Ian, Erin, Jules, Newt, come here." Sheila gestured with her chin while holding up the container of spelled serum. When I approached, she took a generous daub and smeared it on the center of my forehead.

"Gross, that's cold," I said. "Warn a person." I lifted my curls away from the serum. "Will that soak in?"

Sheila ignored me, then moved on to similarly treat everyone else.

I moved to the back window and looked out.

I worried I wouldn't know the wraith when I saw it, having no real concept of what it would look like.

I needn't have worried.

The wraith floated, surreal and horrific in a Lovecraftian way. It hung in the air. A cross between an octopus, the darkest storm cloud I'd ever seen, and one of those spatial anomalies they use so often in science fiction shows. Black and gray shot with ultraviolet purple, roiling, formless, yet of a shape that somehow seemed more coherent the longer I watched. I'd expected something humanoid, with arms and legs and even a head. Or insectoid like a literal tick. But I couldn't see a head, eyes, anything recognizably sentient. The wraith looked more like a dense vortex that shifted and spawned appendages, sometimes reaching and sometimes trailing toward the ground like jellyfish tentacles.

Just as Sheila said, the wraith appeared small, with its central cloud about the size of a basketball. Nevertheless, chills crept up my spine and I felt the desire to flee—to run and hide from something so obviously inimical. And hungry.

I stared at the horror floating next to the still-yellowed early spring grass and trees starting to bud, the brick red henhouse and white chicken wire surrounding its yard. As I watched, a Rhode Island Red hopped out of the coop onto the grass and started pecking at the grass. The wraith floated closer, lower to the ground, and a small, smoky pseudopod stretched toward the chicken. The hen stumbled and turned its near-fall into a sit. The churning wraith seemed to spark at the contact, to crackle with deeper blackness, before it drifted back toward the tree line while the chicken sat still and stared into space. I didn't think it was dead.

"My God," I said.

Eliza swore under her breath. I felt Newt move closer behind me, like a shield at my back. Still applying serum at the kitchen table, Sheila set her jaw, though her face showed paler than usual.

Ian and Erin received the focus serum last, and their faces reflected horror at the sight of the wraith hovering on their property.

I broke the silence again. "Okay. I understand now why we have to take care of this, even with Carson still missing."

The expression on Eliza's face reminded me of her wolf, eager and keen, her human form full of barely subdued violence. Her body pulsed with contained energy and my skin felt tight, like my wolf wanted to respond to her call. Sheila, in contrast, bore slight frown lines and seemed all business. I could see ridged burn scars edging out of the neckline of her sweater.

Focus, I told myself.

Sheila said, "Now that everyone can see the wraith, I need to put serum on your teeth and claws, anything you might use as a weapon, so you can touch the wraith. I'm not sure if you need to change shape first or…?"

"I can't change. The moon's not full enough," I said. Erin, a waxing moon herself, spoke up and said she didn't think she'd be much help in a physical fight.

"Ian and I can shift and fight," Eliza said. I glanced sharply at her and wondered if I imagined a note of bragging in her voice.

"I don't think the focus serum will work on my fire. Will it, Sheila?" asked Newt.

They both considered for a moment but decided it wouldn't be possible to coat his flames in serum, even if he materialized them in his hands first, then tried to throw them. Erin, Newt, and I were stuck with conventional weapons if we were needed in this fight.

Eliza decided she and Ian should be in wolf form to make sure their teeth and claws were fully coated. Shadows in the room seemed to twist and part to reveal their wolves, Ian's dark fur contrasting with Eliza's buff wolf. Eliza patiently bared her teeth, lips spread awkwardly, and allowed Sheila to slather her mouth, then claws. Chamomile, pearls, and salt must not have suited the wolf palate because Eliza immediately drooled in ropey strands. She stood there for a moment, while Sheila applied the serum to Ian, and then pawed the ground.

"Sheila?" I said. "I think Eliza wants to know if it's okay to change form now, if the serum has set or whatever."

Sheila peered at Eliza and nodded in assent.

"All right, Jules. For those of us who can't change form or lob fire, what are our options for conventional weapons? I have a gun, but what about you all?"

"You brought a gun on the airplane?"

Sheila spoke with exaggerated exactness. "Why yes, Julie Hall. After we were almost killed by the mafia and after I was nearly burned to a crisp by Salamander cultists, I've decided to travel armed when in the company of Werewolves, especially when we're dealing with unknown kidnappers."

Probably reacting to the stricken look on my face, Sheila reached out and took hold of my arm. "Just taking sensible precautions, Jules," she said with a much lighter tone and a wink.

"Right." I tried to match her manner.

"I checked my gun on the plane, followed all the precautions with security. I didn't bring anything for you, though. Wasn't thinking you wouldn't be able to change form. I'm used to assuming you Weres *are* weapons."

"I don't have a weapon. If this is going to be my life," I gestured to indicate the entire paranormal realm, "I suppose I need to think more about weapons."

"It's a small wraith. Probably two Weres and a gun is overkill. You don't need to worry about other weapons. You three can watch." Eliza's smile bared more teeth than necessary, and I felt the skin on the back of my neck tighten at her display of dominance.

Sheila glanced up with a frown and jabbed a finger at Eliza. "Behave," she said.

"Whoa," said Ian, stretching and bouncing on his toes as if getting ready for a track meet. "We're on the same team here. Except for the wraith."

"Let me just get these ready," said Sheila. She dipped her bullets in the serum very quickly and then waited for them to dry. Once the serum had evaporated, she brushed off any remnants of chamomile, salt, or dirt. At my quizzical look, she explained, "As soon as it's dry, the spell is set. The bullets will be able to hit the wraiths."

Newt said, "I wish we could do that with my flames, but the three of you should be able to handle it. Besides, wraiths aren't expecting anything to actually touch them, so you'll have the element of surprise in your favor."

After a quick conversation, they decided on a plan.

Sheila approached the spirit tick first to distract it. Its tendrils flicked toward her once, twice, and then the body changed direction and floated slowly toward her. Meanwhile, the wolves circled the edge of the yard. Sheila stopped about ten feet from the wraith, just close enough to hold its attention while the wolves prepared. Black tentacles reached for Sheila, but she backed to a safe distance.

Eliza crouched low to the ground with her weight on her haunches as she moved ever closer to the menacing cloud. Even from inside the kitchen, I heard her growl, and anticipation raised the hairs on the back of my neck. Ian approached from the opposite side, his black fur the yin to Eliza's buff-colored yang.

The wraith's darkness whirled, pseudopods extending in all directions—including one Sheila avoided by sliding farther away. The wraith must have sensed the Weres, for it hovered a moment, then swooped decisively toward Sheila, the closer target.

"Should we do something to help?" I asked Newt, standing by my side at the kitchen window.

He shook his head. "Can't without conventional weapons coated in the focus serum."

Damn it.

I knew Sheila was a better shot than I. She had to be the one holding the gun, but—once again—here I stood, helpless, while my friends moved toward danger.

"I want to get closer," I said. "Just in case they need me."

Newt raised an eyebrow but didn't object. I crossed the kitchen, opened the door, and stood on the back steps with Newt close behind me. Erin stayed in the kitchen and watched through the window. The wraith hovered about thirty feet away from us, as both Weres crept in and Sheila danced tantalizingly close to its reach before darting back.

This close to the wraith, I felt static electricity building in the air. My ears popped at the pressure change and my sinuses gave a sudden throb deep in my head. I wasn't sure how the wraith sensed people— could it see? Did it smell? Was it using some sort of electromagnetic force like Salamanders? Did it sense life energy itself? How did it choose targets?

The wraith extended and retracted cloudy tentacles. Flashes of what looked like black lightning flickered within its roiling mass.

Sheila held her gun at the ready. Eliza crouched on

the far side of the wraith, Ian on the left-hand side. The spirit tick hovered in the center of their vague triangle. The bulk of it heaved restlessly. I held my breath. Now or never.

A gun with a silencer wasn't actually silent, but sounded like someone slammed a giant book onto a counter. Loud enough to make people jump if their nerves were tightly strung. Like mine.

The shot pierced the wraith, leaving a gap in its black cloud, a space that slowly closed as the wraith spun in tumult and disruption. Spots of darkness spit from its center and the wraith reared up like a grizzly bear, spilling large tentacles in all directions.

With a growl, Eliza launched herself at one of the biggest tentacles. Her focus serum-coated teeth sank into the wraith and she growled deep in her throat. She worried the tentacle, shaking it back and forth with her heavy head like a dog playing with a stuffed animal. With a sudden pull, she twisted her head to the side and the tentacle popped off the wraith's body. As soon as it tore loose from the center, it disappeared into puffs of gray cloud and I heard Eliza's jaw snap together, now clenching nothing. She shook her head. The wraith churned with energy, like a beehive, then shot a mass of tentacles toward the buff-colored wolf.

Another gunshot cracked through the wraith. This puncture closed more slowly, and I wished once again I had a weapon, anything to help. Eliza snarled and pounced on pseudopods. Ian lunged and raked his claws through the center of the body, then snapped his jaws into the core of the wraith. I saw him fall back to the ground and shake himself hard before regrouping to attack again. Eliza's attacks slowed and I saw the effort she made to lunge and snap, lunge and snap.

Sheila shot again, above the heads of the wolves and right through the densest portion of the gray miasma.

The wraith died. Its body burst into bits of foggy fluff and faded into nothing, like it never existed.

Both Eliza and Ian pulled on shadows until they were covered in darkness, then emerged in human forms. Their transformations lagged, taking the space of two full breaths instead of happening between one blink and the next.

Sheila raised an eyebrow. "You Weres gave the wraith a nice meal before it died."

"We'll be okay. Weres heal fast, even from a wraith." Back in human form, Eliza sat on the grass for a moment. She breathed hard.

"I didn't realize it would touch you as you fought," I said. "Are you both okay? Eliza? You gnawed on that thing."

She smiled at me. "I'm tough."

After a moment, I returned her smile. Detente. Maybe. Hell if I knew.

"Not sure I've ever felt anything like that," said Ian. "Like fighting through the fog of exhaustion, like everything in the world lost some of its color, turned gray."

"Well, it's dead now. As long as you Werewolves are sure you'll heal quickly, I need to scry again and see what else I can discover about Carson," said Sheila.

As she said his name, a physical ache welled up in me, a need to hold my son, to feel him against me. I crossed my arms across my chest and hugged myself instead. As if that could fill the void. As if that could save me from shattering into pieces.

"Are you sure..." I cleared the tears out of my voice and started again. "Sure you're up to it, Sheila? You've just done two spells in a row. And killed a wraith. After being up all night on airplanes."

"I'll be just fine, Jules. How about you make me a cup of tea while I cast? Earl Grey, if they have it."

"Absolutely," I said. I frowned at the fine lines creasing Sheila's forehead. Only the urgency of the situation kept me from admonishing her to rest before scrying again.

We filed back into the kitchen, Eliza heaving herself off the ground. After a glance at Erin and a nod from her, I busied myself in the cabinet with the tea canisters and set the kettle to boil. It gave me something to do, which, knowing Sheila, was half the reason she asked.

"I need to update the Full," Eliza said with her head through the kitchen door. She stood in the yard with her cell phone out.

Get new instructions. Like a soldier. Like the pack held her in thrall. I frowned as I added honey to the mug and waited for the water.

An entire pack of Werewolves, helpless against one Pneumaphage, unable to find my child. Seemed to me Sheila's witchcraft helped a lot more than anything the Weres had done so far. I watched our resident witch set out the materials for her scrying spell, the silver bowl, spring water, lilac candle, and small stone. After she arranged everything, she sat still for the space of several breaths with her eyes closed. Dark circles shadowed her eyes and she looked paler than usual—she'd used a tremendous amount of energy already today. I looked at her hand and her arm where she pushed up her sleeves, the reddened scars livid against her pale skin, then averted my gaze. She really needed to rest after this.

Eliza burst back into the kitchen and brought in hair-raising energy with her. Sheila startled. Ian said, "Whoa, Eliza!" I felt a rise in the heat from Newt, beside me, and knew he'd accessed his powers in response to her charge.

"Indiana," Eliza said. "Carson's in Indiana."

Chapter Seven

Paranormal senses stymied, the pack had turned to mundane detective skills and the help of their members on the police force to access surveillance cameras from all nearby locations. Turns out Greybull, Wyoming, home of eighteen thousand people, also housed more cameras in public places than I would have suspected. Banks, four fast food parking lots, two supermarket parking lots, the police station, and five free-standing ATMs. With the backing of Lily Rose, in her capacity as mayor, the local police confiscated every minute of footage from the forty-eight hours, narrowing in on the window of time Carson disappeared. They hit pay dirt.

The video caught a black SUV with rental plates and a quick view of my toddler inside, a vague glimpse of another figure in the driver's seat, sunglasses and the brim of a ball cap obscuring his face.

After Eliza's news, we rushed to the police station to review the footage. Carson. The freeze-frame captured him asleep in an unfamiliar car seat, wearing his green shirt with the polar bear skiing, his wispy toddler hair falling into his eyes because I hadn't had the heart to give him his first haircut yet. Pacifier in his mouth. Whoever took him cared enough to buy a car seat and bring his pacifier. Or they knew enough about him to know how to keep him quiet. Had they watched us? Had they waited until I left town? Had they planned this kidnapping for a long time?

I turned away from the grainy, blown-up shot on the computer screen.

Sheila put one arm around me. "Do you have any coffee?" she asked, and an officer jumped up to pour each of us a cup. Stale and slightly scorched, but I held my Styrofoam cup gratefully.

Lily Rose stood on the far side of the room with her gaze targeting me. I'd avoided speaking to her so far. Our group filled the conference room in the police station: me, Newt, Sheila, Eliza, Lily Rose, and one officer, who was pack. Lily had ordered the MacGregors to stay at their house and contact pack members.

"We traced the car back to the airport rental company and got ahold of the contract, made out to DeVossen Mindspring and Holistic Wellness in Evansville, Indiana."

"Evansville? Where is that?"

"Southwest corner on the Ohio river. Small city, about three hundred thousand people in the larger area."

"How did they get Carson back to Evansville, though? They—he—whoever—wouldn't be able to board the return flight with a strange baby," Newt said.

Sheila said, "Pneumaphagy. Some kind of obscuring spell, just like he used on all his traces at the scene. And for however long he's watched you. It's likely no one else knew Carson was on board."

"He's been taken across state lines," said Ian. "That makes it a federal crime."

"We don't want to involve the FBI or the police. We're keeping this footage to ourselves," said Lily Rose in a tone that allowed no argument. "Pack business."

"Not just pack," Newt said.

Lily turned on him with a narrow-eyed glare. "You're here on sufferance, Salamander."

"Actually, he's here because I want him here," I snapped. "Same with Sheila, who's been more helpful so far than anyone in your pack. My son, my decisions."

Eliza made a small noise in her throat. I couldn't tell if she was angry or entreating me to be quiet.

"These decisions affect everyone in our pack, Julie Hall. Not just you and your son. If some Pneumaphage learns Weres are an easy target, who knows who will be the next victim?" Lily's taupe eye shadow shimmered in the overhead lights as she moved a step closer to me. I fought the urge to back up.

"Have you notified the Council?" I asked.

Silence.

"Julie—" Eliza started.

"No, if this is about more than just my son, if this is about some danger to all Weres, I want to know. Lily, have you notified the Council?"

"The pack can take care of our own."

The bitter coffee now sat like molten acid in my stomach. I set the Styrofoam cup down gently.

"Yeah. That's what I thought. You don't want the Council to think you're weak, that you can't protect your own pack members. You'd rather never find Carson than admit weakness—especially after one of your pack members shamed the whole pack by allying with the mafia, by siding with humans against his kind. And then I stood up against the Council last fall. No love lost there, and no proof that you've brought me or

Carson under your control or your protection."

I looked around the room. Sheila stood up as our gazes met. Newt hovered by the door with his strawberry-blond hair flashing copper in the lights; I knew he was ready. I knew he had my back. He always did.

Eliza appeared to hold her breath.

"Julie." Lily Rose's voice sounded cold and sharp. "I realize you are under immense emotional strain and, therefore, I will not hold your words against you. We will find Carson. We would never let him go missing. Right now, though, you need to leave this room. Go home and rest until you can gain some composure."

Fists at my side, I shook in fury at her patronizing words. I wanted to yell, to explain I was *not* over-emotional and I would feel this way even if it weren't my own child. But somehow anything I said would reinforce her points, her interpretation of my words.

Instead, I stormed across the room, yanked open the door, and walked away. Away from Lily Rose. Away from the pack.

I knew Sheila and Newt hurried after me, but I didn't stop and wait for them until I'd left the building.

Outside, the sun warmed my head and the air smelled like spring. Robins hopped this way and that on the court house lawn, while the state flag flapped in the breeze. My inner storm clouds wished the skies echoed my distress instead of broadcasting the joys of new growth and blossoms. I stood on the walk halfway to the street and stared at the sky.

Newt reached me first and wisely didn't try to touch me or get too close. He must have known I might snap.

"You okay, Jules?" he said.

"Yes. No, not really. I am so sick of Werewolves. Sick of pack posturing and pride and arrogance."

Sheila said, "I know you are, Jules."

"I don't know what to do about it, though. What do I do? And how do we find Carson in some crazy Indiana city?"

Newt shrugged and sunlight glinted off the freckles sprinkled across his cheeks. "First step, we go to Evansville, Indiana. Second step, we find Carson and get him back. We've got a Were, a Witch, and a Salamander. How does one Pneumaphage stand a chance? Let's get back to your house, pack some bags, and buy plane tickets. Let the pack do what they will."

"Newt? How did the Pneumaphage even know about Carson? If this guy lives in Evansville, Indiana, why did he travel all the way here to kidnap my son? How did he learn about us and why does he want Carson, anyway?"

He shook his head slowly. "Those are really good questions, Jules. I don't have any answers. But we'll find out after we rescue Carson. First things first."

He took a step toward me and held out his arms in invitation. I moved into his hug, clung to him, and sighed into his shoulder. He kissed the top of my head with warmth that shot through me.

When we parted, Sheila looked at me with one raised eyebrow.

"Thanks for being here," I said. "Without friends like you, I'm not sure how I could handle this."

I may have emphasized "friends." Just to remind myself.

****

Half a block from my house, my palms started to sweat on the steering wheel and my stomach jumped. My body reacted before my brain could even interpret the sensory input.

Tony.

In wolf form, he lay on the grass in my front yard. As we drove up, he lifted his great, black head from his front paws and then raised the rest of his body. He extended his forelegs out in a huge stretch, then shook before trotting to the driveway. His gait looked stiff, unlike the fluid movements I expected from him.

I glanced in the rearview mirror and smoothed my curls down with one hand as I brought the car to a halt. No time for lip gloss. Damn it. He was a wolf. No one cared about my lip gloss. Why had I even called him? I didn't need this distraction—I needed to save Carson.

Newt never cared about my lip gloss.

Sheila said, "Tony looks exhausted."

I made a noncommittal noise and did not allow myself to look in the mirror again before I opened the car door. By some unspoken accord, neither Sheila nor Newt got out of the car right away.

"Hey, Tony," I said, "Come on inside."

Tony thrust his cold nose into my hand, which I found totally disconcerting even now that I was a Werewolf. I patted him on the head and tried not to be too awkward. As I led the way to the door, Sheila and Newt got out of the car and joined us. They both murmured hellos but saved any real conversation for inside and human forms.

As soon as we all stepped into the living room, Tony called darkness, which crept out from under the sofa and the corners of the room to veil him. The tattered bits of shadow hung in the air for several moments before slowly dissipating. Tony stood in human form. Cut shorter than I'd seen it, his dark hair lay sweat-soaked against his olive-toned skin. His T-shirt likewise hung damp with sweat, his jeans and sneakers muddied. The scent of him—not just sweat, but the pheromones, the musk, the scent of Tony himself, his skin, his hair—overpowered my Were senses and I almost took a step toward him. I stopped myself with a small shake, swallowed hard, then mustered a smile.

"Long trip, huh? You look exhausted," I said.

Tony shrugged. "I'm fine. Any news about Carson?"

"Your throat sounds awful. Let me get you some water," said Sheila. She went into the kitchen while the rest of us arranged ourselves in the living room. I sat on the rocking chair, while Newt and Tony took opposite sides of the couch. Newt stretched out his long legs and watched Tony.

"Yeah, news. A Pneumaphage kidnapped Carson and also used the life force of an unwilling victim—Liam—to summon a wraith. We killed the wraith. The Pneumaphage took Carson to Evansville, Indiana. We have no idea why."

Tony's eyes widened as I spoke. Sheila came back into the room and handed him a glass of ice water, then perched on the arm of the couch.

"Oh," I added. "Also, I've pissed off Lily Rose, Eliza, and probably the entire pack. I accused them of only caring about Carson because he's such a strong Werewolf. I told them they're afraid to involve the Council because they don't want to expose their weakness to other packs. I said they'd been useless so far and our resident Witch was twice as helpful as they were. Maybe not in those exact words. Lily said I was emotional and overwrought. She kicked me out of their meeting and told me to rest."

"Are you going to rest?" Tony asked.

"No. Hell, no. I'm going to Evansville, Indiana. Just as soon as we can get tickets."

Newt said, "On it, Jules. I knew you'd say that and I searched during our drive back. We can fly out of Cody this afternoon. It'll cost us, mind you, but I don't think we can worry about expenses right now. The Evansville airport's really small so we change planes twice, in Salt Lake City and in Chicago."

"Here," I dug in my purse, pulled out my wallet, and tossed him my credit card. "Charge all the tickets on this. I mean…if any of you are coming?"

"You know I am," said Newt.

"Absolutely. And I can buy my own ticket," said Sheila.

"I didn't come over 550 miles to housesit while you rescue Carson." Tony stood up and stretched. I heard his vertebrae pop as he twisted. I averted my gaze from the muscles flexing in his shoulders and arms.

"How the hell did you run that far, anyway?"

"Hopped a train for a large part of it. I need to detour back to my place for clothes, though. Brought absolutely nothing with me."

I nodded. Tony kept a small studio apartment over the garage of another pack member. He spent hardly any time there and didn't own much, but I thought of the studio as his pledge not to spend another five years as a wolf. One small foothold in the human world to anchor him.

"We can fly out at 5:30 on a red eye. I'll book it now," said Newt. "Better go get your stuff, Tony, and we'll head to Cody."

"Do you want to use my car?" I asked Tony. "You might need something other than your four legs."

"That would be great. Do you want to come with me?" Tony's amber eyes met mine. I wasn't sure why he asked—he didn't need help to pack clothes or take a shower or whatever else he needed to do—and I knew I didn't want to be alone with him right now, so I shook my head.

Sheila stretched and sighed loudly. "Good thing I didn't unpack. Heaven knows I hoped to take another overnight flight today." She started to do hand stretches and I worked hard not to avert my gaze from the reminder of what happened the last time we were attacked by unknown enemies.

"I wish I had a gun. My own gun. With a permit, so I could bring it on the plane," I said.

Tony frowned. "Haven't your powers grown enough for you to shift at this time of the moon?"

"No," I answered, stung.

"Sorry." He held up his hands as if to indicate he meant no offense. "We can talk about increasing your training later."

"Increasing my training?" My voice rose.

"Jules, are your car keys in your bag?" Newt said.

Grateful for the interruption and needing something to do other than yell at Tony, I nodded and grabbed my purse. I found the keys and tossed them to Tony so he could be on his way, then I escaped upstairs to grab some clothes and necessities. About five minutes later, Sheila followed me upstairs and found me sitting on the bed staring at nothing.

"Newt's making coffee," she said, taking a spot next to me.

"Thank God for Newt."

"In more ways than one." She twisted to look into my face. "We'll find you a weapon, you know. Once we get to Indiana."

"Okay."

"And we'll find Carson. You know that, right? You, me, Newt, Tony—no Pneumaphage has a chance."

"I hope you're right." After a pause, I asked, "Do you think I'm right to go off without the pack? Without Eliza?"

"Do you think you really have a choice?"

I thought for a minute. Could I go back to Lily Rose? Apologize? Ignore their treatment of Carson as a tool, instead of a person? Did I want Carson to grow up like Lily Rose? Like some of the other powerful Weres I knew? More obsessed with power and status than with doing what's right. Willing to let other people make their decisions. To follow orders.

I needed to make sure Carson grew up knowing every person was important—human, Were, Witch, Salamander—and to judge people based on their actions and their character, not their powers.

"No," I said. "I don't have a choice, if I want Carson to grow into his potential as person. Not just as the 'strongest Were.' "

Sheila nodded. "Right. So let's stop second-guessing, get your things packed, and go find him."

"Do you think Eliza…" I shrugged, unable to finish

the sentence.

"She was raised in the pack, Julie. No gray in her world. She might love you and Carson, but I don't think she can defy Lily Rose."

I nodded. "She did once, though. When we went to Las Vegas to hunt down Mac's killer. The pack didn't know—Lily Rose forbid her to go."

"And she paid for that, didn't she?"

"What do you mean?" I asked.

"Hasn't she ever talked to you about what that cost her? The consequences with Lily and the pack?" Sheila said.

"No," I said. "No, she never said anything. What happened?"

"Not my story to tell, Jules. But if you two get through this, you should ask her."

As I pulled out clothes from my dresser and exchanged them with the dirty ones I'd had at Newt's house, Sheila continued.

"On another note, what's up with you and Tony?" she said.

I paused and shot her a look intended to shut down this avenue of conversation. "Nothing new."

"He hasn't been around for months, then thinks he can walk back in and order you around? Criticize you and question your 'training'? If he wanted to make sure you learned how to be a Werewolf, he could have stuck around to do it."

"Yet the one who did teach me—Eliza—also runs around doing Lily Rose's bidding, serving as her spy, and acting like the pack can do no wrong. Twice now, she's followed orders instead of prioritizing our friendship and people's needs." I shrugged. "It's just so…confusing."

"You still like him, don't you?"

"Who?"

Sheila gave me a long look until I relented.

"I don't know," I said. "No. And it doesn't matter because he's not interested."

"Hmmm." Sheila looked at me for a long moment, then raised her eyebrows and smiled. "Let's focus on Carson for now and worry about your love life later."

"Or never. My love life's nonexistent and it's going to stay that way."

"Whatever you say, Jules."

Chapter Eight

On the way to the airport, Newt researched DeVossen Mindspring and read some of the highlights to the rest of us. Their website listed services including hypnotherapy, past life regression, trauma recovery, energy-centered counseling, and targeted herbal therapies. And Pneumaphagy? We speculated wildly, but we needed more information to reach any conclusions. At least we knew where to start.

We sat scattered about on the planes, but managed to sketch out some plans during our drive to Cody and our wait at the airports. I also slept for a few hours, sorely needed. Tony conked out the minute his head hit a seat and woke up each time we arrived at a new airport. His long run from Canada must have exhausted him. Sheila slept, too. I worried about her, after expending so much power and taking red-eyes two nights in a row. After a ragtag assortment of flights and a long night, we landed in Evansville at 9:34 a.m. As soon as we stepped off the plane, I took a deep breath and met Tony's eyes. He nodded.

"Carson was here," I said to the others. "His scent."

The faintest whiff of my baby lingered throughout the airport. Sheila's eyes widened and she glanced around, as if we might see Carson toddling across the carpet or held in someone's arms. Newt set his jaw, giving his face an unusually grim look. His freckles began to pick up their characteristic Salamander glint as he gathered power, just in case.

The Evansville airport was smaller than any I'd been to, with just a few gates. After we collected our bags, we walked a short distance to find a counter with a couple of car companies, one of which happily rented us a vehicle. We'd all done our share of searching the internet while sitting in the airports: Sheila booked a hotel in the middle of downtown Evansville; Tony and I combed through a few weeks of the local *Courier Press* newspaper but didn't find anything that seemed relevant.

Still too early to check in to our hotel, and I was impatient to find Carson, therefore tempted to drive right to this Mindspring place and demand my son. However, I wasn't about to forget one important detail.

"I need a weapon. Now," I said. "I can't shift with the moon as it is and I need to find some kind of weapon. No way will I go into this situation unarmed."

A frown of concentration on his face, Tony thumb-typed into his phone for a moment. "In Indiana, you can't buy a gun if you have an out-of-state driver's license. Well, you can, but they have to ship it to your state. No waiting period, but that doesn't help."

He looked up at me abruptly, his amber eyes startling in their intensity, reflecting his wolf. I felt my face flush but refused to drop my gaze.

"How are you with a knife?" he asked.

"What?"

"Any experience with a hunting knife? Knife fighting?"

"Uh, no. You see, librarians don't often learn knife

fighting."

Tony frowned. "I can teach you the basics. Your Were reflexes will help. Better than nothing. You should have spent the last six months learning to defend yourself."

I opened my mouth, but Newt interrupted before I said something I might regret.

"Perhaps Jules can be the brains of this group and let the rest of us deal with the combat," said Newt with a light tone. "She's learned a lot over the last six months."

Tony wheeled on him. "She needs to protect herself!"

"Whoa there, big boy." Sheila's smile showed too many teeth and her eyes narrowed with anger. "I believe everyone here cares about Julie's well-being, not just you, Tony. I say, yes, let's get some hunting knives. If we have time later, I can do a few quick spells to enhance speed, coordination, aim—things like that."

"What exactly are you implying about my coordination?" I said in mock-outrage, hoping to defuse the tension now that my initial flash of fury settled.

Newt slung his arm around my shoulders, the warmth from his body soaking into my tense muscles like a welcome heating pad. "We all know you're the picture of grace, Julie Hall."

I relaxed into him and smiled up at his freckled face.

"I found a hunting store that will probably have what we need," said Tony, looking up from the phone with a frown that deepened as he looked at me and Newt. He strode to the car and opened the driver's door.

He handed his phone to me, along with verbal instructions to navigate. After a glance at Sheila, I peeled Newt's arm off my shoulders and hopped into the passenger's seat, leaving the other two to get in the back.

Following the directions on Tony's screen, I successfully directed us to the outdoor store, where Tony took the lead in purchasing several wicked-looking knives. I held one in my hand, hefted the weight and turned it this way and that, before it met with his decisive approval. The knife seemed foreign in my grip and I felt dubious about my ability to use it. I reminded myself to add knife practice to my training with a gun, and also resolved to figure out the right kind of permits so I could travel with a handgun. I dearly hoped to settle into a life that involved no violence, but, if my last year was any indication, life as the mother of the strongest known Werewolf didn't seem conducive to peace and contemplation.

****

"Jules!" Sheila said. I glanced into the backseat to see her thumbs dancing along her cell phone. She looked up at me in triumph. "Tim's going to fly here to meet us."

"What? That's great," I said. "Is that okay with his job? Like…"

"Well, he didn't share details with the Council. He told them he has a family emergency—totally true, because you and Carson are family—and needs to get back to the States. He'll be here late tonight."

"Tell him thank you *so* much," I said. "I'm grateful. He'll be a huge help."

Sheila gave her sunniest smile. "He will! And I

can't wait to see him."

All right. We had this. My whole team would be here soon. Next stop, DeVossen Mindspring and Holistic Wellness.

Tony commandeered the driver's seat again and, with a pointed glance, indicated I take the other front seat. Our route to Mindspring's address took us downtown and along the Ohio River, sitting high within its banks, wide, and muddy with early spring rains. April in Southern Indiana felt twenty degrees warmer than Wyoming, and blooming reddish-purple trees, daffodils, tulips, and forsythia dotting the surroundings proved we'd advanced about four weeks into spring during our flights. Our road followed the curve of the river. Fronting its banks, a wide paved path held quite a number of people strolling, jogging, and walking dogs or strollers. We passed a riverboat and then some sort of monument where I noticed a group of teens hanging out and smoking.

"Tony!" Sheila yelled.

Tony's foot hit the brakes slightly as he swore. The car jerked to one side before he corrected.

"Sorry," she said, her voice still high and excited. "But there's a wraith—a wraith hanging over that path. A big one. Can you pull over?"

The divided road didn't have parking on the side, so Tony proceeded another block or so and pulled off the road. He parked the car in a small lot surrounding a pagoda-like welcome center that looked a bit out of place on the banks of the Ohio River. Newt and I craned our necks in the direction we'd come from. We looked for the wraith, even though we both knew the focus serum had worn off. Sure enough, I saw nothing.

"Where was it, Sheila?" I asked.

"Back near that monument," she said. "A big one."

"How much bigger than the one we fought?" I asked.

"Four times as large. Maybe more."

Newt gave a low whistle.

"Sheila, we can't fight it right now. We don't have focus serum to see it. Our weapons aren't treated. And it's broad daylight with a bunch of people around," I said.

"I brought the rest of the serum," she said. "Okay. I know you're right, but as soon as we can, we need to come back to the riverfront and kill it. With this many people to feed on, it won't move far. We'll be able to find it later." As if pulled, her whole body leaned in the direction of the wraith and I saw how hard it was for her to walk away from that magnitude of public threat.

"We'll come back for it." Tony nodded and restarted the car. "Sheila, is there a way to lure it away from other people so we can kill it?"

"Hmmm. I think there might be. Wait."

I watched in bemusement as Sheila typed frantically into her phone. Looking for Wraiths "R" Us? I had no idea.

"Here!" She fumbled with her cell phone and dialed. As the phone rang, she took a few deep breaths and rolled her shoulders. She gave the rest of us a big smile. "If I'm going to keep hanging out with you Werewolves, I'm going to need to study harder. I should—"

"Hello, I wondered if you recharge crystals? I have three black quartz crystals that have been drained and— Yes, I can hold. Thank you." Sheila nodded and fell silent for a minute.

Newt and I exchanged a puzzled glance.

"Hi! I have three black crystals—Yes. My name is Sheila, I'm in town from Oregon, and I just saw a wraith. Do you—No. Yes, I'm sure. Another one? What do you—Wow. When do they get back? Yes, well, I have backup I can use, if you have some supplies, maybe a lure? You do? Great. Okay. Ask for Josie." Sheila held out her hand and snapped her fingers at me. I mouthed, "What?" and she mimed scribbling. She nodded thanks as I rummaged, then handed her a random receipt from my purse, along with a pen.

After another minute and some further unintelligible comments, Sheila hung up the phone.

"Who was that? Do you really need to recharge a crystal to fight the wraith?" I asked.

"What?" Sheila looked at me blankly for a minute. "Oh. No, that's just code; asking to recharge three crystals identifies me as a fellow Witch. I mentioned black crystals which means it's an emergency."

"But who were you calling? And how did you reach them? Certainly not under 'Witch' in the phone book?" I pressed.

"Under psychics with an E name because we're in Evansville. Any larger city with a Witch will have a helpline for just this type of situation." Sheila cut off my further questions with a shake of her head. "Let's find Mindspring first, check out the situation. If we have time later, we'll gather supplies and go kill the wraith. That Pneumaphage's up to something—the wraiths must be connected."

****

DeVossen Mindspring and Holistic Wellness

Center occupied a spacious restored home from the late 1800s on a corner lot in an area of old cobblestone streets just south of downtown. They'd painted the Victorian building bluish-gray with lots of white gingerbread trim and cobalt blue accents. Three stories tall, the building featured a large front porch, balconies on both upper floors, a rounded corner tower with a pointed gable, and three bay windows lining the opposite side of the house. The closely manicured lawn sported spring-green grass with daffodils lining the walk and a large bed of what appeared to be irises just starting to leaf. A small bubbling pond with a waterfall cascading down ornamental rocks occupied part of the yard. I saw a turtle balancing on one stone to absorb the early spring sunlight.

"Whoever DeVossen is and whatever Mindspring actually does, clearly they have money," Sheila said.

"And Carson's here," I said. "At least, I think he's still here—his scent is thick. Tony?"

"Yes, I agree."

"Okay." I frowned, considering. "Tony, how about you and I call shadow and sneak around the exterior of the building? We can scout for entrances, see if there are open windows, maybe catch a direction for Carson's scent."

Newt said, "Sheila and I can watch the house. We'll be the lookouts."

"Jules," said Sheila.

"What?"

"Wraiths. More of them." She didn't sound nearly as freaked out as she had the first time, as if they'd become somehow commonplace. She seemed almost resigned.

"Them?" I echoed. "Plural?"

"I see two and I think there's one in the house." Sheila pointed toward the right-hand corner, near the bay window. "A small one just came around to this side of the yard. It's about the size of the one in Wyoming. The medium-sized one must have been behind that porch furniture because I didn't see it at first. But it's on the porch. And I'm pretty sure I see one inside, in the gap between those curtains." She indicated the large bay window on the first floor, where white sheer curtains left a crack of about four inches at the center.

"What the hell?" Newt said. "We're going to need a hell of a lot more spirit serum."

"We can't check out the premises if wraiths will follow us and attack," said Tony. "We'll attract too much attention fighting them off."

"But…" I trailed off, realizing he was right. As much as I wanted to find an entrance, rush into the house, and grab my son, we had no chance against incorporeal spirit ticks *and* a Pneumaphage of unknown abilities.

"Okay," said Sheila. "We need more spirit serum and we need a lure. Let's go round up an ally."

****

After twenty-five minutes of following directions on Sheila's cell phone, we parked in front of the strip of stores housing Madame Evangelina's, our friendly Witch-contact listed under E in the phone book. The psychic was sandwiched between a pizza place and an adult bookstore. A large neon crystal ball flashed in the window, but the storefront was otherwise swathed in purple curtains.

The front room resembled a reception area:

couches and armchairs in various shades of purple and green, a fountain gurgling in the corner. Signaled by the door chiming our entry, a woman pushed aside a hanging curtain of beads and stepped into the room.

"Good afternoon," the woman smiled, "Can I help you?" Gray-streaked hair hung limply behind her ears and nearly reached her waist; kindness radiated from her blue eyes.

"Yes." Sheila modulated her tone to match the woman's. "I'm looking for Josie. Is she here?"

The woman's brows raised slightly, then relaxed. "Yes, she's in the back. Can I tell her who's calling?"

"My name is Sheila Martin. I'm a friend of the family."

Newt nosed around the room, picking up an angel statue here, a polished rock there.

"Wait one minute, please," the woman said, after assessing our group. She ducked back through the beaded curtain. In a moment, she re-emerged to usher us down the hallway, where we passed two closed doors before she gestured us into a back room.

As we entered, a young girl of perhaps ten years greeted us.

"Hi, I'm Josie and I guess you're Sheila. I'm sorry my grandma isn't here to meet you—she always likes to meet visitors—but, like I said on the phone, she and the others are out of town right now. Big meeting in Indianapolis." Josie's gaze darted between us.

"Josie," Sheila said, with a hand gracefully extended, "these are my friends Julie Hall, Tony Blythe, and Newt Sanders. Josie's of the Bywater lineage and has kindly offered to assist us while her grandmother is out of town on coven business. Josie,

Julie and Tony are Werewolves. Newt is a Salamander."

Josie's mouth formed an O of surprise, either at our identities or at our cooperation as a team. Then she held out her hand for each of us to shake, an oddly adult gesture.

"Please," Josie said, "have a seat. Would you like some tea?"

We declined politely and took seats around the table in the meeting room, probably used for small groups, or perhaps even for séances held by the famous Madame Evangelina. Josie was in a lanky stage, all legs and long hair. Two dark braids hung over the shoulders of her T-shirt, pink with hearts and cartoon monkeys wearing blue eye shadow. She fiddled with one of her braids, twirled it around her fingers, and brought it up to her mouth, only to suddenly drop it and smooth her hands downward.

"Josie," said Sheila, "Can you tell me more about wraiths in this area? You said your grandma destroys them regularly. I haven't encountered many wraiths in my life, but is this normal for the area?"

"Kind of. She and some of the other Witches from nearby probably deal with one every couple of weeks."

"Every couple of weeks!" Sheila echoed.

"Is that unusual, Sheila?" I asked.

Sheila shook her head in bewilderment. "I've never heard of anything like it. Josie, how long has there been this much wraith activity in the area?"

"I'm not sure. I've only seen a few myself and they were pretty small. I'm not allowed to fight them yet. My grandma put in a call to the coven up in Bloomington. They're going to come down next week and help us investigate."

"Have the wraiths been hard to destroy?" I asked.

"No," she shot a look at me, before continuing to address Sheila. "Of course, they aren't corpo...corplo...um...the wraiths don't have bodies, but once my grandma and the others spell their weapons to affect spirits, my grandma said it's a piece of cake. As long as they're small."

"You said your grandmother might have a lure we can use? And some extra spirit serum?"

Josie smiled and fished in a backpack next to her chair. "I got it from her things already. Here!" She held out a sealed plastic container and large piece of rose quartz. "My grandma charmed this crystal with a lure spell to attract wraiths. Sometimes she needs to use it if the wraith is in a really busy area."

"Great idea." Sheila took the dusky pink crystal from Josie and gave a nod of approval. "Do you know what your grandma uses in her serum?"

"Salt, pearl dust, some kind of herb...I could look it up if you want?"

"No, no, that sounds perfect. Thank you very much. This will be a great advantage in our fight. We'll get rid of the wraiths we saw so your grandmother doesn't have to worry about all of them on their return."

Josie sat up straighter in her chair. "Shall I come with you and help?"

I noticed the corner of Sheila's mouth quirk slightly, but she gave a solemn answer to the eager girl. "Thank you for the offer, but I wouldn't want to infringe on your time without your grandmother's permission. I believe my friends and I can handle the wraiths. You said your grandmother and the other elders will return in two days? I'll be sure to call and give her a full report so they can keep track of these occurrences."

Josie covered her disappointment well and saw us to the door. Newt, who remained silent through the exchange, winked at her as we left, sparking an enormous grin. Through the front window, Josie watched us pull away from the curb. She chewed on the end of one of her braids, but quickly whipped it out of her mouth when she saw me glance back.

"She's awfully young to deal with things like this, isn't she?" I asked.

Sheila shrugged. "Her grandmother's the head of the coven and she's probably as experienced in the craft as I am."

"Think about what Carson will be like at ten," Tony said.

I decided *not* to think about that.

"What's the plan?" Newt popped his head between the front seats of the car. "Do we head right back to the DeVossen place, use the serum, kill the wraiths, and find Carson?"

Sheila shook her head. "We need to make sure we know exactly what we're up against first. Let's check into the hotel room. I can scry for Carson again—maybe we'll figure out exactly where in the house he is. We can try to get some rest and go back tonight, when it's dark. We also need to take care of that large wraith on the riverfront."

"Four wraiths. One Pneumaphage. And a baby Werewolf to save. We got this, peeps." Newt squeezed my shoulder. I twisted around to look at him. His blue eyes looked intently at me, but he gave me an enormous grin, causing a smile to spread across my face, too. In the shade of the car, his freckles seemed to glow.

"Now," he stroked his chin as if pretending to be an evil mastermind. "Can someone figure out how to make my fire affect these wraiths?"

Chapter Nine

A couple of hours later, Sheila flopped back on the hotel bed and flung her spellbook onto the comforter beside her. We'd checked into two rooms in a generic chain hotel near the downtown area with the idea of resting for a few hours and regrouping in the late afternoon when we might be able to accomplish something. I lay down on the bed and—despite my stress and worry—promptly fell asleep for two hours. When Sheila saw her audience was awake, she sighed dramatically and raised her hands in frustration.

"Did you rest at all?" I asked. "You kind of look like crap and you've spent the last two nights in airplanes."

"Gee, thanks, Jules. I always love being told I look like crap."

I shrugged and rolled onto my side to face her.

Sheila raised her left hand and started to work through some exercises to stretch the scar tissue. She opened and closed her hand a number of times, then worked on each individual finger and her wrist movement. When she looked at me, I quickly tried to adjust my facial expression so she wouldn't give me a hard time about feeling guilty about her injuries. Of course I felt guilty. If it weren't for me, she wouldn't have burn scars over nine percent of her body and still struggle with normal function.

"But seriously, did you get any rest?"

"Yes. A little. I'll be fine. I hoped to find something in this spellbook to help Newt join our fight. The closest I can come…well…"

"Well?"

"Looks like there might be a way to make *him* incorporeal." At a startled noise from me, Sheila explained. "It's a complicated spell and I've never tried it. Well, obviously, I mean it's not the kind of spell you'd use often. But if the spell worked, Newt could become incorporeal like the wraith, which means anything he does would affect it and he could use his fire. The spell kind of synchs them into the same plane of existence. Or the same phase of matter. Hmmm…" Her voice slowed and she paused her hand exercises. "I wonder if incorporeal things are just in a different matter phase? You know how theoretical physicists always say particles are all potential energy and can be in multiple places at once, until an observer's involved?"

"Uh. Theoretical physics is not exactly my forte, but I'll take your word for it."

"I wonder…" She frowned up at the ceiling and started flexing her fingers again.

"Sheila?"

"Hmmmm?"

"Theoretical physics aside, you can make Newt— and his fire—incorporeal? And then he can fight the wraiths?"

She nodded. "But like I said, the spell's complicated. Would take time to learn and cast."

"I don't think we should send Newt alone. He might need backup."

Sheila paused to consider. "Tony?"

Now that would be a sight to see.

"Somehow, I don't think they'd make the best team. And you're our crack shot with a physical weapon that can affect the wraiths in this plane, as long as you treat your bullets. It should definitely be me."

Sheila raised one eyebrow. "You'll use those hunting knives to fight the wraiths?"

"Uh. Yeah," I said.

"Because you're a great knife fighter and you've been hiding your talents from me?"

"Okay, you don't need to mock me."

Sheila sighed and rubbed her forehead. "You're right. Sorry, Jules."

"Besides, if I try really hard, maybe I can shift form at this phase of the moon. Tony seems to think I should be able to." I heard the note of bitterness in my voice and shook my head in annoyance. "Anyway, someone needs to go with Newt and I'm the most logical choice."

As Sheila continued to look at me skeptically, I gave in and uttered my real reasons. "Sheila, I want to do this. If I'm incorporeal, I can walk right through the walls and find Carson. I'll be able to figure out exactly what's going on, where he is, and how to rescue him."

Sheila swung her legs over the side of the bed and sat up, mirroring me. She leaned across toward my bed.

"Jules, I'm not even sure I can do this spell without some practice."

"What's the worst that can happen? It just wouldn't work, right?"

Sheila gave a dramatic full-bodied shrug, raising her hands for emphasis. "I have no idea! I don't think it would hurt you…but…"

"We should try."

Sheila pushed her heavy blonde hair over her shoulders, twisted it up on the back of her head, then let it fall again. "Okay," she said, finally. "Go get Tony and Newt."

She picked up her spellbook again and started studying it with a slight frown on her face. I bounded off the bed and went to knock on the guys' hotel room to collect the rest of our team.

Newt answered the door immediately.

"What's up?" he said. "You look excited."

"Sheila found a spell to help us. She can turn you and me incorporeal, so we can interact with the wraith."

"What? Wow. That's kind of crazy. But cool. Okay, let me come hear the details."

"Where's Tony?"

"In the shower," Newt said, with a tilt of the head toward the bathroom door. "I am not sure that guy likes me."

"Did he say something?"

"Didn't need to. He did have a lot of questions about why you came out to visit me in Colorado and everything we did."

"Damn him. Like it's any of his business."

Newt shrugged. "Enough of that. I want to hear more about turning incorporeal."

We entered my room and saw Sheila had moved to the hotel desk. One hand propping her spellbook open, she scribbled on the courtesy notepad. As we walked closer, she looked up, her forehead creased with those lines she hated between her eyebrows—the ones she got when she concentrated hard.

"We need supplies and some of them might be hard to find," she said. "Also, I need to practice this several times. The full casting takes about twenty minutes and if I make one mistake, I'll have to start over. Also, I want to go over some of these warnings with you—there are notes in several different hands. Lots of do's and do not's for the incorporeal beings."

"Like what?" I asked.

"Like knowing what things are in your phase and what things you can move through. And paying attention to warning signs that you're about to return to corporeal state, so you don't end up stuck in something."

"Oh." I glanced at Newt, but he didn't seem to find her words as concerning as I did.

"Julie, do you really think you'll be able to change form this time of the moon? You said yesterday you couldn't," Sheila said.

"Yes. I can. I will. We're only a week away from the moon being full again. As a half moon, I should be able to. And I'll have the hunting knives in case I need them. We can even treat the knives with serum in case I snap back to this plane suddenly or something. I'll be all set." I gave her my firmest nod. I wasn't convinced the knives *or* my Were form could help me, but I didn't care. I'd do whatever I needed to do in order to see my Carson.

"How long will it last? How long will we be incorporeal?" Newt asked, bouncing on his toes.

"Somewhere between twelve and twenty-four hours, depending on the purity of the materials we can find."

"What do we need?" I leaned over her notepad and

tried to decipher her notes. For someone full of grace, poise, and style, Sheila sure had awful handwriting.

She sighed. "Mercury. About half a cup. That will be the hardest to find. Sand, as finely ground as we can get. Matches and lichen, preferably an olive drab lichen."

"Wow," I said. "Okay. Sand? We can probably buy fine, clean play sand at a toy store. They'll have the kind used in sandboxes. Do we have to find the lichen ourselves? Harvest it outdoors? Or could we get it from a garden store or a craft store where they sell things to arrange flowers?"

"We don't have to harvest it, thank goodness. But it can't be artificial."

"I have no idea how to get mercury, though. From a thermometer? A bunch of thermometers, if we need half a cup…"

Newt said, "I don't think they even sell real mercury thermometers anymore."

"I've been wracking my brain," said Sheila. "And the only idea I've had is to search the local university. If only we were in Oregon, I could probably find some way to, shall we say, liberate some from one of the chemistry labs on campus. The University of Southern Indiana is here in Evansville. I think we'll have to break in and steal some."

I took a deep breath and let it out slowly, while I thought. A knock on the door interrupted us so I peered through the peephole, confirmed it was Tony, and let him into our planning session.

"What did I miss?"

"Sheila found a way to turn me and Newt incorporeal, so Newt's fire can kill the wraiths and I can find Carson. But one of the ingredients is liquid mercury. Not sure there's any way to get some unless we break into the chemistry lab at the local university and steal it."

Tony's eyebrows shot up and his amber eyes seemed to darken. "Sounds like an errand I can accomplish. I've not heard of a spell to make people incorporeal—sounds very high level."

"Probably the most challenging spell I've attempted. Ingredients are easy—the ritual is very complicated and precise. You three can get the ingredients, but I need to study," Sheila said.

"Now that sounds like a plan," said Newt. "Where should we go first?"

Tony said, "Maybe you should stay here and guard Sheila while she prepares, just in case the Pneumaphage knows we're in town. Julie and I can handle getting the mercury and whatever other materials we need."

Newt looked at me as if for guidance.

"That makes sense," I said, feeling a hesitation I couldn't quite name. Did I think we'd need Newt with us? Did I just not want to be alone with Tony?

"I think I'll be fine on my own," said Sheila. "I'm just going to stay in the hotel room."

"We don't need three paranormal creatures to break into a storage room at the university. Overkill," said Tony.

"I could go back to DeVossen Mindspring. Nose about. Keep watch. See who's going in and out," said Newt.

"Not alone, you can't. You wouldn't even be able to fight any of the wraiths if they come after you." I shook my head adamantly. "Either you stay here or you come with us. We shouldn't split up into more than two groups."

"Sheila shouldn't be left alone." Tony took a step to stand right beside me and put one hand on my shoulder. I jumped slightly at his touch, as if an electric current ran through me. "Julie and I can handle getting the ingredients."

I swallowed through a suddenly tight throat. "I guess that does make sense."

"You're sure?" Newt asked. I couldn't read his expression.

"Yeah."

Sheila had continued frowning at her notes while we discussed plans. She now transferred her frown to me, along with a full set of narrowed eyes. "Jules, check in with Newt every half an hour so we know you're okay. And that you're not doing anything stupid." Her eyes gave the quickest flick toward Tony and I felt heat rise in my face.

"I won't do anything stupid. Promise."

"Well," drawled Newt, "I, for one, trust your judgment, Jules." He dropped me an ostentatiously cheesy wink, and I felt his smile like sunlight on a winter day.

"Okay, then. Let's go." Tony's voice held a hint of a growl.

I leaned over to hug Sheila. "Don't get too stressed. If you have time, catch another nap or something, okay?" To Newt, I said, "I'll text you within the half hour." I leaned into his body for a hug, lingering a moment to savor the feeling of safety I always had when he was near. Newt dropped a kiss onto the top of my head with a loud "mwah" sound that made me snort.

Tony gave an impatient huff and walked toward the door.

"Okay. Sand, matches, lichen, and mercury. We got this," I said, before following Tony out of the hotel room.

"Before we search for any of those ingredients," said Tony. "I want to teach you some basics about fighting with knives."

"Uh, okay." I said "Where?"

****

Every one of my preternaturally-sharp senses prickled with the awareness of Tony's nearness. We were alone together for the first time in a very long time. His scent filled the car—male, musky, overlain with hotel soap, and clean clothes. I clasped my hands tightly together in order to quell their traitorous desire to touch his hair, to feel the texture of his skin. I shifted in the passenger seat, well aware that my rise in body temperature and the flush on my cheeks was easily detectable by another Were. Even now, I smelled Tony's desire, which spiked my own into a cycle of anticipation and interest that spiraled between us.

That was what I couldn't understand about Tony. He so obviously desired me. And yet he ran away every time. Clearly, nothing more than physical attraction bound us and I refused to have a fling with him when I'd just feel rejected afterward.

Tony drove us to a local park, where we took a left and followed a narrow road past a baseball field and into a wooded, private area. Too private. As we got out of the car, I rubbed my suddenly-sweaty palms on my jeans. Tony's scent wafted toward me with his movement and I fought the urge to step closer to him. Instead, I held my spine straight and walked onto a cleared grassy spot. I was stronger than my body's treacherous urges. We would practice with knives, pick up the spell materials, rejoin the others, fight the wraiths and the Pneumaphage, and rescue Carson.

Tony followed me and my skin went tight and tingly with his nearness. He handed me two knives, keeping a set for himself.

"First, let me see you hold the knives," he said.

"Tony, I'm pretty sure we're not allowed to have knives in a public park," I said. I felt the back of my neck creep with nerves, as if a squad of police officers would descend upon us out of the tree line.

"Julie," Tony said. "If we see someone approach, we'll call darkness."

"Oh," I said.

"Now let me see you hold the knives."

The blades were black and slightly curved. They looked wicked sharp. I wrapped my hands around the grips and held up the knives.

"No," said Tony. He adjusted my hands on the knives. "Move your thumbs like this, to support your hold on the blade. Better. A forward grip gives you better control with this type of blade."

My hands felt the warmth of his touch long after he adjusted my hand. I cleared my throat, then moved the knives around a bit and adjusted my fingers until the weapons felt easy in my hands.

"Now, you're not an expert," he said.

"Gee, really?"

He frowned at me. "If you end up in a fight, your primary focus should be survival and defense. Got it?

No crazy heroics."

"Got it," I said. "Survival and defense sound good."

"If we had more time, we'd practice with markers."

"Markers?"

"Great stand-in for knives and you can see where they hit you. That's how I'll teach Carson in a few years."

I dropped my hands to my sides and looked at Tony. "Tony, Carson's not even a year and a half old."

"He can walk, he can hold things. As soon as possible, we need to make sure he can defend himself. Just think, if he'd been able to fight off the Pneumaphage, we wouldn't be in this position."

"Tony! He's a toddler."

"Right, so we have plenty of time to train him. Julie, I'm not sure you really understand Were life or how many people will come after him once they realize what a powerful Were he is. Dethroning him will consume those who seek power."

"Great. So we'll teach him knife fighting before he can spell his name," I said.

"Yes. We will."

My sarcasm seemed lost on Tony. I shook my head to dispel the distraction.

"Teach me what I need to know," I said. "Just the basics, because, hopefully, I won't need them."

Tony moved behind me and adjusted my grip on the knives, then moved my hands. He nodded, so close behind me I felt the movement.

"Is that right?" I said.

"Yes. I missed you, Julie," he said, his voice a low murmur at my ear.

"Sure, yeah, missed you, too. You're doing important work, though."

I turned my head and found Tony staring at me. So close I could...

And I did. I leaned toward him and found his mouth with mine. The world exploded with the taste of him, the feel of his lips.

"No!" I yanked back, breathing hard. "No, Tony. Sorry. I don't want that. I didn't mean to."

"Julie..."

"Teach me about the knives," I said. "Just the knives."

For the next thirty minutes, Tony demonstrated various holds, thrusts, and parries. I pushed aside everything else. I practiced just enough to feel sure I'd mess up royally and stab myself by accident but pretended to have more confidence. One good thing— my Were reflexes, speed, and balance gave me some advantage in a fight—at least enough to defend myself, disengage, and get out of the situation. I hoped.

Chapter Ten

After our brief knife training session, we turned to the errands at hand. I chattered incessantly to fill the silence between us, telling stories about Carson, about the Were archives, relaying any bit of pack gossip I could remember. As the navigator, I led us first to a toy store for fine-grained play sand, then to a craft store, where we raided the flower arrangement aisle to find the perfect shade of olive-green lichen. I even texted a picture to Sheila to confirm our best choice—and to assure both her and Newt we were fine.

Next stop, the university. A quick internet search told us we'd find the Chemical Distribution Center on the second floor of the science building, easily located via the online campus map. This late in the day, we hoped the building would be relatively empty—empty enough that we could break in with some magical darkness and elbow grease.

The University of Southern Indiana sat by itself off a main highway on the west side outskirts of Evansville. We drove into the roundabout as I squinted at the campus map on my phone.

"Looks like the science building is attached to this big complex on the right," I said, and pointed Tony to pull into a mostly vacant parking lot.

We sat in the rental car for a moment, watching three students walk down the sidewalk toward a campus bus stop.

"I'll call darkness just to make sure no one spots us," Tony said.

"I can call my own darkness."

His eyebrows rose. "No need for both of us to use power; you should rest. Save your strength in case it's needed."

"I have plenty of strength to call some shadow when the moon is almost three-quarters full." I barely stopped myself from snapping at him. My eyes flicked up to the sky, my gaze drawn to the spot where the moon would rise in several hours.

As I lowered my gaze, Tony's eyes caught mine and I found myself staring at their amber depths, all else forgotten. I wrenched my attention away after the space of several heartbeats, during which I'd inadvertently taken a half step closer.

"Never mind," I said, clearing my throat. "You call the darkness. Silly for both of us to do it. Let's go."

Without another word, I walked up the cement walkway to the building. I heard Tony follow me, felt his presence close behind cause a prickle on my neck. Darkness gathered around us, creeping from the shadows, condensing from the haze in the early evening air, a flickering dimness that didn't obscure so much as caused people to avert their gaze, to not notice us. At least, I hoped. We made our way into the foyer of the building and walked up the central staircase, then turned to get into the science wing. The maze-like corridors gave us a momentary puzzle, but we finally wound our way to the Chemical Distribution Center, identified by the sign at the door. Next to the door, a sliding metal panel, now closed flush with the counter and locked, covered a window meant to disperse supplies. The heavy, wooden door to the facility didn't appear to have an alarm and I saw no security cameras, though I couldn't be positive.

We'd passed a few students studying together at tables, but this hallway was deserted. At least for the time being.

"We'd better hurry," I said to Tony in a low voice. "No clue if there's a late class or something nearby."

He nodded without taking his gaze off the door, the distribution window, and the surrounding area. "I can break these locks fairly easily, but then we couldn't disguise our entry. I think we ought to enter a different way."

At my baffled look, he pointed upward. I looked. The ceiling was composed of lightweight tiles, held by a grid of metal-looking strips.

"Um…doesn't that only work in movies?"

Tony laughed, a deep resonant sound that ran through me and brought an echoing grin to my face. I found myself laughing along with him.

"I know, I know. But I'm serious. Do you really think we should go into the ceiling? Isn't that dangerous?"

"Julie Hall, if crawling through a ceiling is the most dangerous thing you do this week…" Tony's voice trailed off, and he lifted one eyebrow at me in a teasing way that made my stomach tighten. Damn it.

"Ha. Okay. You're right." I looked up at the ceiling tiles. "So…how do we do this?"

"We don't. You do. This one's all you, Julie."

"Me?"

"You're lighter. I'll boost you up. Once you're in

the ceiling, make sure to stay on the firm areas or even slide along the pipes. We don't want you to come crashing through the ceiling."

"Very true. That's the last thing I want." I surveyed the surroundings.

Dubious, I nevertheless stepped into his cupped hands. I balanced myself with one arm on his shoulder and then, at his gesture, put one foot onto that shoulder as he lifted me higher, his Werewolf strength making it seem easy. Tension arced between us where we touched, but I pushed it away to focus. I frowned at the ceiling, looking for the best spot to climb in.

Before I could move again, though, Tony pulled me down and toward him. His arms closed around me, the smell of him surrounded me, and then all I felt was his body pressed against me. His mouth met mine. Hot and demanding. I felt his breath against my lips. For a moment, a long moment, I kissed him back.

I pulled away from him so hard I slammed against the side of the hallway. "I don't want this, Tony."

"Don't you?"

Damn it.

We both stood in the hall, breathing hard. The smell of our mutual lust spiraled around me and I straightened my spine against its lure. Tony gazed at me with amber eyes nearly glowing with intensity.

"You can't avoid me for months and then just kiss me like that," I said.

"Don't you like the way I kiss?" His voice rumbled through me.

"Damn you, Tony Blythe. We have work to do. You and I are friends, friends and allies. I appreciate your help, but I don't want anything more."

He looked at me in silence. I glared back, not moving from the wall, not saying anything that would make this easier for him.

"Is it because of Newt?" he asked.

"Newt?" I echoed. "Why, what…no. I mean. No. Why would you…? No, of course not."

He looked at me.

"This is just about you and me, Tony. About us being friends. Just friends."

"Okay," he said. "Sorry. It won't happen again."

"Good," I said.

He nodded and gestured toward the ceiling. He laced his fingers again and I forced myself to approach him. This time, I stepped up as quickly as possible and reached for the ceiling. Especially given my flustered state, I felt grateful for the Were coordination that allowed me to easily keep my balance as I reached toward the ceiling, pushed up on a large ceiling tile, and slid it to the side. My Were vision parsed the dark space—several sets of pipes, beams with sprayed insulation that looked like wet, chewed up cardboard. I looked in both directions and saw the upper space wasn't blocked by walls. Should be a straight shot over and down into the Chemical Distribution Center.

"Okay," I said, hoping my Were grace wouldn't fail me now. "Going up."

I pushed off from Tony's hands and shoulder and guided myself into the ceiling space with both hands. I hadn't been sure if the ceiling braces, the ones that held the tiles in place, would hold my weight, so I aimed for a central metal beam about two feet above the dropped ceiling. I caught it easily and slid my body onto the tiles. I spread out my weight as much as possible and centered each hand and knee over the braces. The ceiling held. Thank goodness.

I'd entered the ceiling about four feet from the wall separating us from the storage room, so I didn't have to travel far. I paused to replace the ceiling tile, just in case someone ventured down our hallway. Grateful for my Were-powered vision, I moved about eight feet, following the course of the metal beam so I could grab it if the need arose. When I was sure I'd traveled far enough, I pried up a ceiling tile and moved it aside. Staring down, I saw the top of a large metal shelf full of jars, boxes, and assorted equipment, including scales, glassware, containers, and some items I couldn't identify. Not wanting to crash down on top of the shelf, I moved over three feet and opened that tile to find clear floor space below me.

Giving a mental shrug, I positioned myself and dropped to the floor. If I'd still been a human, I'm pretty sure I would have twisted an ankle or otherwise hurt myself in the fall. With my paranormal abilities, though, I landed on my feet with flexed knees and a soft thud.

Outside the room, Tony said, "Julie, are you okay?" Low in volume, the rumble of his voice nevertheless carried easily to my keen ears.

"Yes. Give me a minute to find the mercury."

"Do you want to open the door for me?"

I frowned, looking around the storage room. "No, I can do this. You stand watch."

One of the best things about being a Werewolf was not even needing a flashlight. Rows of metal shelving filled the space with piles of varied equipment and plastic containers full of both dry and wet substances, from what I could tell. Tanks of gases. I walked quickly around the perimeter of the room, trying to decipher the organization system. I'd hoped for something easy, like an alphabetical ordering of the chemical substances with mercury clearly in the M section. No such luck.

I stood near the door and did a 360-degree turn, scanning the area. Distribution desk, rolling carts, bulletin board with posted safety regulations. Computer. Rolling chair and tall stools pulled up to a workbench-like table on one side of the front area. A door marked "Hazardous." Mercury was hazardous…I crossed to the door, wishing the glass panel allowed for a view inside instead of presenting a frosted front. Locked, I learned with a jiggle of the door knob.

I walked back to the desk at the distribution window and started opening drawers. Just as I hoped, amid the detritus of pens, notes, and paper clips, I found a key ring.

"Any luck?" Tony's voice from the other side of the door startled me and I almost snapped at him before I regained composure.

"Maybe. Hold on."

So much for university security. The fourth key I tried actually opened the door, which swung inward to reveal a smaller storage room, about ten feet on each side. Shelves lined two of the walls, but the right side held four cabinets that—upon testing—I found locked with keyholes on the handles. Hoping my luck would hold, I tried every key on the ring to no avail. I quickly inventoried the rest of the room but didn't see any mercury.

Damn it.

I really didn't want to leave clear signs someone

had broken into the distribution center, but my options dwindled quickly. And my Were strength did come in handy, right?

Four cabinets, each with metal doors meeting at the front and handles locked, each with a toxic chemical symbol on the front. No match for my Were strength. I did a quick one-potato-two counting rhyme in my head, chose the second cabinet from the right, and grabbed the door handle. I twisted it until the lock engaged, then gave a sudden flick of my wrist and heard a ping, followed by a sharp crack inside the locking mechanism. Swung open, the door revealed shelves full of bottles, metal containers, and jars full of varied substances, but I didn't see any mercury.

I hit pay dirt in the second cabinet and found a plastic container with a red label that said, "Mercury. Danger. Do Not Open." Smaller symbols dotted the container—health hazard, toxic, corrosive, environment. In all caps, the bottle reminded me, "Fatal if inhaled. May damage the unborn child. Causes damage to the kidneys and central nervous system through prolonged or repeated exposure if inhaled or absorbed through the skin. Do not eat, drink, or smoke when using this product. May be corrosive to metals. Keep only in original container. Toxic to aquatic life with long lasting effects."

Great. What exactly was Sheila going to do with the mercury? Because I did not want to drink, touch, or breathe this stuff.

I shook off my trepidations and gingerly unscrewed the lid of the plastic container. Holding my breath so I wouldn't inhale anything dangerous, I peeked in the top to see another, smaller plastic container within to hold the actual mercury. The large container was half-full of what looked like kitty litter with the smaller plastic container nestled in it. Red labels covered the inside container, too, just in case I'd missed all the other warnings. I tightened the outside container again. It seemed secure enough to transport and the cat litter should provide cushioning; I guessed that was its purpose. I closed the cabinet doors on the two I'd forced opened, hoping no one would need dangerous chemicals soon or otherwise notice the broken locks.

I covered my tracks as much as possible before leaving the Chemical Distribution Center, including climbing a shelf to pull the ceiling tile back into place. The front door wasn't locked from the inside, so I whispered a head's up to Tony before pushing the door open and stepping into the hall. His amber eyes caught me in their gaze, and he nodded after assessing that I was, in fact, okay.

"Got it," I said, holding up the container with its vivid danger markings. I suddenly wished I had brought a bag or something to stash the mercury in because I felt extremely conspicuous standing in the hall of the science building holding obvious contraband.

"Good job," Tony said. The low growling approval in his voice chased a flush into my cheeks and I took another half step away from him. "Let's go back and see what Sheila will do with all of these ingredients."

He called shadow to wreathe us in flickering darkness and we left the building.

Chapter Eleven

When we got back to the hotel, Newt met us at the door with a finger at his lips. I couldn't meet his eyes for some reason. He stepped into the hall before speaking.

"Sheila's finally taking a nap," he said. "She's been reading and mumbling to herself and reading more and mumbling more. Plus taking notes. Let's give her a few minutes to rest."

We filed into the other hotel room to wait.

"Jules, are you sure you want Sheila to make you incorporeal, too?" Newt asked. "I'm the one who can't affect the wraiths on this plane—there's just no way for my fire to hit them—so it makes sense for me to try it. You could stay here with Tony and Sheila."

"I'm sure."

The more I thought about it, the more I wanted to try this spell. With Newt. I'd be able to walk through the house, travel wherever I wanted, freely search for Carson, and observe the Pneumaphage...

"Yesterday you said you couldn't change into your wolf," said Tony. "You'll be helpless against the wraiths in your human form."

"I won't be helpless. I have those knives. Besides, today's one day closer to the full moon," I snapped back.

"All right. Show us." Tony crossed his arms in

front of his chest and waited.

"Show you?"

"Show us you can change form."

"Fine!"

I crossed to the window, which luckily faced in the direction the moon would rise. I felt her, mother moon. I tried to clear my mind, tried not to think about Newt and Tony watching me. Tony, waiting for me to fail so he could say something about my lack of training and come up with a reason to keep me out of this fight. I took three deep breaths, filling and emptying my lungs completely.

My wolf was with me always. She shouldn't be caged. I was my wolf and my wolf was me.

My thoughts brought Eliza to mind and I pushed down a flash of mixed sorrow and anger. I couldn't get distracted. I closed my eyes and relaxed my body, feeling for the moon, feeling for my wolf, feeling for that moment of change, which finally came as a rush of warmth and twisting and pulling as I dropped into fur and four legs.

I did it!

I shook myself, feeling the weight of this body settle over me, and sat back on my haunches to look at Tony and Newt.

"Nice!" exclaimed Newt. "Good job, Jules." He reached out a hand and ruffled the fur on my head.

As a wolf, I smelled him even more clearly, a hint of flame and ozone accompanied by the scent that was purely his. I preened against his hand a bit, before I reluctantly pulled back, then drew shadow over myself and stepped forward in human form—always an easy shift for me.

"All right," said Tony. "You can become incorporeal with Newt."

"I don't remember asking for your permission, Tony."

He reached out and grabbed my arm, his skin hot against mine. I pulled away from him.

"You know all I care about is your welfare. You and Carson."

"I'm the best judge of my own welfare. Not the pack, not Tony Blythe. I need friends, Tony, and I appreciate when my friends care about me. But I don't need anyone to protect or control me. Not anyone."

Tony's mouth twisted in a grimace. "You're right. I apologize."

I stood there waiting for the "but," where he'd defend himself or explain. Yet he said nothing else.

"Okay," I said, after an awkward moment. "Thanks. Apology accepted. Let's see if Sheila's ready to wake up. Then let's grab some food, become incorporeal, and head out to fight wraiths and rescue Carson."

****

After a quick bite to eat in a restaurant down the street, where we made a conscious effort to engage in normal conversation instead of discussing paranormal danger, we crowded into our hotel room. I collected ingredients.

Finely-ground sand, olive-green lichen, a packet of kitchen matches, and a sealed plastic container of mercury ringed with red hazard markings. Next to the items, Sheila placed a glass from the hotel and a chopstick she sometimes used to pin up her hair.

"Sheila, what exactly do you need to do with the

mercury and is it safe for us?" I asked.

"Jules." Sheila leaned back in the desk chair and looked at me as I perched on the edge of the bed. "We've traveled to Evansville, Indiana to fight a Pneumaphage and an unknown number of wraiths. Do you really think we went to all this trouble just so I could kill you with mercury poisoning?"

Newt laughed and came to sit by my side. He threw an arm loosely around my shoulders. "When you put it like that, I think we'll trust our resident witch and see what happens. Right, Jules?"

I shrugged. "I do trust you. I just don't want to drink or inhale that stuff. Or paint it on my body. Did you see all those warning labels?"

"She saw the warnings. We all saw the warnings. Sometimes we must do what must be done, regardless of the personal cost," Tony said.

A flash of annoyance ran through me as I straightened from my lounge against Newt's shoulder to shoot Tony a glance that was not an eye roll. It might have been close but definitely not an eye roll.

"Wow, very astute," Newt said.

"Tony, no one in this room wants to rescue Carson more than I do. At any 'personal cost.' Sometimes talk is just…talk. To lighten the mood. But I don't want to find Carson just to poison him with mercury."

"As I was about to say"—Sheila cut into the rising tension—"the spell will change the mercury's properties. Once I'm finished, it won't be toxic, and it won't really be mercury."

"Great. When can we start?"

"Now. But I need you and Newt to understand some things about this spell first."

Newt dropped his arm from around me and we both nodded, intent on her words.

"This spell is complicated and dangerous and not because of the mercury. Basically, I'm transmuting the materials to make a potion, which will allow you to shift and become incorporeal. You know the theory of multiverses? Parallel dimensions? It's kind of like you're in a parallel dimension that occupies this same space and time, but it's off-sync physically."

Newt shook his head. "Okay, I've seen this kind of thing in science fiction shows and it doesn't make sense. If we're off-sync from everything, won't we sink through the floors? And the ground itself?"

"Yes and no. This is exactly what I wanted to talk about. Natural objects—trees, plants, rocks, earth—they project through all dimensions. That's why you don't fall through the ground into the core of the Earth or something. However, you're right that you would sink through floors in buildings. That's why my family's spell includes a variant that makes you float. Like a ghost. Like, well, like the wraiths we saw."

"So we'll be incorporeal and we fly?" I asked.

"Not fly exactly. But you'll hover. You need to pay attention to where you want to go and direct yourself there mentally."

Newt and I exchanged a look. This sounded more and more complicated.

"You'll be able to affect other incorporeal things, like the wraiths. Newt, you should be able to use your fire against the wraiths and, Jules, you should be able to attack in wolf form. Or with the knives you brought through on your body."

I nodded. "Let's get started, then. We need to kill

those wraiths, get into the house, and find Carson."

Sheila directed us to pull the two full beds as close to the walls as possible, clearing a space in the middle of the room. She sat cross-legged on the carpet, took several deep breaths, and rolled her shoulders—just about as much evidence of tension as I'd ever seen in my competent, unflappable friend. She wrapped a scarf loosely around her nose and mouth. She set the glass in front of her and took a handful of sand. After pouring half into the glass, she tossed a dusting toward each of the cardinal directions, clockwise. Finally, she brought her hands together as if in prayer and rubbed the last sand off. I heard grains of sand grating between her palms.

Next, Sheila took the lid off the mercury, then pulled out the inner container. She uncapped it and tilted the container until a small amount of mercury trickled into the glass. The mercury looked almost alive, reflecting the room's lights on its quivering surface. The drops of liquid metal gathered together over the sand. Sheila repeated this pattern—sand in the glass, tossed to the four directions, rubbed between her palms, and a stream of mercury into the glass—five times. She ended with a final round of sand.

The collection of sand and mercury in the cup didn't mix, but seemed to stay two distinct things— pockets of sand and balls of mercury snuggled next to each other, yet remaining separate. I looked at Newt, who moved his shoulders as if to indicate he knew nothing more than I did. All of a sudden, I longed for Eliza. I could imagine her skeptical look and the shadow of a wink she'd drop me as if she mocked the seriousness of witchcraft, even as she was secretly impressed.

Sheila next used the chopsticks to stir the mixture, her movements following a specific pattern. I saw her brow crease in concentration as she bent closer to the mixture and started...whispering? Whispering something I couldn't catch, except for the sibilant sounds that hissed through her voice at regular intervals. I shifted my weight back and forth restlessly as this continued for quite some time. The mixture continued to appear non-cohesive, as the mercury and sand stirred together but did not integrate. When she set down the chopstick, it still looked perfectly clean, with no residue left from the mixture. She picked up the moss, held it close to her face, breathed in deeply and blew directly into the cupped handful of olive-green strands, which she then placed into the glass on top of the mercury and sand.

Sheila glanced at her notes lying beside her and hummed five repeated notes as she took out a match. She lit the match and held it above the glass until the flame nearly reached her fingers, all the while humming, then dropped it into the center of the moss. The moss caught fire in an instant and the entire glass flashed red-hot, so bright I closed my eyes and still winced from the light behind my eyelids. A sweet smell rose into the air, evoking in me a fierce nostalgia for something I could not name, something I might remember or maybe only ever dreamed. My eyes welled with tears of longing and I blinked them away, wiping my face with the back of my hands. When I could focus again, I saw the glass.

"What is that?" I said, leaning forward for a better look.

"The potion," Sheila said.

The liquid swirled with an opalescent glow, as if it caught and refracted every bit of light in the room and kept it for its own purposes. No hint of mercury, sand, or moss remained. The potion looked like pearls, mostly cream with a hint of pink, and it moved in the glass, flowed and twisted around as if alive.

"It's moving," I said.

"That's about the coolest thing I've ever seen," said Newt. He knelt on the floor to look more closely at the glass. With a nod of permission from Sheila, he picked up the potion and held it close to his eyes. "Is it alive?"

"Ew. I'm not drinking it if it's alive."

"Jules, it's not alive." Sheila said, "I'm a decent hand at witchcraft, but I can't bring inanimate objects to life. No witch can—the most we can do is to animate something so it can move. But this isn't even animated like that. I think the movement happens because it exists on many different planes at once, in different phases or however you want to think about it. That's why it allows you to become incorporeal."

"That smell..." Newt's voice trailed off as he inhaled deeply. I saw him swallow hard and close his eyes for a second. I felt an echo of that earlier rush of longing and I wanted...something. I reached out a hand and Newt enveloped it in his, warmth spreading from his Salamander frame into my cold fingers.

"I don't like it," said Tony, his voice jolting me out of reverie. "It's like a plant that puts out sweet perfumes or pheromones to attract bugs. And kill them."

"Wow," I said, "Way to ruin things. I can't believe

you're here, looking at that potion, smelling that smell, and you immediately think it's some kind of enemy."

He shrugged. "One of us has to keep his head."

"My head's fine, thanks," I said. "Sheila, do we drink it now?"

"Not until we're at Mindspring and ready to fight. I'm not sure exactly how long it will last, but we want to make sure not to waste one minute of it. This should be enough for two doses each. You need three mouthfuls."

Tony stood up and stretched his broad shoulders, his neck. "Eight o'clock now. Probably a great time to get rid of those wraiths with few bystanders. Then we can investigate the property, see if Carson's kept there or somewhere else."

"And get him back," I said.

"Yes, we'll get him back. But before we go back to Mindspring, I want to show you some of what I found on DeVossen's website," said Sheila. She opened her laptop and frowned at the screen.

"Why? What did you find?"

"Just trying to get an idea of who our Pneumaphage is. People sure seem to love him. Listen to this testimonial," said Sheila. " 'Kenneth is the best therapist I've ever met. It's like he can see into your soul and bring you true, lasting peace.' "

"Kenneth?" I said.

"That's DeVossen's first name."

"His patients call him Kenneth? Not Dr. DeVossen?"

"They aren't patients, Jules. They're 'seekers.' "

"What?"

"Look." Sheila turned the screen of her laptop to

face me and pointed to a section on the Mindspring website. " 'We welcome all seekers of healing, peace, and enlightenment. Seekers should peruse our full menu of services to find what will help them most.' Those services, by the way, include hypnotherapy, past life regression, group meditation sessions, chakra treatment, spiritual alignment, and inner truth seeking."

"I don't know what half those are. Is this guy even a doctor?"

"Hmm." Sheila clicked on the "About" page and followed links to get to DeVossen's background. "Lots of spiritual retreats. Let me see…Yeah, he has a PsyD from some place I've never heard of. And a Master's in Social Work, too. Uh, and he lists his studies with several gurus and 'inner development guides.' This guy…"

"What else do his patients say?"

She clicked a few times and brought us back to the page full of testimonials. " 'Now that my chakras are unblocked, I sleep like a baby without any anxiety. I've recommended Kenneth to all my friends.' Well, good. Maybe he can unblock our chakras, huh, Jules?"

"Look here," I said, pointing to the screen, " 'My son used to be hyperactive and struggle with impulse control. After regular sessions with Kenneth, he's an entirely different kid! His teachers keep telling me he's the calmest kid in the classroom. He'd sleep all day if I let him.' "

"Hmmm," said Sheila.

"Hmmm, indeed," I said. "He sounds like a complete nutcase, but…well, not what I expect from an evil Pneumaphage who goes around kidnapping babies."

"It's always the ones you don't expect who turn out to be the most dangerous," said Sheila. "After a serial killer gets caught, the neighbors always talk about how polite and quiet he was. They're so surprised, they had no idea."

"I think it's creepy. All these people saying he brings them peace and relaxation?" Newt shook his head. "Creepy. Let's go take him out."

Chapter Twelve

Sheila insisted we take care of the large wraith at the riverfront first, before it could harm more people. The Pneumaphage must want Carson alive—killing him would have been easy—so he shouldn't be in imminent danger like the unsuspecting populace of Evansville, Indiana. I agreed, in theory, and somehow kept myself from screaming that the only person who mattered was my baby. We'd dispatch the large wraith first before it killed any people.

We drove along the Ohio River and noted Tony was right. At this time of night in April, the walkway and riverside were mostly empty.

"If there's enough potion for four doses, should we all become incorporeal and just kill all the wraiths that way? Instead of using the focus serum for you two and your weapons?" I asked Sheila.

"No," said Tony. "We need to affect things on this plane. Subdue human enemies. Deal with the Pneumaphage."

"Right. Sheila, how long 'til Tim gets here?"

She glanced at the time on the car radio. "He lands at 10:43. He'll call us as soon as he's on the ground."

"Should we wait for him?" asked Newt.

"No," I said. "I wish he were here already, but if we have the chance to find Carson, I don't want to waste any more time."

Tony pulled over and parked near the pagoda that served as a visitor's center. Sheila pointed in the direction of the monument where we'd seen the wraith earlier. Still in the car, Tony pulled on shadows and emerged as his wolf, large and black, with amber eyes gleaming in the streetlights. Sheila carefully dabbed the focus serum on his forehead, teeth, and claws, then readied herself and her gun the same way. I wasn't sure how useful a gun would be in the middle of the city, even if the riverside was largely empty and she had a silencer.

"Come here, you two. I want to give you more serum, too," she said. "The incorporeal potion should last at least twelve hours, maybe longer. But just in case it wears off suddenly, this serum should let you see the wraiths for a full day. I just want to be extra careful in case something happens and you pop back to this plane unexpectedly. Julie, let's coat your knives, too."

Her speech did *not* fill me with confidence.

Newt carried the potion in a travel cup. He and I looked at each other for a long moment.

"Are we doing this?" I asked.

"Remember," said Sheila sharply, "Jules, no going through natural objects, okay? You need to direct yourself mentally while hovering. Might take some practice. Newt, got it?"

"As much as possible without ever having been incorporeal," Newt said, "Right, Jules?"

"Right. Let's get out of the car first."

"Three mouthfuls each," called Sheila as we stepped out.

Newt's freckles shimmered and I felt heat emanating off him—the only sign he might be nervous.

My own heart raced and my throat suddenly felt so dry I wasn't sure I could even swallow the potion. Newt rolled his shoulders, bounced on his toes, and gave me a huge grin. Raising the cup in a toast, he brought it to his lips and swallowed. I watched as a strange look spread across his face, leaving him momentarily unguarded, his charm and humor erased by an expression of wonder. He swallowed twice more, quickly, and handed me the cup. His eyes widened in surprise.

"Does it work right away? Do you feel…" My voice trailed off as Newt seemed to shimmer for a second and then suddenly hovered above the ground. "Holy crap."

"It worked! It really worked." Sheila popped her head out of the open car door. "Wow, that's the most complicated potion I've ever made and I'm so glad it worked."

"Uh, Sheila? Your surprise is not reassuring. Did you think it wouldn't work?"

"Not exactly. That is…I thought I'd done everything right. Just glad for the proof."

Tony pushed past Sheila and jumped lightly to the ground. His furry bulk pressed against my legs. Energy prickled my skin and I reached down to stroke his ears, my hands reaching for him like iron filings drawn to a magnet. His amber eyes looked up at me as I ran my fingers through his coat, thick and soft against my skin. He made a low grumble in his throat, butting his head against me, and I said, "Yes, I'll be careful."

A thrill of adrenaline ran down my spine and tightened my muscles as I raised the travel mug full of potion. Three mouthfuls. How was that a measurement? As much as I could fit in my mouth? Or the amount I'd usually drink? What happened if I drank too much or not enough?

Damn it. Before I could overthink "mouthful" any more, I popped open the cup and took a healthy sip. My mouth flooded with the sweetest flavor I could imagine but not cloying sweet. A pure, fresh sweetness like clear rainwater, like dew off a spring flower. I took another sip and immediately the third. Warmth spread through my chest and I began to tingle as if every nerve woke from sleep. I quickly set down the coffee mug so it wouldn't follow me into the incorporeal realm. I stared at Sheila, then startled as my feet left the ground.

"Crap!" I said.

"Can you hear me yet?" asked Newt.

"Yeah. Hi."

"Hi."

"Sheila and Tony can still see us, right? Because of the focus serum on their foreheads."

Newt nodded. "I don't think they can hear us, though. I was trying to talk to you all earlier."

"Sheila?" I said, but she didn't respond. Instead, she turned to Tony and said something to him. I saw her mouth move but heard nothing. Tony nodded his wolf head, then raced into the darkness after a fleeting glance in my direction from his amber eyes.

Sheila looked at me and Newt, then pointed up the walkway and moved away.

Now that I paid attention, I noticed all the ambient noises of the city had dropped away. Cars drove by silent as ghosts. I guess we were the ghosts, though.

"This is really…strange," I said.

Newt nodded. "But cool. And we're here together, Jules." He reached out one lanky arm and I rested my hand in his, thankful for the contact.

"All right. Let's follow them and find the wraith."

When I moved to walk, I realized my feet weren't actually touching the ground. Which I knew, of course, because Sheila clearly said we'd hover. Or do something like hover. I lifted my foot and then put it down, wondering what to do next.

"Come on, Jules," Newt said, tugging at my hand and swinging me closer to him.

With a waggle of his eyebrows, he started to glide forward without moving his legs. My hand still in his, I followed him. At first, I shuffled my feet back and forth in some semblance of a walk, but I soon realized how unnecessary the movement was. As long as I thought about moving in a particular direction, I did. When Newt glided through a parked car, though, I stopped short and yanked my hand from his.

He stood within the car—literally superimposed on it—and grinned at me. "What's wrong, Jules?"

I reached my hand out and watched it pass through the solid metal door, as if the car were a projected image, as if it didn't exist. A dandelion grew from a nearby crack in the pavement, so I knelt and touched it. Firm. Real. I could interact with the plants and the ground—a theory I tested by patting the dirt—and yet not the pavement. My fingers went right through the asphalt and hit the bare ground underneath.

"Newt?" I asked, straightening from the ground. "If wraiths exist in this incorporeal phase and we're now in the same phase, what other kinds of creatures naturally exist here? It can't be a plane populated with just plants and dirt and rocks and wraiths. Can it?"

Newt took his time answering. "I'm not actually

sure, Jules, and I kind of wish we asked that question earlier. But hopefully if anything else does live here, it'll be glad to make friends? And remember," he held up his hands and wreathed them in dancing orange flame, "Now that we're incorporeal, all my powers will work on anything we encounter, just like your wolf strength. Do you want to change form? Would you feel safer?"

"Not until we see our target, I think."

We drifted onward in the general direction of where we'd seen the wraith. I ventured to glide through a car, a garbage can, and a concrete wall. The wind stirred the air, whipping nearby trees into whispers of movement that broke the quiet. The rustles grew into something more than wind—an eerie keening interspersed with crackling like static electricity. My ears popped.

Newt and I exchanged a glance. I nodded, then dropped into my wolf.

All right, my transformation wasn't quite that smooth, but I did manage to shift form with less trouble than back in the hotel room, which boosted my confidence. Bring on the wraith! The sound we heard must have come from the large wraith. With my sensitive ears, the noise was so eerie I shook my head several times before gritting my jaw and trying to ignore the wailing. I poked my nose into Newt's hand and he gave me a quick rub on my head, pulling one ear.

He whispered, "Keep to the shadows."

In response, I pulled on the shadows and veiled myself, then loped down the path toward the source of the ear-splitting noise.

This was one time where I regretted my wolf's sharp senses because the keening, wind-like whistling, and pops of static electricity became so loud I laid my ears tightly back against my head. A low growl formed in my throat in anger at the noise. I slowed down as I got closer, pulling the shadows closely around myself. I stopped at the side of the path and had a clear view of the wraith. Nearly the size of a small car, it spun in the air, hovering near several pillars that made up a monument on the waterfront. The wraith spit out bits of black lightning and extended tendrils in a flowing motion, like squid ink blooming in water.

Crouched about ten feet away, Tony watched the wraith with his lips curled up to reveal his fangs. His fur stood at the back of his neck, just like mine did. I didn't see Sheila and I couldn't smell her—or Tony—the curious lack of scent was strange, as I'd gotten used to my super Were senses giving me lots of information at all times. Come to think of it...I took several deep breaths. I smelled subtle background scents of river and trees. I smelled Newt walking up behind me, his particular scent of warm male conjoined with the Salamander smell, lit matches and sunbaked rocks. I smelled the wraith too, ozone and a bitterness I could almost taste.

With a sudden jerk, the wraith moved. It shot away from the river, toward the sidewalk. As I tracked its movement, I saw Sheila standing at the crosswalk. She backed away, to the other side of the street, and the wraith trailed her. Newt and I followed at a distance, while Tony raced to the left of us, around the wraith, and toward a narrow passageway between two office buildings. Sheila must have decided to lure the wraith to…a dark alley. Okay. I shook my head to dispel my amusement at the cliché. That sounded like a good plan. We'd attack the wraith in a dark alley.

When we reached the opening of the alley, I saw Tony crouched at Sheila's side about forty feet away, next to a pair of dumpsters. The wraith hovered in the air between our two groups. Writhing pseudopods of darkness stretched out in all directions.

Suddenly, the wraith shot toward me and Newt. I snarled in surprise. Perhaps, since we stood—or rather hovered—on the incorporeal plane, we made a more tempting target than the others, even with the lure. Whatever the reason, the wraith jolted quickly toward us. It moved about fifteen feet in just a couple of seconds.

Behind me, I felt a surge of warmth as Newt called his fire. I hunkered down, prepared to lunge, and growled low in my throat. Purple light flickered in the corner of my eyes and then arced overhead as Newt lobbed his flames at the wraith. Its keens turned shrill and piercing as it hurtled through the air, closing the distance to reach Newt.

I leapt as the wraith came into range and slashed at one smoky pseudopod with my fangs. Even knowing we were on the same plane, I half-expected my teeth to snap through the storm-like body, yet my jaws closed upon it, rubbery in my mouth. I bit down hard and pulled, like pulling on a jellyfish or a chewy bit of taffy. The wraith's body swelled and rolled in my mouth and grayness flooded my senses, colored the air around me, and choked me with amorphous regret and despair.

White-hot flames burst above my head and I ducked, then rolled to the side. The wraith shrieked, a formless sound drowned out by the roar of flames that grew taller, brighter. Fire consumed the wraith as it jerked and stretched, melted into a bubbling mess of char and bruise-colored taffy, then disappeared into nothing.

Newt's flames snuffed out.

Silence.

I shook my head hard, my ears flapping against the sudden stillness of the night after the wraith's keens. After I collected my thoughts, I pulled on shadow and released into my human form.

I sat up.

"You okay?" asked Newt. "Not sure biting that thing was the best idea. You look a little gray."

"I'm fine," I said, still sitting cross-legged on the ground. "Starting to feel better already. Though I vote for using your fire against *all* the wraiths from now on. That was pretty effective. Incredible."

Newt grinned. "Did you see it kind of melt and bubble at the same time it burned? Like one of those charcoal tablets that grows into a snake when you put a match to it."

"Both gross and cool all at once."

Sheila ran over to us, pointed at Newt, and made excited jazz-hands in the air.

"I think Sheila liked the flames, too," said Newt.

Tony's amber eyes glinted with reflected streetlights. He sat like a statue in the deepest shadows. Sheila pointed to herself and Tony, then back down the street where they'd left the car. After nods and thumbs-ups from me and Newt, Sheila left with the wolf padding by her side.

Newt reached down a hand to pull me to my feet.

His hand gripped mine like it was the only other real thing in the universe, and I held onto him even after we stood next to each other.

"Julie…"

After a long pause, I prompted, "Yeah?"

Newt's blue eyes looked deeper and darker than usual, as he held my gaze with his for another moment.

"I'm glad we're here together," he said.

"Me, too. This would be creepy alone."

"I think Tony and Sheila headed in the direction of the Pneumaphage's Mindspring. Shall we join them?" He squeezed my hand and let go, swooping one arm in a courtly bow.

"Definitely. If your fire can do that to the wraiths, this will be a piece of cake." I frowned, looking back in the direction of the car. "Do you know where we're going?"

"We follow the river, turn left on Cherry Street. Once we get into the historic district, the house will be easy to find."

"If you say so."

Newt and I moved in the direction he indicated, our feet skimming over the ground. Every time we passed through a cement post or a car, I felt a small thrill. We detoured through the Evansville Museum, and I mean literally through, just because we could. I pushed myself to move faster, feeling the wind rush past my body as I approached the speed of running. Newt kept pace with me. I glanced over to see his freckles gleaming like copper in the half moon and I laughed into the night, just for the joy of moving, of magic, of freedom. I was on my way to rescue Carson. Newt swooped through a parked pickup truck in the museum parking lot and I mirrored him, rushing through a car of my own. People appeared on the sidewalk near the museum, a couple walking hand in hand, deep in conversation.

"Watch this!" yelled Newt back in my direction, as he passed right through the people.

I stopped short, then allowed myself to drift closer to the couple. I reached out one hand and watched it pass through the man's arm, clad in a jean jacket. A shudder passed through me.

"That...that is really eerie." I backed up, shaking my head. "I definitely feel like a ghost now."

I looked up at Newt, who'd moved to stand next to me. I slid a few inches closer to him and breathed in his scent.

"Newt? What if we stay this way? What if something was wrong with the potion and we're incorporeal forever?"

"Jules." He wrapped his arm around my shoulders and pulled me into a hug. "We're not going to be incorporeal forever. You gotta trust Sheila. So far, everything's happened just the way she said it would."

"Yeah." I leaned my head against his shoulder and closed my eyes. "It feels like you and I are the only real things in the world."

"Julie..." Newt cleared his throat and his arm tightened slightly. I felt tension creep into his muscles and looked up at him.

The freckles sprinkling his face gleamed gold; the blue of his eyes shone like sunlight.

"Can I kiss you?"

Surprise jolted through me and I found no words. Newt?

Kiss Newt?

I…

I tilted my head, pulled him closer, moved toward him as he leaned down and we kissed. His mouth felt hot against mine, my lips tingled with his Salamander power and something else, some desire I hadn't dared to recognize before. My arms twined around his neck and I pressed myself into him, aware of nothing but the two of us, everything else unreal, everything as immaterial as ghosts themselves. We kissed softly at first with a swift growth of intensity that left me shaking with desire, our breaths and lips and tongues mingling in a haze of heat.

I pulled back after several minutes and looked up at him. "Wow."

"Wow?"

My cheeks hurt from the huge smile stuck across my face. Joy bubbled inside me and my stomach swooped like I'd crested a rollercoaster. My whole body clenched with desire.

"Wow is good, right?" said Newt.

"Shh, no talking. Come back here," I said and pulled his head back down to mine.

Chapter Thirteen

When I finally peeled myself away from Newt, I still didn't want to stop touching him. I held his hand, that simple touch sending shivers of need through me. Newt's eyes were nearly black in the night, his pupils swallowing the blue with desire.

"Um. Let's go find Carson and get back to this," I gestured between the two of us, "Later."

"Absolutely." Newt squeezed my hand.

My heart pounded as we glided through the still night toward the Pneumaphage's lair. Two blocks west of the Mindspring mansion, we came across the parked rental car. Sheila and Tony had arrived ahead of us. I kept forgetting we didn't need to hide in the shadows, we were incorporeal, so only wraiths could see us. And anything else that lived on the incorporeal plane or used focus serum. Or saw us by a different method. Okay. I needed to stop thinking that way or I would freak myself out.

I rubbed my thumb along the back of Newt's hand to ground myself. Freckles glinted down his arms, signaling he was ready to call fire at any moment.

The old house occupied by DeVossen's Mindspring sat silent on its lot with lights on in several windows, but no people visible. On the incorporeal plane, I couldn't smell anyone or anything, which really disconcerted me now that we tried to scope out the building. My Were senses easily pierced a patch of darkness near the next door neighbor's fence to see Tony—surprisingly enough in human form—and Sheila hunkered down, watching the house. I pulled Newt in that direction.

As we approached, Tony stood up abruptly and turned toward us. Instantly, I dropped Newt's hand. Tony took half a step back, then dropped into his wolf in the space of a blink. He sat down and stared at me.

Sheila's blue eyes took in this interaction and she raised an eyebrow.

"Julie?" said Newt.

"I'm sorry," I said.

"Are you and Tony…?" He made a vague gesture toward the black wolf.

"No! Nothing's going on with Tony."

I still smelled the desire hanging in the air between me and Newt. I wanted to kiss him again. And I'd kissed Tony just hours ago, even though I didn't want to. But I did. Kind of. Even though I didn't.

"Are you sure?" Newt asked.

"Yes."

I spoke firmly, but Newt moved further away from me and a frown creased his forehead.

"This is bad timing," he said. "Let's just focus on what we need to do."

I nodded, feeling a twinge of panic race through me to join with the whirling ball of anxiety and fear for Carson. Had I messed up things with Newt already, before they even started?

Sheila waved to get my attention, motioned us closer then spoke.

We couldn't hear her. I shook my head in

frustration and held up my hands to show we didn't understand.

Sheila mouthed a curse. Now *that* I understood. She said something to Tony, whose black ears flicked toward her before pointing ahead again. She frowned, then tried to communicate with her hands. She pointed at us, then at the house, mimed ignorance, and wiggled her fingertips. Oh. Flames. She meant Newt's fire.

"I think she wants us to go in first and kill any wraiths we see," Newt volunteered.

"Good job interpreting," I said. "Okay. Sounds like a reasonable plan."

I nodded at Sheila and held up my hand in a peace signal, for lack of any better way to communicate. She blew me a kiss, followed by a saucy wink that embraced both me and Newt and brought a flush to my cheeks. Tony sat and just looked at me. The fur on the back of his neck stood up.

I gave Newt my sunniest smile and vowed to put the sulky Werewolf out of my mind. "Let's go inside."

Leaving Sheila and the Were in their patch of darkness, Newt and I glided smoothly across the yard toward the house. At least, we would have glided smoothly if I hadn't forgotten that natural objects still existed for us and bumped into a large ornamental rock, stubbing my toe and crying out with a combination of surprise and pain. I caught my balance, though, and hoped Tony hadn't been watching. Not that it mattered.

"You okay?"

I reassured Newt with a nod and focused on where we were going.

Into the house, into the home of the Pneumaphage.

We came to the porch steps and I consciously

guided my body up so I didn't just walk through the foundation. Unlike what we'd seen in the daytime, I didn't see any wraiths outside the building. However, as we reached the front door, I heard the keening sound that signaled our incorporeal enemies were within. The noise wasn't as loud as the earlier wraith, but it was enough to guide us.

"How about I go take care of the wraith, or wraiths, while you try to find Carson?" Newt suggested. "Unless you don't think you should go off on your own?"

"Sounds good. Now that we know how the wraiths sound on their home plane, I'm not worried about one sneaking up on me. And if I know it's there, I can shift and fight it off. Or use these so I don't have to touch it." I tapped the two knives stuck in my belt. "I'll find Carson. Just yell if you need me?"

Newt paused and gave me a look that left me tingling down to my toes. Gods, I wanted to kiss him again. We parted. He dropped through the floor of the porch at an angle to follow the sound of the wraiths, which seemed to come from the basement.

I slid through the front door into the dark waiting room of DeVossen Mindspring. I blocked the wraith sounds from my mind in order to focus on my task: Find my son. My Werewolf eyes saw the plump couches, soft chairs, and coffee table draped with a purple and teal tapestry. On the end tables sat two Himalayan salt crystal lamps—the kind that glowed pinkish-orange and people purported cured everything from migraines to allergies to memory loss. I smelled the salt hanging in the air. Curious, I reached out to touch one and my fingers made contact with its smooth, slightly warm surface. The salt was close enough to its natural form to have presence in the incorporeal realm.

I passed through the door and into a hallway. An alcove held a desk, copier, and printer, lined with file cabinets behind. I poked my head, literally, into several empty therapy rooms and offices, a kitchenette, and a bathroom. Staircase.

Hmm. Rather than move toward the stairs, I directed my attention upward and willed myself to rise and did. This incorporeal stuff was not getting old yet. I rose through the ceiling/floor and into a library.

Bookshelves lined all four walls, even below and above the windows on two sides of this corner room. The center of the room held a large dark wooden L-shaped desk with intricate carvings on the sides. Piles of books, notebooks, and papers crowded the surface. I rose slowly through the floor, taking in the rest of the room. Floor lamps, heavy draperies fell to the floor around the windows, a couple of guest chairs. I drifted upward and moved first to examine the crowded desktop. My hand passed right through the top book as I tried to flip the pages. Damn it.

A large book titled *Ancient Druidic Rituals and Traditions* rested on a pile of notebook pages. The book sat open to a section on using standing stones as a source of power. On a corner of the desk lay three books. When I read the titles, I realized they were all pop-psychology and inspirational books. Weird. A half-drunk cup of tea sat on its saucer in the midst of the papers and notebooks on the desk. I floated to glance over the bookshelves, noting that about half the titles were printed in English, the rest in various languages. The books appeared to be grouped by subject, which pleased the librarian in me. Natural history, astronomy, political history, mathematics. I found an area with art books and another section with music scores. Whoever used this office, and I'd bet it was DeVossen himself, was clearly educated and had eclectic interests. Two prominent shelves were jammed with business and self-help books that promised to teach the secrets of making deals, winning friends, and influencing those in power. I stood before those books for a long moment, trying to find some significance in the "inspirational" pablum of their titles.

None of this helped me find Carson. No spellbooks, as far as I could tell. I glanced at the top papers on the desk again, just to make sure I hadn't missed a vital clue, and moved on.

This time, I chose the traditional path and glided through the door into the upstairs hall. The hallway was lit, the first lights I'd found turned on. I must be getting closer to where people might be.

Wait. If I found DeVossen, would he be able to see me? Did he have some ability to see incorporeal creatures like the wraiths and, well, me? After all, he obviously had some uncanny relationship with the many wraiths in this area, judging from our experiences with him and the presence of wraith screams in his house.

I inched down the hall. I looked in the first door on the left—some type of guest bedroom with blue walls above white wainscoting—an obvious nautical theme complete with hanging nets and glass balls and white wicker furniture. Yuck. Also, empty of people. I glided down the hall to the next room. As I approached, I saw light shining from beneath the door of a room further down, but I decided to check every door instead of rushing to the light like a moth. That way, nothing could surprise me from behind.

When I moved through the next door to take a look, I saw Carson.

"Carson!" I yelled, then clapped a hand over my mouth before I realized no one could hear me anyway because I was incorporeal.

I zipped through the air to stop beside his crib. Carson lay asleep on his back, his chest and stomach rising and falling gently with his breaths. He looked pale and the smooth baby skin around his eyes was bruised with fatigue.

"Hi, sweetie," I said, unable to help myself. He couldn't hear me. I reached down, wishing to touch him, but stopped right before my hand passed through his body. I didn't think I could stand that reminder of how separated I was from my baby—separate, though standing right next to him. We were planes apart. Parallel universes away. Separated by quantum realities.

My hand hovered over him and I smoothed the air near his head, making shhh-ing noises until I realized tears leaked down my face. I wiped my eyes on my sleeve and cleared my throat. He was okay. Here was Carson, alive and fine, generally unharmed, even though his pallor alarmed me. His pacifier lay next to his cheek, as if he'd spit it out while sleeping, and I desperately wished to hand it to him. A small frown crossed his baby face and he kicked a foot. His mouth made a sucking movement, his hands clenched, and he let out a huge sigh. He turned his head the other way and settled back down.

"I'm right here, Carson," I said. "I know you can't

hear me. I know you can't see me. But I'm here and I'm coming for you and there's nothing anyone can do to stop me. Just as soon as I'm back in my body—or whatever—I'll crash in here and I'll rescue you and I'll be able to hold you again."

I leaned over the crib, noticing that my body passed right through the bars, and inhaled deeply, hoping to catch the scent of his hair, his baby sweat. Nothing, because smells couldn't seep into the incorporeal world, either. I knew that. I stood by the crib for what seemed like hours, caught by the desire to hold my baby, knowing I should leave and continue my search.

Finally, I shook my head and said, "Pull it together, Julie Hall. Time to check out the lit room down the hall."

Now that I'd found Carson, adrenaline surged through my body. The Pneumaphage must be in that room with lights and I would find him. I took a few deep breaths to prepare myself and unsheathed my knives, just in case.

As I was about to slide into the hallway, Newt popped through the wooden door. I jumped and nearly lunged forward with my knives but managed to stop myself at the last moment.

"Holy crap, you startled me." I lowered my knives and gestured behind me to the crib. "Newt, I found Carson. But we can't even touch him. My own baby and he doesn't know I'm here. We can't rescue him. I can't stand it. But I think he's okay. He looks really tired but not hurt."

"I found…I'm not sure what, Jules. I think you need to come see."

I frowned at the note of barely-contained alarm in his voice. "Is it wraiths?"

"Yes, but not the way you think. It's like…I think they're trapped. Or being held."

"I think there's someone in the room down the hall. There's a room with lights on."

"The Pneumaphage?"

"Probably," I said. "I haven't looked yet."

Newt considered. "Let's leave that for now. I want you to see the basement first."

We drifted through the floor to the ground level then to the basement stairs. The stairs ended in a room with a concrete floor, exposed beams and pipes running along the ceiling. An old clothesline stretched from one corner to the other, along with a few forlorn clothespins. At least three rooms led off this main area, two doors to the right and an opening to what looked like a larger area on the left. The basement was dark, but a gray, flickering light emanated from the open area to the left. I heard the keening screams of wraiths— multiple wraiths raising an eerie cacophony, though the sound seemed somehow muffled.

I looked at Newt with raised eyebrows and he nodded in the direction of the light. In the dim basement, his freckles gleamed like copper and I felt him gather power. I debated shifting shape, but, damn it, my human form was just more comfortable. I sent mental apologies to the wolf trapped beneath my skin and promised to shift if there were real danger. But Newt would have warned me if I needed to prepare.

We approached the doorway. The gray light lent an eerie perspective to the basement and it flickered like a broken television. I felt like I was in a creepy movie and fought the shivers running up my spine. I wanted to rub my ears and block out the noise. Wasn't this the point in the horror movie where the audience wanted to scream at the characters not to go in the room? I glanced at Newt for reassurance.

When I looked through the doorway, it took me a few moments to parse what I saw. The square room must have once been a laundry area, judging from the pipes and hookups along the left wall and the drain in the middle of the floor. No one used the space for laundry now, though. The source of light was in the center of the room, taking up nearly all the space and emanating that flickering gray illumination. A bubble of light, of energy, of something that made the hair on the back of my neck up straight, occupied the room. And inside were wraiths. Not one or two, but a veritable sea of them swarming around and testing the boundaries of the bubble. The surface of the gray-lit cage swirled with energy, just as the wraiths seethed within.

"Definitely a Pneumaphage," said Newt, and gestured to the floor.

Around the gray bubble were three lines, one drawn in what looked like chalk, one in a black greasy substance, and one a dark color that—judging from appearances—might have been clotted blood. I swallowed hard, not wanting to think about that, just glad it wasn't my baby's blood on the floor. God. I hoped it wasn't my baby's blood on the floor. Carson hadn't looked physically injured. I pushed the thought out of my mind.

Interspaced at regular intervals around the exterior of the three circles were seven white candles. The candles weren't lit at the moment, but had clearly been burned recently, judging from the small pools of wax anchoring them to the cement floor.

"Why would anyone want to capture wraiths like this?" I asked over the noise of the trapped swarm.

"Good question. I wish we had the answer."

"Is this..." I stood behind the circles and reached a hand inside toward the gray barrier. As I approached, I felt the draw of tension on my skin, as if a storm approached. All my hairs stood on end and I fought the urge to snatch back my hand and rub it against my pants. I braced myself and touched the gray wall. Though I pushed, I couldn't break through. "It's impenetrable and in the incorporeal realm. Like us. Or in both realms somehow, like the wraiths."

The wraiths churned in our direction, crowding the gray barrier as if they sensed us and wanted to feed. Their swirling pseudopods reached out then shrank back from the wall enclosing them.

"What is this? Why are they held captive? Where'd they come from and why are they here?" I asked.

"Excellent questions and I don't have answers," said Newt. "Maybe Sheila or Tony have some ideas. Or Tim, when he arrives, which should be soon."

"Before we go ask them," I said. "We need to check out that room upstairs. Do you think the Pneumaphage can see into the incorporeal realm?"

Newt paused to consider then shrugged. "No idea. Guess we'll find out. Let's be really careful."

Chapter Fourteen

With Newt by my side, I floated up through two ceilings until we reached the second story. Light still shone beneath the door at the far end of the hall. Before we checked it out, though, we took a detour through Carson's room to make sure nothing had changed. My toddler had rolled onto his side and now clutched his pacifier tightly in his plump little fist. Other than that, he looked the same—pale and tired but not visibly injured.

After we'd looked at him for several minutes, Newt said, "Okay. Let's go check out the other room."

"All right. Any game plan? In case he can see us."

We both spoke in low voices.

After a moment of thought, I said, "Let's use being incorporeal to our advantage. We should pop in an unexpected way—definitely not through the door. Actually, we could even float outside and look in the windows."

"Now that's good thinking. We don't need to pay attention to regular limits. We can pretty much go anywhere we want." Newt grabbed my hand and laid a big kiss on my knuckles. Even in the midst of raiding a Pneumaphage's house, his gesture comforted me.

I tugged him toward me, gently, and he floated closer then closer still until I tilted up my face and kissed him.

After a brief second, he pulled back. I wasn't sure how to interpret the look on his face.

"Pneumaphage," I said, and he nodded.

Plan set, we floated out of the house—right through the walls. Even though I knew I wouldn't fall, it felt incredibly weird to hover twenty-five feet off the ground. Weird but good. Kind of like dreams of flying I had from time to time, the ones where I ran through a field and suddenly took off, soared into the air without the least bit of effort. When we dreamed, did we access some other quantum reality?

We glided slowly down the length of the house. From the outside, we clearly saw our target room; light shone around the edge of the blinds in two windows. We inched closer and I put out a hand to brace myself on the house before remembering I couldn't touch anything. Instead, I mentally maneuvered myself until my eyes were level with the edge of the windowsill, just where the blind didn't come all the way down.

I peered into the room to see a man lying in bed, reading a book propped up on his knees. He didn't look like a Pneumaphage. He looked perfectly normal, like someone I wouldn't give a second glance if I saw him at the grocery store. White, middle-aged, mousey brown hair cut short. Dark eyes behind gold, wire-rimmed glasses. He frowned at the book, looking intent, then flipped a page. I read the title of the book and saw he read a pulpy crime novel, one I'd seen multiple copies of during our time in airports. The bed jutted out from one wall and ran parallel to the window toward the corner of the house. An ornate dresser of dark wood and two bedside tables made up the remainder of the room's furniture. Everything looked mundane, down to a dirty shirt and some socks crumpled in the corner near what I assumed was a closet door.

Newt placed his hand on my shoulder and I jumped, before glaring at him.

"Sorry, Jules," he whispered. He studied the room and the man. "Do you think he's the Pneumaphage?"

"No clue."

"Can you smell him? Could you smell a Pneumaphage? I know you can tell Sheila's a witch, now that you're a Were."

"I can't smell anything. We're not in the same realm. Or quantum reality. Or whatever."

Newt swore under his breath and we drifted away from the window to confer.

He said, "Okay. If that's the Pneumaphage, at least we know he's not up to anything tonight. Looks like he's turned in for the night. Carson's sleeping and should be safe for now."

"I hate leaving him here."

"Maybe we don't have to. Maybe Sheila and Tony can rescue him, if we can keep an eye on the probable Pneumaphage."

"Should we try to figure out whether he can see us?"

Newt and I both considered, until I finally answered my own question. "Maybe not," I said. "If he sees us, he'll attack and we aren't ready for that. I don't want to start a fight before Carson is safely with us."

"I agree. Let's go tell Sheila and Tony what we've found."

****

When we rejoined the others, however, we couldn't actually communicate. Newt and I were still very much stuck in an incorporeal state. After staring at each other—thank goodness for focus serum—and using a combination of pantomime and exaggerated lip movements to no avail, I finally had a good idea.

"Ha!" I took out my cell phone and flourished it.

Newt frowned before he said, "I'm not sure how that will help. I bet we don't get reception here. Although the idea of a magical phone that can connect between this realm and our regular state..." His voice trailed off and I cuffed him gently.

"Focus. I'm not going to call them. I'm going to text on my phone and show them the messages."

Sheila had been following our exchange with a puzzled look on her face, which cleared as I started thumb-typing on my phone. She moved to stand behind me and look over my shoulder at the words. As I typed, I watched her mouth the words to Tony, who sat in wolf form about eight feet away and stared at me with unblinking amber eyes. I explained what we'd found in the house—Carson, upstairs in a bedroom. Tony's ears cocked at that and he looked like he might pad closer but remained seated. With Newt's help verbalizing the strangeness of the basement, I explained the gray magical barrier full of wraiths.

Sheila gestured for me to hand her the phone, then grimaced and took out her own instead. She typed several questions about the basement and the set up. I explained the candles, the rings, and described the barrier, its sheen, the static, the sense of reluctance I felt to touch it. She nodded at each point and then stared into space, obviously lost in thought.

Finally, she tapped her phone decisively and typed out curt instructions. She and Tony would approach the house, try to enter through the back door, go up the stairs, and find Carson. Newt and I could keep watch in the incorporeal realm and attack any wraiths that might show up. We all agreed the guy we saw must be the Pneumaphage. No one else would have wraiths locked in their basement for some unknown purpose.

Tony called on shadow and wreathed himself and Sheila in darkness before he padded around to the back of the house, Newt and I following. His cocked ears rotated this way and that. The ring of silence in the incorporeal realm was so loud I could barely stand it. I wished I could use my Were senses, but there seemed to be nothing to find. Nothing that shared physical space with me and Newt, at least. I reached out and grabbed his hand, just to remind myself I was real, that I could touch and be touched. Newt's fingers felt at home in my own, his active Salamander powers sending a hot tingle across my skin. I felt the tension in my shoulders ease, until Tony glanced back at us and I froze.

Newt dropped my hand. I grimaced and muttered to myself, "Focus, Julie, focus."

Tony stopped at the base of the stairs up to the back door. The fur on the nape of his neck stood up. Sheila said something to him then moved toward the door. She placed her hand on the doorknob, then jerked it back as if burned. She shook her hand for a moment before reaching back toward the door. This time, she didn't touch anything, but held her hand about two inches from the knob then passed her flat palm across the door. She shook her head and said something to Tony.

"What?" I said. "Newt, what's going on?"

"Jules, sweetheart, I know what you know." He made a large gesture to catch Sheila's attention then moved his arms in the universal "what" gesture.

Sheila moved quickly away from the house and gestured us to follow her back to the car, parked a block away. Tony stayed in wolf form, either because he was more comfortable or because he wanted to avoid human emotions. He kept his back turned to me and Newt. I couldn't even catch his gaze. Sheila leaned on the side of the rental car and typed on her phone as quickly as her thumbs allowed.

Some kind of spell around the house. I can't get in. From the feel, I think it wards off anyone who's not invited. Obviously not in the incorporeal realm, since you and Newt poked around. But Tony and I can't get in unless I can break the spell. Can't do that cold. Might have something in my books. Not sure. So now what?

I typed back. *When will Tim get here?*

Sheila typed. *Hour and a half.*

I thought for a moment before typing back. *I think we should go back to the hotel, wait for Tim and get him caught up, see if you can find anything useful in your spellbooks. Then tomorrow I think you become the latest client at DeVossen Mindspring. That's one way to be invited in, right?*

Newt laughed as he looked over my shoulder. "I'm not sure Sheila seems like the type to go to a place like that. Past life regression and holistic healing?"

"She's a Witch and you think that's so different than holistic healing?"

"Point taken. You think she can pull this off?"

"I think she has a better shot than any of the rest of

us. You and I are incorporeal, besides, the Pneumaphage knows what I look like. Tony? No way. Can you imagine him seeing any kind of therapist or letting himself get hypnotized? Same with Tim. So it has to be Sheila."

Sheila spoke to Tony, who twitched an ear before making his wolf shoulders shrug. She swatted him angrily on the top of his head and he jumped up, hackles raised. I watched the scene play out in pantomime. Sheila shook her finger at the wolf and spat some sharp words, the wolf stared at her with baleful amber eyes and then, with evident reluctance, pulled on shadow and emerged in human form. He glanced at me and Newt before turning to Sheila, and I flinched at the anger I saw in his gaze. The next moment, I felt answering rage surge within me. How dare he act upset right now. I couldn't believe he wanted to make everything about him when we needed to focus on Carson. He acted upset now when he'd had months—months!—to discuss a relationship with me and decided to roam northern Canada instead. Ugh. I wasn't sure why I'd ever found him attractive. Tony was...exhausting.

Sheila gestured toward the car and pantomimed driving then held up her hands in the universal questioning gesture.

"Newt?" I said. "How are we going to get back to the hotel?"

He frowned. "Well, definitely not in the car. Um. We could just glide there?"

"Actually," I paused as an idea began to coalesce. "Do we even need to go back? I mean you and I can't sleep in a hotel room. We'd fall through the floor as soon as we fell asleep and stopped focusing. I guess we could sleep on the bare ground. Maybe we could stay here at Mindspring. We can make sure nothing else happens tonight."

Maybe I could stay in Carson's room. Watch him. I could stay up all night to make sure he was okay and no one hurt him before we rescued him. At the very thought, I gave a huge yawn. Stupid red-eye flight, I needed to stay awake. I wished for some incorporeal coffee.

"Jules," said Newt, "If we stay here, what happens when we shift back into the real world? We just all of a sudden pop into view in the middle of the lawn or standing in the Mindspring house?"

"Damn it. I wish we knew exactly how long the spell will last."

"Yeah, twelve to twenty-four hours is a pretty large time span. More certainty would be good."

"Still," I said. "I don't want to leave Carson. Now that we know where he is, I want to stay here and watch over him. I don't want to go to the hotel and leave him alone again."

"Okay. We stay here."

I typed the message to Sheila, who proceeded to have an argument with Tony about it, an argument that ended with Tony turning his back on her and stalking off toward the car. She gave me her biggest I've-got-this smile, flipped her blonde hair behind her shoulders, and walked after Tony to slide into the driver's seat. Before they drove away, she mouthed a distinct "be careful" to us both.

Without needing to confer, Newt and I both drifted into the house and up to the bedroom where Carson still slept. I peered over the crib at my toddler, wishing more than anything to touch him, to smell his head, to hold his lax sleeping form against me. Damn it. I reached out a hand and traced his cheek in the air. I watched his chest rise and fall with his breaths, watched his pulse beat in a small vein that crossed the side of his forehead. He was okay. I would make sure he was okay.

"Jules," Newt said, "Since we know the wraiths aren't a threat right now and you're here watching Carson, I'm going to check out all the other rooms in the house. See if I can find out anything more about DeVossen."

I nodded and fought the urge to reach for him— something solid in this otherwise intangible place.

"Hey," he said. "I'll be back in a few. Don't worry."

****

I discovered I could float on my side and rest. My eyes kept sliding closed in spite of my best intentions to stay awake, and I wished I could pace or something. Floating aimlessly around the room didn't help me stay awake. After about half an hour, I started wondering where Newt was and why he hadn't returned yet.

The door to Carson's room opened.

"You're back," I said, then realized Newt wouldn't be able to move a door.

I cursed and started to zoom backward toward the window, but I didn't get there before the man—the Pneumaphage—came into the room.

I froze.

The Pneumaphage didn't even look in my direction. He walked over to Carson in the crib.

"Don't you dare," I said. "Get away from him. What are you doing?"

I knew he couldn't hear me—if he couldn't see me, he couldn't hear me—but the words poured out anyway.

I grabbed my knives and moved closer. Futile. I knew it was futile. I couldn't stop him from doing anything he wanted—I wasn't able to interact with him at all.

"Newt!" I yelled at the top of my lungs.

The man frowned and looked at Carson. He didn't touch him. He didn't do anything else. He looked at him then turned and left the room, pulling the door shut. I zipped through the door after him and followed as he went back to his bedroom. He climbed back into bed, placed his glasses on the bedside table, and turned off the light.

"Julie?" Newt called from the hallway.

"In here."

"Are you okay?" Newt said as he floated next to me.

"Yeah. I just thought…The Pneumaphage came in to look at Carson. I thought he was going to hurt him."

"Is Carson all right?"

"Yeah, I guess he was just checking on him before going to sleep."

The Pneumaphage's actions seemed so parental I felt even angrier than before. I knew he didn't care about my son. He just wanted to use him for some evil pneumaphagy purpose.

"Damn him," I said.

"I guess he can't see us, then?" Newt asked. "That's a good piece of information." Newt moved in front of the Pneumaphage's bed and snapped his fingers then called out, "Hey, Pneumaphage." DeVossen didn't move. Newt shrugged. "Okay. So he may have some specific link to the wraiths, but he can't just perceive everything that's incorporeal."

"Yeah." I slowly floated out of the Pneumaphage's room and back to Carson.

"Jules, we should get some rest," said Newt. "No idea what we're up against tomorrow."

"Okay."

"I think we should go outside and try to find a soft spot on the ground to sleep for a while."

"What if something happens? What if..." I looked at Carson, lying so still in the crib. Hot tears flooded into my eyes and I blinked wildly to keep them from trickling down my face. I crossed my arms across my chest to keep myself from reaching out to my son.

"We could rest right near the door. We could even split up—one of us at the front door and one of us at the back."

"Newt." I shook my head. "As long as we're incorporeal, we wouldn't even hear them if something did happen. And they could walk right through us. DeVossen could pick Carson up, walk right through my sleeping body, and take him God knows where."

Newt floated closer.

"I know you're worried," he said. "I'm worried, too. But DeVossen's sleeping. He's unlikely to get out of bed in the middle of the night and do anything at all. If we don't get some rest, I'm not sure we'll be able to do what needs to be done tomorrow. How about we take turns? You sleep for a few hours while I stand watch in Carson's room then we switch."

"Okay."

Newt went with me to find a place to rest then pretended to tuck me in on the patch of grass I'd chosen to hover above. I grabbed his hand as he turned to leave.

"Newt? Are you mad?"

"Mad?" he echoed. "No."

"Then..." I gestured between the two of us.

Newt sighed. He sat cross-legged next to me, hovering just above the ground. "I'm not going to fight for you, Jules. I know there's something between you and Tony. There's been some kind of attraction since the moment you two met. I guess I thought you'd made your choice and you didn't want to be with him. But now I'm not sure you know what you want."

"I do know what I want," I said.

"Do you?"

I started to speak again, but he held up a hand to stop me.

"Don't answer now," he said. "If you and I are going to date, if we're going to be more than friends, I need you to be absolutely sure I'm the one you want. Not Tony. I don't want to play games or have some long, strung-out soap opera drama. I'll understand if you decide you want to be with him. I know he's pack. I just don't want things to go any further until you know for sure, one way or another."

I gazed at him, blue eyes dark and serious in the night.

He squeezed my hand and moved away, promising to wake me in four hours so we could trade watch over my Carson. My mind whirled with a mess of fear, anxiety, and confusion. I didn't think I would sleep.

Chapter Fifteen

To my relief, Tim arrived with Sheila and Tony in the morning. I gave him my biggest smile, waved, and then added some jazz hands to properly express my gratitude. Sheila pointed to herself then to Mindspring. I nodded.

We'd passed an uneventful night with some amount of rest. Carson still lay in his crib with no changes at all. Still asleep, which I could hardly believe. I pushed the worry out of my mind and reminded myself we were doing everything we could to rescue him. Newt zipped toward the second floor, where I knew he'd watch Carson while I watched Sheila. Tony and Tim pulled on darkness and waited on the front porch for whatever happened next.

Sheila walked up to the door with a flip of her long blonde hair and a quick straightening of her coat. I watched as she set her shoulders into a relaxed stance and adopted her brighten-the-world smile—the one that stopped most people in their tracks and charmed the surliest of clerks in any store. I hoped she wouldn't pour it on too thick. She needed to act like a panic-ridden woman who believed in past life regression, for Pete's sake.

Sheila pushed open the front door. No shield, nothing stood in her way, either because an appointment served as an invitation or because the shield dropped during the day. The front room looked even more peaceful than last night with the two salt lamps glowing pink and a fountain now burbling in a corner. I could actually hear the water in the silence of my alternate dimension since it was a natural element, and I said a quiet thank you for the relief from silence. Sheila hovered in the entranceway for a moment before sitting in an armchair. I saw her take in the room. A dark-haired woman with copious freckles and winged eyeliner—an employee who we'd watched arrive about an hour earlier—came in from the hallway to greet Sheila and hand her some paperwork. She bustled out of the room and came back a few moments later with a cup of hot tea in a lavender-colored mug.

I hovered over Sheila's shoulder and noticed she wrote fictional contact information on the intake papers. Under "Reason for Visit," she wrote, "anxiety and a change in my aura—need to get back in balance." I snorted.

She handed the paperwork in and drank some tea while we waited.

When Dr. DeVossen walked into the room, I said out loud, "Oh, come on, now." Today, he wore one of those hippy-looking tunic tops, billowy azure cotton embroidered at the neckline with bright gold thread. I used to live in Ashland, Oregon so I was accustomed to the sight of wanna-be hippies, but not ones also purporting to be doctors. With a name like Mindspring, though, what did I expect?

DeVossen took Sheila's hand and held it for a too-long moment, his gaze fixed on her face, his large blue eyes seeming to well with empathy and well-wishes. He reminded me of a certain type of guy I would have found so sensitive and enlightened when I was about nineteen years old. The type of guy who was actually rather predatory and narcissistic but knew how to sway naive women into falling for him.

Creepy.

Sheila laughed and smiled, but I knew her well enough to see the lines of distaste around her eyes that signaled she wished she could yank her hand away from this guy. Instead, she followed him down the hall and into one of the smaller therapy rooms, with me floating close behind.

One side of the room held a desk and chair, computer screen turned on but locked, papers and books stacked on nearby shelves. The other end of the room contained a sitting area with a couch, armchair, and recliner surrounding a coffee table covered in a tapestry with candles, polished rocks, and a set of varied bells arranged on top. DeVossen indicated Sheila should take a seat on the recliner, which she did. They spoke for a while. Sheila gestured expansively and the man nodded while he took notes. I tried to read what he wrote, but he must have been using some sort of shorthand system because I couldn't decipher it. Sheila's gaze darted in my direction a couple of times, but she primarily kept her eyes—and her charm—on DeVossen. After a while, she nodded and reclined her seat. I hovered in the corner, wishing I could hear what Dr. DeVossen said to her. Sheila's eyes closed and her breathing became slower, deeper. DeVossen picked up one of the bells from his table and struck it with a soft mallet. Once, twice. He struck a larger bell then continued to pick up different sizes and ring them every thirty seconds or so. I tried to read his lips as he continued to speak but gave up. Damn this aspect of being incorporeal! After about five minutes, DeVossen leaned forward, hovering over Sheila. His speaking paused and he put down the bell in his hand.

Sheila didn't move.

I floated closer.

"What the hell are you doing, DeVossen?" I said out loud into the silence.

Sheila looked asleep.

DeVossen nodded once, turned, and slid open his desk drawer to withdraw a small jar. A jar...

I zoomed forward. Okay. Yeah. The jar had a tiny wraith in it.

"Sheila?" I said, even though I knew she couldn't hear me. "Sheila!" I reached out to grab her shoulder, to shake her awake, but slowly drew back and cursed my helplessness.

Sheila continued to lie motionless in the leather recliner. Her chest moved slowly up and down with her breathing, but other than that she was utterly still.

DeVossen reached over to a side table and picked up three candles I hadn't noticed before. Gray candles like the ones around the wraith-pen in the basement. He placed them in a triangle around Sheila. One on the coffee table in front of her, one on the windowsill to her right, one on the table to her left. He lit the candles as I watched in horror, wondering what would come next and how I should intervene.

He reached inside the triangle of candles and unscrewed the lid of the jar. It looked like a Mason jar, which was horribly incongruous given the nature of the dark, writhing mass inside. As soon as he unscrewed it, I heard the wraith's high-pitched keen. I'd not seen a wraith this small before. I think I could have reached out and cupped it in one palm. Not that I wanted to. Because, regardless of its size, it was a wraith and looked like something one should smash into oblivion, not hold in one's hand.

The wraith squeezed out of the jar and hovered for a moment. Its inky, miniature pseudopods writhed in the air—several shooting with purpose toward me. I drew back, afraid to draw the Pneumaphage's attention. After a second of internal debate, I pulled out my knives. I would kill it, if Sheila was in danger. A shrill and tinny hum emanated from the small wraith, interspersed with static-like crackles as it flashed and turned within the triangle of candles. DeVossen spoke and gestured with his hands, oddly formal movements. The wraith jerked in response and sped toward Sheila, where it hovered over her face. One flickering tentacle reached out and touched her forehead. The wraith pulsed and grew brighter, like it swallowed, like the stretching of a snake's scales as it reshaped its body to force down a mouse. Sheila's breathing slowed and her skin lost a bit of luster.

Shit. Should I...? My hand tensed around the knife, while my mind raced through options. If I killed it, he'd know I was there and I wasn't ready to fight him alone. But I couldn't allow the wraith to hurt Sheila...

The wraith retreated while I stood there paralyzed with indecision.

It had nearly doubled in size, now approaching the size of a small soccer ball though much less regular in shape.

DeVossen's mouth moved as he intoned something. His hands sketched symbols in the air and slowly, slowly the wraith moved toward the Mason jar and stuffed itself in. This time, the wraith filled the jar to capacity—its swirling blackness encompassing every square inch of the space. DeVossen reached into the triangle and placed the lid on the jar. Then he blew out the three candles. He picked up the jar and brought it close to him, holding it like I would a baby or, well, let's face it, my first cup of coffee in the morning. His hands cradled the jar as he moved it toward his face. With his eyes closed, head canted toward the pulsating glass jar, he spoke. My wolf eyes widened in alarm as I watched the wraith shrink again.

As wraith shrank, DeVossen seemed to glow. His face looked exalted, like a televangelist in prayer, and when he opened his eyes, the blue of them nearly dazzled my senses. The man hummed with energy. The wraith bumped around in its glass prison and DeVossen patted the jar, as if acknowledging a dog. He put the jar back in his desk drawer.

I lowered the knife in my hand but didn't put it away. Sheila continued to lie in the recliner. Her face looked pallid and her breath hitched into a huge sigh before falling back into the even rhythm of sleep. I thought she would be okay. I hoped she would be okay.

Wait a second. If the wraith was trapped in the Mason jar that meant...

I reached my hand through the wood of the desk drawer and groped until I felt it—cool, slick glass under my fingers. The jar existed in at least two dimensions and must have been spelled to imprison that wraith.

I really wanted to talk to Newt, but I didn't want to leave the room until I knew DeVossen had no further tricks up his sleeves.

The Pneumaphage pulled out his cell phone and started tapping away, like he was a regular guy and this was a normal day and he hadn't just sucked life out of my friend via wraith. I hovered at his back and looked over his shoulder. Social media. Yeah. He was on some social media site scrolling past memes and family pictures and random posts. Okay. Awesome. This was normal.

After about ten minutes, DeVossen glanced at the time and clicked his phone off. He leaned forward to look closely at Sheila and for a moment—for a sickening moment—I thought he was going to reach out and touch her. Luckily, he sat back in his seat. DeVossen picked up the largest bell and rang it three times, then clapped his hands together. Sheila startled and opened her eyes. I saw a puzzled look cross her face and her gaze flicked to me before she nodded at the Pneumaphage and carried on a short conversation. She yawned three times during their exchange, then they both stood up, shook hands, and Sheila walked out of the office with slow steps. After shooting DeVossen one more glance, I floated after her and out of the house.

Sheila stopped on the front walk to talk for a few minutes with a middle-aged woman walking into Mindspring. I floated behind the other woman and gestured impatiently to Sheila, mouthing, "Come on!" I pulled out my cell phone, frantically punched letters, and waved it at her. She shot me a glance with one eyebrow slightly raised then wrapped up her discussion and parted from the next client.

Sheila got into the rental car and I zipped through the metal door onto—well, partly through—the seat next to her. I held up my phone, which said:

Are you okay?

Yes, she typed back. *But what the hell happened?*

He stole part of your life force! He put you to sleep, unleashed a wraith to eat you, and then sucked the energy right out of the wraith and into himself.

Sheila looked at me in horror.

Do you feel okay? I typed.

Sheila paused in thought then shrugged. *Really tired. That woman on the walkway told me she feels totally relaxed after a session, that she always sleeps well the night after. She said DeVossen completely removes her anxiety and leaves her at peace. She called him a miracle worker.*

Yeah, if the miracle uses his wraiths to slowly devour his clients.

Something moved outside the window next to me and I jumped—would have hit my head if I weren't incorporeal.

Tony. He stood just outside my window, his amber eyes looking right at me. I gave him a weak smile and he gestured for us to unlock the doors.

I tried, and my hand passed right through the car. Oh.

Sheila clicked the locks. Tony yanked the door open and got into the car. Tim stood outside. Sheila spoke to them and, I assumed, brought them up to speed. Tim placed his hand on Sheila's shoulder, somehow expressing more love and tenderness with that small gesture than most people ever showed. Her hand crept up to cover his. I watched their mouths move for a few minutes then gave up in frustration.

I'd go find Newt. I could talk to him.

Chapter Sixteen

I floated through the car door and toward the house. I was not running away from Tony, I reminded myself firmly. Not at all. I just needed to find Newt. Not being about to communicate with people or interact with the physical world was becoming more of a drag than an advantage. I needed to talk to someone. I needed to do something. We needed to rescue Carson.

"Newt!" I yelled. My voice rang out in the incorporeal realm. He'd promised to stay with Carson while I watched Sheila's appointment, so when he didn't answer right away, I moved up toward the second floor and cruised through the wall into that bedroom.

Newt turned toward me from his spot by the crib where Carson lay sleeping. Still. Now that I watched DeVossen with Sheila, I thought I knew why.

"Jules? You look pale," Newt said. "What happened?"

"Sheila had her appointment with DeVossen. He put her to sleep—hypnotized her or something—and brought out a very small wraith." I gestured with my hands to indicate peach-sized. "Which drained her life force. And the Pneumaphage absorbed it from the wraith."

"Wait. What?"

"I know."

Newt listened intently. Halfway through, he took

my hand and clasped it. The feel of his skin on mine grounded me. Together, we would face it all. "So," I said, as I finished relating the details, "I think that's why he kidnapped Carson. I think he's doing the same thing—using wraiths to drain Carson and then, in turn, draining the energy from the wraiths into himself. Except he could take even more, knowing that Carson will heal himself within a short period of time. He could drain my baby, allow him to heal back to a usable state, and drain him again."

After I finished, Newt and I stood and looked at my son. Deep shadows blotted the fair skin near his eyes and he looked almost transparent around the edges, as if he faded from sight.

"DeVossen's using the wraiths like...batteries or something. Charging them and storing them in his force field. Using them when he wants the power," I said.

"That's a creepy image."

"But true."

"I think you're right," said Newt. "Carson's such a strong Were. DeVossen can take more energy from him than a regular person. Or even a regular Werewolf. And he heals quicker."

I looked down at Carson, sleeping so still.

"How did he know about Carson? He's not a Were and Weres don't talk about their own. How did he know to come to Wyoming and kidnap my son? Carson's powerful and he's helpless. Just what the Pneumaphage wants. A toddler. God damn him. Damn all of them— damn everyone who wants to use Carson instead of letting him grow up and become his own person."

"Including the Weres?" Newt asked.

I frowned and didn't answer, suddenly aware

something had changed. In the next moment, Newt's eyes widened and I realized what happened. I could hear. Traffic on the road outside the house. Footsteps downstairs along with the creak of turn-of-the-century hardwood floors.

Speaking of floors, I felt solid ground under my feet.

"Newt," I whispered.

"Yeah," he said. "It's good to be back. But now we've gotta get out of here."

Wait! I sucked in a breath as the enormity of my return to corporeal form slammed into me.

Carson.

I could touch Carson.

I held my breath and reached for my son. When my hands touched him, felt his solid form, tears formed in my eyes and I had to blink rapidly and swallow through a tight throat.

"Hey, Carson, hey, sweetie," I said in a low voice. I stroked his cheek, felt the softness of his baby skin against my fingers.

Carson stirred in his sleep and his mouth made sucking noises before he lapsed into stillness again. I picked him up, his body lax and warm and heavy in my arms. Balancing him on my shoulder, I grabbed his pacifier from the crib and held it to his lips until he gave a sleepy sigh and opened his mouth to take it.

"Okay," I said to Newt. "Let's get out of here."

I called darkness to cover the three of us, coaxing shadows from the corners the room, from the air itself until we were wreathed and hidden. Now we just needed to stay silent and make it out of the house without encountering the Pneumaphage. I didn't want to get into a paranormal fight with my sleeping son on my shoulder.

With a nod at Newt, I opened the door, thankful it didn't creak on its hinges. I stepped into the hallway, Carson snuggled against me, holding him tight with both arms. Padding down the hall, I felt power radiating off Newt, walking close behind me, and I knew he readied his flames, just in case.

At the top of the staircase, we paused and I listened, giving silent thanks for my heightened Were senses. Voices murmured in the waiting room, someone's fingers clicked on a keyboard in a downstairs office, and I heard a male voice—DeVossen?—coming from one of the treatment rooms. At least four people in the house, then. I whispered as much to Newt then crept down the stairs with him close behind. I stayed by the edge of the steps, but nonetheless a board creaked loudly underfoot. We froze and I pulled more darkness, hoping to obscure us in a haze that would confuse the eye of anyone who heard us. After a few moments, we continued.

When we reached the main floor, I pointed my head in the direction of the back door and Newt nodded agreement. We snuck down the hallway. At that moment, Carson stirred in my arms. His eyelids fluttered and I stopped in my tracks to look down at my son. He blinked once, twice, then spit his pacifier onto the floor, opened his mouth, took a huge gulp of air, and screamed.

At the first sound from Carson, Newt whirled around and looked at me with frantic eyes.

"Shhh!" I bounced him on my hip. "Carson, it's okay. I'm here. Settle down."

Newt gestured wildly down the hall.

"I know, I know," I said under my breath. I broke into a run, just as a door opened behind us with such force it crashed into the wall.

Fire wreathed Newt's hands. I looked back over my shoulder to see DeVossen. He stood in the hall, looming taller than his actual height, suddenly menacing in his blue hippie-top. The air crackled with power as he stared down the hall into the darkness I furiously summoned to obscure his vision. Carson let out another ear-piercing scream, his pale face turning red with rage. I felt my arms prickle as he tried to gather power—I knew he wanted to shift form, but he didn't—he didn't, because he was too drained. I'd never known him not to shift when he wanted; alarm rose next to my relief. All this raced through me, time stretching out as I bolted down the hall toward the back door, toward where Newt stood, toward escape.

DeVossen spoke, spat out words I didn't understand over the blood pounding in my ears.

Out of nothing, a wraith appeared in front of me, in front of the back door, between me and Newt. I crashed against the wall to stop myself from running right into it. Carson sobbed and grabbed at me with cold hands and one part of me soothed him, bounced him, made meaningless shushing noises, while the rest of me fumbled with a numb, panicked hand toward the knife at my side. Newt released a stream of fire at the wraith, but the flames passed through it—of course they did, of course. Incorporeal. The wraith reached out with ropey tentacles of smoke and malice, latched onto Newt and pulsed as it sucked his life into itself. Newt jerked.

"Get out!" I yelled. "Go! Just go."

He looked at me with wide eyes—wide with pain, with fear, with exactly what I wasn't sure. Then he pulled away from the wraith, yanked open the door, and pushed his way out.

I stabilized Carson on my hip and gripped my knife. I held onto the darkness for dear life—literal life. The murky haze of eye-distorting illusion and darkness was the only reason DeVossen hadn't attacked me. The wraith didn't need to see to attack me. It sensed my life force.

Carson buried his head against my shoulder and I held onto him fiercely. No matter what else happened, I would not be separated from my son again.

The wraith spun and pulsed like a bloom of squid ink in the air. Three tentacles shot out, trailing black sparks and reaching for me, for me and Carson. I pivoted to shield Carson and held my knife at the ready, waiting, just waiting for the wraith to come in range. My teeth were bared, and I felt a growl rise up my throat. How dare the wraith attack me and my son?

I lunged, slicing with my knife through the air and through the closest tentacle. I severed the tentacle and it popped into smoke. Sickening, bruise-like colors chased across the wraith and I swore I almost heard it shriek, even though it was completely silent on this plane. Another tentacle trailed across my arm and I almost lost my footing as a sudden wave of nausea and fatigue hit me. The darkness around me faltered and I pulled on the power of the moon to strengthen myself. I jerked away from the wraith and shook my head to clear it then cut across two more tentacles. The wraith jerked, and I seized the moment to run. I careened against the wall as I raced to get past the wraith. I banged my left arm hard, but I managed to keep Carson out of the wraith's reach. A flurry of tentacles flew at me and I screamed in anger, screamed to push away the grayness that flooded my vision. Then, somehow, I passed the wraith, was at the back door, out the door, stumbling down the back steps.

Newt caught me by the arm, his hands so hot they snapped me out of the wraith-induced fog.

"Run!" he said.

We fled across the yard and ran straight to the car where it sat wreathed in the distortion of Were darkness.

Eliza stood next to the car with Sheila, Tim, and Tony.

I stopped short, my brain catching up to the messages from my nose and eyes.

For an irrational moment, I felt a surge of fear greater than that inspired by the wraith, fear that Eliza was here to take Carson from me, fear that she came to claim him. I clutched him tighter as my heart pounded.

"No time," said Newt. "We've gotta get out of here!"

Tim assessed us quickly then gestured Eliza and Tony to a black compact car parked farther down the street.

"Sheila," he said, and she nodded and slid into the driver's seat. Newt and I got into the back, Tim slammed the front door shut after himself, and the car bucked as Sheila stepped on the accelerator. The wheels jolted over the cobblestone street and Sheila sped away, away, away from Mindspring.

"Julie? Report," said Tim.

I nodded, still trying to catch my breath. I twisted

back to stare in the direction of Mindspring, waiting, just waiting for a swarm of wraiths to pour out after us.

But nothing came.

Sheila made several quick turns and merged onto a larger road, putting distance between us and DeVossen.

I realized I was panting through bared teeth and closed my mouth, sought composure. I held Carson to me so tightly he squawked, which made me laugh, the kind of laugh that's really half-crying. I took slow breaths to stifle my sudden giggles and collapsed back into the seat. We'd done it. We were safe.

"Julie? Newt?" said Tim. Sheila's gaze kept flicking to me in the rearview mirror.

"Right," I said, calming myself and trying to stay focused. "Okay. We got out. We got Carson. But the Pneumaphage knows he escaped and he sent a wraith after us and it almost got us—it touched us both—but I used my knife and I somehow got around it and, well, here we are. We got out."

"Sheila, let's get someplace safe and debrief with the whole story," Tim said.

I closed my eyes and allowed myself a moment to enjoy the weight of my son on my lap. We'd done it. We saved Carson and everything was going to be okay now. I slid down in the seat and focused on Carson, Newt next to me, the comforting scent of Sheila—my Sheila who made everything right. "Thanks for coming, Tim. Thank you. Wait." I sat up straight. "Was that Eliza? Did I just make that up? Is Eliza here?"

"Eliza's here," said Sheila.

"Why?"

"Now that's a good question. We don't know much more than you do, Jules," Sheila said. "She pulled up

about five minutes before you ran out of the house—
just long enough to establish a cordial detente and not
long enough to talk about anything else. She and Tony
almost fought, but the moment passed."

Carson collapsed against my shoulder, closed his
eyes, and fell asleep again. I pushed my worry away.
We'd rescued him. He would be fine, right?

We pulled into the parking lot of our hotel,
followed by the other car. As soon as we stopped, I
hopped out of the car—still holding Carson—and
strode over to Eliza's door. Newt stood at my back.

"How did you get here?" I asked.

She shrugged, her fawn-colored ponytail moving
behind her as she got out of the car and leaned against
the side. "You're not the only ones who can book a
flight."

Tony slammed the passenger door and walked
around the car to the rest of us. The air crackled with
energy.

"Eliza, are you here for the pack? Or for yourself?"
I asked.

For friendship? For me and for Carson, I wanted to
add. Or for Lily Rose? For blind obedience or for what
was right? I hated the sharp note of anxiety in my voice,
hated knowing her wolf senses could read my worry
and hurt, even as I read the stress in her own sweat, her
stance that looked so studiously casual. Tony stood as if
ready to pounce.

"Both?" Eliza looked at me, her brown eyes dark
and serious. I couldn't tell what she wanted to
communicate.

"She can't be trusted," Tony said.

"And you can?" Sheila asked from behind me.

Tony growled deep in the back of his throat and I felt his power rise, prickling the hairs on the back of my neck.

"No, I mean it," Sheila said. "I'm tired of tiptoeing around this. Tony Blythe, you think an awful lot revolves around you. You swoop in as if to rescue Julie from the Salamanders last fall, but then you run away when she might actually need an ally to stand with her and face the Greybull pack. You run hundreds of miles when Carson goes missing and then you act like you can waltz back in as the hero of her life or something. You and I both know if the external threat were removed, you'd run right back to Saskatchewan just to prevent anyone from actually relying on you. Just to escape any actual deep, emotional connection. You want to be the hero, but you don't want to stick around for the day to day. You ran out on your brother and sister when your parents died and you haven't stopped running since. And you say Eliza can't be trusted?"

I stared at Sheila in shock. She didn't even sound angry. She uttered this scathing criticism absolutely matter of fact, as if she explained a theory to her college students.

"So. I ask again. Can we trust you, Tony? Are you here to fight all our fights and be a true part of our team? Weres, 'Manders, and Witches alike?" She pointed to me, to Newt, then to herself. "Or are you going to pout about your lost chance at romance, posture like the alpha for a while, and then run off again to avoid anything truly important?"

The tension stretched to the breaking point and I opened my mouth to say something, anything to dispel the strain. But before I could think what to say, Tony shifted form between one moment and the next, landing on the pavement as a huge, black wolf that raced across the parking lot and disappeared between buildings.

"Yeah. That's what I thought," said Sheila. She looked at me. "You okay, Jules? I won't apologize. That was long overdue."

"I'm fine. I mean. I think I'm fine. Do you think he'll come back?"

"Tony's been taking care of himself for a long time," said Newt. "He knows where we're staying if he wants to find us." Newt gradually released his gathered power so the burnished copper gleam of his freckles faded and the temperature of the air around us dropped.

"I didn't know you felt so strongly," I said to Sheila.

She shrugged. "Didn't want to say too much while you toyed with the idea of being besotted with him."

I thought about her turn of phrase for a moment. I glanced at Newt, who looked right at me. His blue eyes seemed to understand me better than I understood myself. I smiled. He winked and I felt him release the last of his power. His insouciance showed in his grin, the kind that made his eyes scrunch up and emphasized the freckles across his nose.

"I guess it built up, then," I said to Sheila. "Your anger at Tony, I mean."

"We have no time for allies that aren't going to be there for us as we rebuild the world, Jules."

"Is that what we're doing? Rebuilding the world?" I asked.

Sheila leaned toward me and ticked off points on her finger. "First, we dismantled pack hierarchy. You walked away from the pack—and not like the typical lone wolf who flees for solitude. You're more like a pack refugee fleeing the pack to find something better. To *make* something better. Second, you assembled your own team: Weres, Salamanders, Witches. You rally people not because of what they are, but because of what they believe. Third...Well, I'm not sure what the third is, but I'm sure there's a third."

"Third," Newt said, "you value humans as much as those of us with paranormal powers. Humans and humanity."

I looked between the two of them, humbled by their confidence in me, gratified they so clearly understood what I believed. Tim stood just behind Sheila, silent, but a solid source of support.

"The world doesn't need rebuilding," said Eliza.

I spun around to face her. My hackles rose with her words and I knew she felt the surge of anger. Our Were powers stretched and collided, putting us both on edge. Newt took two steps closer to my side.

Sheila—reverting to her diplomat role, the role she'd abdicated during her lecture to Tony—said, "Not here. Let's go inside, make sure Carson's okay, and plan our next steps. Eliza, you still have some explaining to do. We all have questions."

Eliza nodded. I could tell from her clenched jaw that she wanted to say more, but she mutely agreed and followed us into the hotel.

First things first.

Carson.

Chapter Seventeen

As soon as we closed the hotel room door firmly behind us, I laid Carson on the bed and attempted to rouse him. I called his name, talked to him, stroked his face, and rubbed his chubby, dimpled limbs. When that had no effect, I unsnapped the front of his footed sleeper. The cold air seemed to work for a moment. Carson stirred. His eyes fluttered a few times before they closed again.

"Why won't he stay awake? This sleep is unnatural. Do you think..." My voice trailed off as I refused to finish the sentence, refused to give utterance to all the anxieties swirling through my head.

Maybe Carson would never wake up. Maybe the wraiths ate his soul. Maybe he would die.

I told myself to stop the spiraling anxiety. I'd seen wraiths feed on people—Sheila, during the appointment, Eliza and Ian during their fight with the wraith. They recovered. I'd felt a wraith's touch myself and I was okay. I looked at Sheila as she sat on the other bed, craning my neck to see as much of her face as possible. She still had faint lines of stress and worry on her forehead, and her skin looked pale. But, really, I could hardly tell that a wraith snacked on her. As I studied her, she yawned and blinked her blue eyes. But she was fine, fine to tell off our resident sulky Werewolf, and fine to plan the next stage of our escape.

Carson would be fine, too.

"Carson," I tried again. "Carson, Mama's here. Carson, big boy, can you wake up?"

Finally, his eyes opened again and focused on me. His face scrunched up and he let out a wail. He sat up on the bed and held his arms out toward me then fell forward into me with a sort of desperate lunge.

"Yes, sweetie, I'm here." I scooped him up. This time, when I held him, he held me back. He still cried, not an upset cry, but as if the trauma of the last days ran out of him at the sight of me. I let him cry until he stopped, patting him on the back, telling him he was safe now.

"Do you think he's hungry?" Sheila asked.

"Probably," I said. "Who knows when he ate last and he needs to rebuild his strength so food's always a good idea."

Sheila offered a few packets of crackers from her purse—she was always prepared—which Carson eagerly crunched. He sprayed cracker crumbs all over the bed, but I didn't mind. We'd go out for a meal soon but first? I had questions.

"Eliza, you said earlier you're here for both yourself and the pack. Did Lily ask you to come?"

Eliza sat on the edge of the bed with her spine straight and her feet planted evenly on the ground. I saw the lines of tension in her body. She shrugged.

"I wanted to come."

I must have made some disparaging expression because Eliza continued more fiercely.

"I did; I wanted to come. I know you don't always understand the pack—how could you when you lived as a dark moon for so long—but you know they want what's in your best interest because, in the long run, whatever's in the best interest of the pack is in your best interest."

I stared at her, so sickened by her logic I couldn't even respond.

Eliza continued, "Lily wanted me to come, both so I could help rescue Carson and so I could help you understand. You're part of our pack. We care about both of you"—she gestured at me and my son—"and the pack watches out for its own. We don't need to involve the Council every time there's a minor threat—it's better to take care of things ourselves."

" 'Minor threat'?" I repeated.

"You got him back, and it's only been two days. He's going to be fine—look at him chowing down on those crackers. Weres heal quickly. We'll go back to Greybull. After we've proven Carson's not an easy target, I doubt this Pneumaphage will bother us again."

"Wait," Sheila cut in. "You think we should go back to Greybull right now? And leave this guy to prey on the people of Evansville?"

"We're not the police force of the world, Sheila," Eliza said. "It's not our job to neutralize all paranormal threats. He's obviously established here, and he's kept himself pretty low key. We needed to protect our own, and we did." She pulled out her phone. "We should try to get back to Greybull as soon as possible. Hopefully today." She frowned at the screen and typed rapidly with her thumbs.

"No," I said.

"What?"

"No."

"What do you mean, 'no'? You rescued Carson. We

need to get him back to the pack where he can be safe."

"We can't leave while this Pneumaphage endangers all the people in this area. Besides, I don't trust the pack to keep him safe. They didn't keep him safe before," I said.

Eliza drew in a long breath. "Okay, I'm going to ignore the last part of that because I know you're still mad and I refuse to get into an argument about the pack right now. But you're responsible for Carson, Julie. Not the whole world," she said.

"How can I teach Carson to live up to his potential if he sees me turning my back on people who need me? How can I go back to Greybull now? Back to life in the pack…going through musty archives, struggling to draw a drop of water from the ground, watching people stare at Carson as if he's God's gift to Werewolves, changing diapers. Back to my daily life. All the while, here in Evansville, DeVossen will use wraiths as tools to drain people's life force. This whole community is at risk from his sham holistic healing set-up. And who knows who he'll target next?"

"It's not your job to stop him," said Eliza. "Why don't we get out of the way, report the situation to the Council, and let them take care of it?"

"So now you want to involve the Council?" My voice rose in anger. I felt Newt go perfectly still next to me. Carson stopped combing the bedspread for cracker crumbs and looked at me with his dark eyes wide in alarm. "Shh, Carson, it's okay. No one's going to hurt you." I picked up my son and plopped him into my lap, feeling his toddler weight against me like a reminder of everything that really mattered.

People. All people. Not just Carson. Not just the

pack. Not just the paranormal world.

"Does the Council police paranormal activities that hurt people? Not Weres, humans," I asked. Eliza shifted in her seat, and I realized I didn't need her to answer after all.

"The Council stops rogue Weres," I said. "They intervene if there's a risk of Werewolves being discovered by humans. But they don't operate as any sort of paranormal peacekeeping force. Do they?"

We all knew I was right.

"Sheila? What about Witches?" I asked.

"Covens keep a close eye on their communities. We'd interfere with black magic or Pneumaphagy, but on a local level. We're more like anarchist collectives. No hierarchy equivalent to Weres. But most Witches would agree with you and I certainly do. We can't leave while the Pneumaphage preys on people."

"Newt, would the Salamander Master authorize an attack against DeVossen?"

He shook his head. "I'm not sure, Jules. This isn't the same as fighting the Eclipsers last fall. They were our problem to solve. Most of the time, 'Manders try to steer clear of other paranormal races. We have enough to deal with policing our own and trying to improve our birth rate so our kind doesn't die out."

"So, who protects humans?" I asked.

"Humans have been doing just fine without us watching out for them," said Eliza. "In case you haven't noticed, they run the world."

"The people DeVossen drains don't run the world," I said. "These people need us."

"Seriously, Julie?" Eliza stood up and crossed her arms in front of her. "You're the mom of the most powerful Werewolf we've known."

"Would you stop calling him that? His name is Carson and it shouldn't matter if he's some uber-Were or a regular fourteen-month-old human."

Eliza continued without a pause. "Your job is to keep him safe."

"I'm staying. Carson's staying. I'm finding some way to stop DeVossen. Who's with me?"

"You know we are, Jules," said Newt, speaking for both him and Sheila.

"Tim?" I asked.

"I'm not leaving," he said, and slung an arm around Sheila's shoulders.

Eliza stood stock still and just stared at me. Finally, she threw her hands up as if in disgust. "I'm going for a run," she said. "I'll go along to protect you all—you know I will—but I think you're making the wrong decision. I'll leave you alone to think more about it. Maybe you'll come to your senses."

After she left the hotel room, I wondered if she really wanted to go for a run, or if she just wanted privacy to call Lily and get new instructions.

"Before we 'think more about it' or make plans, I think we better get something to eat." Sheila pointed to Carson, who had stuffed a corner of a blanket in his mouth to gum.

I looked closely at her. She still looked peaked around the edges. Maybe food would help her, too.

****

Main Street, Evansville, turned out to be home to quite a number of restaurants and we soon settled in at a local Italian place. With Carson gnawing on garlic knots and the rest of us waiting for our lunch pasta specials, we discussed plans.

"Not sure if DeVossen will come looking for us or if he'll expect an attack at his base," said Sheila.

I glanced at Carson, now biting on a spoon and mumbling nonsense syllables. He looked to be recovering quickly from being kidnapped and drained by wraiths, though he still had dark shadows under his eyes. He seemed a lot more energetic than he had been. Thank all the gods.

I did not want him put in harm's way again. But I didn't have any options.

"Do you think I'm crazy for not just grabbing Carson and running back to Greybull?" I asked.

"I think you're brave. Not crazy," said Newt.

"But I'm endangering Carson."

Sheila said, "Carson's always going to be a target for anyone who fears—or wants to use—such a strong Werewolf, at least until he's old enough to use his powers to fight back. And, by the way, that will happen sooner than you think. You're raising a kid who could destroy another kid on the playground over a small disagreement. If he doesn't learn to use his power wisely—to fight for what's right rather than what's convenient or self-serving—then what kind of damage will he do? Who will be able to stop him? How better to teach him what's right than by modeling it yourself?"

I closed my eyes in gratitude for my best friend's words, which were exactly what I needed to hear.

"If there were some way to keep him out of the fight, I would," I said. "But I think we're all needed. And I'm not leaving him with Eliza—she'd probably hop on a plane and fly away with him."

"What about Tony?" Newt asked.

A beat of silence.

"I'm not even sure if Tony will come back," I finally said. "He might run all the way to Saskatchewan."

"I think he'll be back," said Newt. Sheila raised an eyebrow and gestured for him to continue. "He's fighting himself, you know. He's terrified to need anyone."

"I don't think he *does* need anyone. He lived alone as a wolf for five years. He spent a total of maybe two and a half weeks in Greybull since last fall. He hardly spent time with his sister, even," I said.

"We all need people, Jules. He just wishes he didn't. He's coming to terms with his own…humanity." Newt shook his head at the word, indicating the irony. "He's afraid."

"He would hate us to think he's afraid," I said.

"Doesn't mean he's not," said Sheila.

"He'll come back, Jules. I'd bet money on it," said Newt.

The food arrived and we all dug in. I felt like I watched health and energy flow into Sheila with the nourishment. Carson made a royal mess eating macaroni and cheese with his fingers, but I didn't care. I pushed away all thoughts of Tony and Eliza. My heart felt full, surrounded by Sheila, Tim, Newt, and my son. This was my family.

This was my pack.

"I'm not going back to live in Greybull, you know. Ever," I said.

Conversation at the table halted.

"I know," said Sheila.

"What will the Weres do?" I asked Tim.

He shook his head, spread his hands wide. His eyes looked even darker than usual, fixed on me with somberness not usually found on his mild, pleasant, you-can-trust-me face. "There's no precedent. Will you declare yourself a lone wolf and still abide by the Council's will?"

I chose my words carefully. "Not necessarily. I need to follow my own moral compass."

"They'll declare you a rogue," Tim said.

"Will they? Are those the only options? I can be part of a pack structure, I can be a lone wolf who follows all Council dictates, or else I'm a rogue and they need to neutralize me? Kill me? Would they kill me?"

"Frankly, I'm not even sure you have all those options. I don't think they'd allow you to be a lone wolf," said Tim. "You're mother to the strongest Werewolf they know. They want to keep Carson under their control. If you take him out of the pack structure, you're setting yourself up in open rebellion to the entire Were society."

"Am I?" I asked. "That's not what I want."

"I think it's exactly what you want." Tim's voice sounded more serious than I'd ever heard him.

Was this what I wanted? Did I want open rebellion against the Council? Did I imagine myself some sort of…Martin Luther, nailing tenets on the cathedral door?

I shook my head to clear it. "Okay. Never mind that right now. Let's get back to DeVossen. What are we going to do?"

"I've been thinking about it," said Newt. "If I can become incorporeal again and if we can find some way for me to penetrate that gray force field then I can destroy all the wraiths with fire. My flames seemed particularly effective against them. That might not help in the immediate fight against DeVossen, but it will prevent him from using them as magical backup. He'd be limited to whatever power he currently has."

"Good idea," said Tim. "The three of us can focus on the Pneumaphage himself."

"With Eliza or Tony, if they show up to help," I added.

"Sheila, do you have anything that can get me past that force field?" Newt asked.

"Describe the scene to me again," she said. Sheila closed her eyes, forehead creasing in concentration as she listened to Newt explain the precise set up of the room, the position of the candles, and the concentric lines encircling the shield.

"Okay," she said. Sheila reached into her purse and pulled out a butter knife, then waved it in the air. "Last night, I spelled this knife to cut through the force field surrounding Mindspring so we can enter the building."

I leaned closer to study the knife, which looked absolutely ordinary.

"I'm pretty sure this same spell will break into the wraith's prison." She slid the knife back into her purse then nicked one from the restaurant to join it. "I can spell this one when we go back to the hotel. But, Newt, as soon as you break the enclosing spell, the wraiths will scatter in all directions and attack you. You'll need to strike right away."

He nodded. I wished we had backup to send with him, but Newt was right—the rest of us were better battling the Pneumaphage on our current plane.

"Can DeVossen be killed like an ordinary human?

No super strength or regeneration?" I asked.

"He'll have whatever extra magical strength and life force the wraiths have provided him. But Pneumaphages aren't inherently regenerative or immortal or anything like that," Sheila said.

"Do you have any attack spells?" I asked Sheila, already anticipating her answer.

She shook her head. "I won't use my craft to hurt people."

Tim reached over and took her hand, while Newt and I nodded.

"I have a gun, though. And somehow, no moral qualms about attacking with normal weapons." Sheila flashed a grin and a wink. "Last night, I prepared some other spells to help us. I made good luck charms. And I made a sleeping potion, if we can get close enough to the Pneumaphage."

"Wow, you were busy."

"I slept too, Jules. No worries."

"So a sleeping potion? Like…we need to hold him down and make him drink it? How can we do that?" I asked.

"No, it works on contact. Here," Sheila said. She handed each of us a small bottle—she'd apparently emptied the hotel shampoo containers and filled them with the sleeping potion.

I unscrewed the lid of mine and brought it up to my face to smell.

"Jules!" she said, halting my hand with her urgent tone. "Don't. Do not touch it, smell it, drink it. Just put the lid on and be ready to throw it on the Pneumaphage if you get the chance."

I carefully threaded the lid back on as tight as

possible and shoved it deep in my pocket.

"I'm not as skilled at calling madness as Eliza is," said Tim, "But if I can get close enough to touch our Pneumaphage, I should be able to call enough mental cloudiness that he'll be unable to cast spells. That might give us time."

"Good." I ran through new scenarios in my mind.

Tim leaned forward and tapped the table. "We don't have any idea what this Pneumaphage can do. But we know he doesn't share Sheila's moral qualms against using his powers to harm others. This will be a dangerous fight."

"What should I do with Carson?" I asked. "I can't just bring him into battle. He'll turn into a wolf and attack the guy's foot or something. He'll get killed. I can't control him while I need to be fighting."

I left out the part where I wasn't sure exactly how I'd contribute to this fight. I could call darkness. I could bite and pounce like any Were, even if I wasn't as skilled in wolf form. I had knives. Yeah. That all sounded really helpful.

"Jules," said Sheila. "Maybe you should stay at the hotel and protect Carson."

"What?" I stared around the table. No one else spoke. "No way. It's my fault everyone's here. And I'm the stubborn one insisting that we neutralize this guy instead of fleeing back to Wyoming."

"We all agree with you, Julie," said Tim.

"Still. There's no way I'm cowering in a hotel room while you all take the offense."

"Wait!" said Newt. "What if we turn Carson incorporeal? And he goes with me?"

"What?"

"We turn Carson incorporeal so he doesn't turn into a wolf and go after the bad guy like it's a game. The Pneumaphage can't target him if he's not on the same plane of existence. I don't need two hands to fight all the wraiths. I can hold Carson and manage my flames at the same time. Or maybe you have a sling for me to carry him hands-free? Or I can just hide Carson somewhere on the other plane, knowing no enemies can find him."

"That's…that's not a horrible idea," said Tim, his eyes half-closed as if calculating new variables. "Actually, I think that's a good idea."

Carson squawked from the high chair at the end of the table and I reached over with my glass of water and a straw so he could drink. He sucked avidly—this was a relatively new skill for him—and pounded a fist on the edge of the table then reached out in the direction of the garlic knots. I handed him another.

Could I turn my baby incorporeal and hand him off to Newt? Newt sat next to me, his solid warmth like a beam of sunlight in the darkened restaurant. He would protect my son. I trusted him, even this much. Maybe…There weren't many people I would entrust Carson to in this situation. Maybe this meant Newt and I…

I fought the urge to look at Newt out of the corner of my eye. Now was not the time. But maybe…

"I think we have a plan, then," I said. "What do we need to prepare?"

"I want to scry and see how DeVossen's reacting to Carson's escape and spell another butter knife for Newt to use," said Sheila.

We finished our meal in a hurry and headed back to

the hotel to find both Eliza and Tony waiting in the room. Eliza sat straight-backed in the hotel chair, while Tony stood against the window watching her.

"Hi," I said into the painful silence once we'd all filed in.

"Have you chosen a side?" Sheila asked. The tension level in the room ratcheted up several notches and the hair on the back of my neck prickled uncomfortably. I shifted my shoulders.

"I'm here, aren't I?" said Tony with a growl in his voice. "I'm not deserting my friends. I gather you want to take down the Pneumaphage instead of returning to Greybull with your tails between your legs?"

Eliza bristled. "It's not cowardice to know when something's not your fight. Sometimes you need to retreat and protect your own."

"We're staying and we're protecting the people who live here. Eliza, are you in or are you out?" I asked.

"I'm not leaving you all in danger. I'll fight by your side," she said. "But I don't agree with your choice."

"Did Lily tell you to stay?"

"What I discuss with the Full is none of your business, Julie."

Great. So she'd been set on us like a watch dog. Well, hopefully we could put her to good use, regardless of her reasons for joining this fight.

"Okay," I said, pushing aside all the weaknesses in our motley team. "Here's the plan."

Chapter Eighteen

Sheila took out a stone she'd remembered to pick up from the walkway at DeVossen Mindspring and used it to scry the property. She reported what seemed to be an unusual lack of activity at the house, especially considering this was a regular workday and the place ought to have been crawling with a string of gullible people hoping for past life regressions, aligned chakras, or hypnotherapy, while secretly being drained of their life force.

Sheila caught a glimpse of DeVossen through an upper window so we knew he was on the property. He hadn't come looking for us yet, but I feared he rallied his wraiths or his powers. He must be up to something.

"Sheila, what type of spells can a Pneumaphage do, anyway?" I asked.

"Pneumaphages and Witches are capable of the same spells, if we have someone to teach us. It's more a matter of which spells meet our moral compass and the source of the powers we use. If I wanted to learn attack spells, I could. But my family has always believed our powers aren't meant to be a source of harm." She shot a quick look at Newt. "No offense to anyone who views things differently."

"None taken," said Newt. "Believe me, I'm much more comfortable using my abilities to protect people. That's why I'm training as a hotshot."

"Pneumaphages power their spells by using other people's life force instead of grounding their spells in the four elements. It's kind of like using a fire hose instead of coaxing a fountain into alignment," said Sheila. "Usually they require long rituals and volunteers to provide the life force, but then the actual casting is instant. Witches don't stockpile power like that; we do the ritual in order to cast the spell and we call on the elements at the time of the casting."

"I've been wondering about that. Who would ever volunteer to give their life force to a Pneumaphage?" I asked.

"People do strange things, Jules. Think about cult leaders. Think about how many people in this world would give up some of their own energy in exchange for connections to the paranormal world. Maybe they're rewarded in some way. And—unless the Pneumaphage drains them too far—people recover their life force. Not as quick as Weres, though."

"Did you say you made us all good luck charms?" I asked. "Did you make the kind you did in Las Vegas?"

"Mmm-hmm," said Sheila. "Didn't take me much time at all. That, scrying, and dream-walking are the spells I've practiced the most lately."

"Dream-walking? To who?"

Sheila blushed and glanced at Tim. "Anyway, I have charms for everyone except Eliza. Sorry, I didn't know you would be here."

"No worries," said Eliza. "I'll make my own luck." Her confident smile caused a surge of irritation in me, but I squashed it down.

Sheila handed us all bobby pins. Enchanted bobby pins. I guessed a Witch worked with what she had and the depths of Sheila's purse yielded bobby pins. Most of us snugged the pins on the collar of our shirts. I placed Carson's on the inside of the pajamas he wore. Sheila twisted her pin into her long hair with some amount of grace.

Newt hoisted the travel mug with the remainder of the incorporeal potion. "I've got everything I need."

"Time to spell the other butter knife so you can break through to the wraiths," said Sheila. "I just need to read for a minute and make sure I don't need to do anything differently this time."

While Sheila settled in with her spellbooks, the rest of us went into the guys' hotel room and strategized. We weren't sure what to expect, but we tried to cover all the most likely contingencies and figure out the best role for each one of us. After a couple of hours, Sheila called us back over. We gathered around and she held out both butter knives.

"Choose your poison," she said to Newt.

"Nice job." Tim smiled and the two of them shared a long look.

"I just hold this and slice the barrier? The knife will penetrate it?" asked Newt. He studied the dull knife in his hand, turning it this way and that.

"Yes. It should pop like a bubble," Sheila said. "The trick will be to keep the wraiths from absorbing too much of your life force in the time between when you release them and when you burn them."

I winced at that image then pushed it out of my mind.

"Okay. If we've done all the preparations possible, let's go," I said.

As we filed out of the hotel room, Tony caught my

arm and held me back a moment.

"We need to talk," he said.

"Now's not the time."

"We're headed into battle, Julie. There may not be another time. I want you to know that I'm sorry I've been away so much. Once we get back to Greybull, I'm going to stay in town. I want us to spend more time together. You feel our connection as much as I do—I want to see where this goes," Tony said.

I stared at him in shock—shock he must have taken as assent because he pulled me closer and bent to kiss me. His scent surrounded me and my heart skipped a beat, my body traitorously melted against him. His mouth found mine, his lips warm and demanding.

I jerked away. "Tony, I'm not going back to Greybull. And if I were, it's too late. If you'd...if we'd..." I shook my head to clear it and took a step away from him. "It doesn't matter now. Look, you're right. We had a connection and I think you're...hot, okay? But I don't want to date you."

"Even though you want me. Julie, I can tell you do." His voice rumbled through me.

I crossed my arms in front of myself. "Not in any of the ways that matter. I don't want to date you."

"Because of Newt."

"Actually, no. Not because of Newt. I am going to date Newt." I added, "if he'll have me" in my head. "But he's not the reason. You and I just aren't good for each other."

He continued to stare at me and opened his mouth to speak again, but I interrupted him.

"I don't want to be with you," I said. Calm, firm, decisive. Even though my insides didn't completely agree.

Tony dropped my arm and I walked away, hoping he'd follow to fight with us and knowing I'd be okay if he didn't. I didn't need Tony Blythe.

****

Sheila parked on the street two blocks away from DeVossen Mindspring. Eliza and Tony pulled up behind us in Eliza's rental car. The separation in our two cars reflected the natural fault line in our alliance, I suppose. At least they were both fighting on our side.

Sheila smeared a new helping of focus serum on each of our foreheads and our weapons. I blew on my knives until they dried, then carefully brushed off the remaining flakes and specks of dirt.

"Bottom's up," said Newt. He raised the travel mug full of shimmering potion. My Werewolf senses caught the smell of it. I watched as his features reflected the wonder and longing brought forth from the potion.

An instant later, he mouthed something at us. I shook my head to indicate we couldn't hear him. He was gone from our realm.

Now Carson. I looked at Newt for a moment and took a deep breath to calm myself. Newt would take care of my son. I trusted him. I poured a small amount of potion into a sippy cup we'd detoured into a grocery store to buy. I estimated three toddler mouthfuls and figured that since this measurement didn't seem exact, we'd be okay. I held Carson on one hip and brought the cup close enough so he could grab it.

"Jules," said Sheila. "Put Carson on the ground first."

Oh. Right. I didn't want him to fall through my body when he became incorporeal. The very thought sent a shudder through me. Not just the idea of him falling, but the thought of my body being permeable to him, the thought of being unable to touch him. Again.

For a short time, I reminded myself. For no more than a day. It was the best way to keep him safe.

I set Carson on the ground, where he bounced on his bottom in excitement. He started to push himself forward onto his hands to stand up then stopped as I brought the sippy cup within reach. I think he could smell it—hell, *I* could smell it and the scent made me want to rip it away from my baby and drink it myself.

Carson held the sippy cup with both hands and tipped it up into his mouth. I watched him swallow until it was gone.

"Newt!" I said urgently.

He was right there, of course. Newt squatted by Carson and talked to him, though I couldn't understand the words. I did understand Carson's body language and the excitement in his movements as he held his arms toward Newt.

"Up on Newt," I imagined him saying. He probably didn't form the sentence that well, though. My Carson was strong but not known for his verbal abilities.

Newt picked up Carson. He pointed toward us and waved. Carson did the same. I made a show of blowing him a really big kiss and smiled broadly. I knew if he saw me upset, he'd mirror me, so I pretended to be all sorts of happy to see my baby on the incorporeal plane.

Newt gave the group a thumb's up and zipped away with Carson through the late afternoon sunlight toward DeVossen's Mindspring. Our group had discussed whether someone else should go with him, now that our team had been enlarged by Eliza and Tony. But none of the rest of us had a clear advantage in a fight against wraiths. Sheila's gun might have helped, but we also knew we might need Sheila's spellcasting abilities. If she didn't have a way to engage the Pneumaphage, she might at least have enough knowledge to parse and deflect some of his spells. Besides, Sheila didn't have enough ingredients to make more potion. Newt would be okay alone, I reminded myself. His power over fire gave him an immense advantage—he was our best bet in the incorporeal realm. He'd be just fine. I just kind of wished I'd given him a good luck kiss. Instead, my lips still tingled from my near-encounter with Tony. Treacherous lips.

"Ready?" I said. At nods from the others, I called darkness to cover our group.

We made our way within sight of DeVossen's house. With a quick gesture, Tim and Sheila split off from our party to make their way to the back door. Tim called darkness to cover them, while Eliza, Tony, and I waited at the front. Sheila would disarm the field around the house so we could enter. She said the spelled butter knife should cut through the shield with a simple stab.

We waited.

After several minutes, Tim let out a single bark to signal the force field was down. I nodded to the others as Tony dropped into his wolf form. I opened the front door and the large black wolf darted past me and into the empty reception room. Eliza and I followed. I engaged every one of my Were senses to look for signs of traps or danger but found nothing. I couldn't even smell the Pneumaphage. I couldn't smell Eliza or Tony.

Uh-oh.

Eliza shot me a look and I nodded with my mouth tight. He knew we were coming.

I dropped into my wolf.

Well, okay, it wasn't quite that fluid, but I did shift quicker than yesterday and I tried not to compare myself to the other Weres. As we'd discussed earlier, Eliza stayed in human form to open doors or deal with anything that needed opposable thumbs. She could change form in an instant once we engaged the Pneumaphage.

I blinked to adjust to my wolf-sight and took a long sniff of the air. Nothing, like a blanket of cotton smothered all normal smells. My hackles rose at the unnatural lack of scent—I might as well be back in the incorporeal realm for all the good my heightened senses did. Tony growled in the back of his throat and I felt my own chest vibrate in response. We wouldn't be able to sniff out the Pneumaphage, but we would find him.

Eliza led us to the door leading into the hallway. When she reached it, she leaned her head on the wood and frowned as she listened. She glanced at me. I shook my head to indicate that I, too, heard nothing. She gestured us to one side and cracked open the door, peering into the hallway. Adrenaline raced through my body, my muscles quivered as if eager to fight. Stay calm, I told my wolf-self. I nosed around the corner of the door and looked into the hallway into darkness, an unnatural blackness even my wolf eyes didn't penetrate. The Pneumaphage must have used some sort of spell. Could he see us? Just in case, I pulled the shadows closer around the three of us. Layers upon layers of darkness. Somewhere ahead of us, Sheila and Tim would enter the house through the back door.

The three of us stepped carefully into the hall. I could hardly see. My eyes blinked and strained at the blackness. At every foot fall, I expected something to happen—maybe the Pneumaphage would leap at us, maybe a wraith would appear, something, who knows what—but the house remained quiet and the tension rose with each passing second. The fur on the back of my neck stood high and taut; a low rumble of unease sounded in my chest. Eliza pushed open doors as we passed them and we peered inside—therapy room, kitchen, bathroom, therapy room. She came to the room where DeVossen met with Sheila and my heart beat faster, but a look into that room found no one.

I sniffed the air, hoping to find a trace of Tim and Sheila, but whatever blocked my sight blocked all my senses and hid everyone, even my friends.

We reached the foot of the staircase and Eliza gestured up. Tony pushed in front of her and padded up the stairs; I took the rear.

As soon as we crested the staircase and stepped into the hall, the wraiths attacked. I couldn't see them, but I felt them—all around us, pressing hungry tendrils against us, sucking energy and color from the world. I lunged and snapped at the air. I relied on instinct as I bit and tore into the wraiths. They dissolved into horrible goo in my mouth and then popped, even as I felt them draining me. I shook my head and charged again with a growl. Eliza—now in wolf form—and Tony fought next to me. I took comfort in their Were energy as we battled in the close quarters of the hallway.

Absolute darkness. Air rasped into my lungs. I couldn't tell how many wraiths we faced. I growled and forced myself to find another target through the gray haze at the corners of my eyes.

Tony growled and let out a sharp bark, echoed by Eliza. I sounded in return and backed toward the top of the stairs. Tony was right. We couldn't keep fighting in the dark with the wraiths draining us. We needed light, we needed to scope out the extent of our enemies, we needed to attack them from a distance. We needed to find the Pneumaphage who controlled them.

From behind me on the stairs, I heard Sheila's voice ring out a fluid sequence of syllables and light permeated the hallway. Light. Three wraiths remained, hanging like cloud vortexes, stretching out their tentacles toward us. A shot rang out, then another. I flattened myself closer to the ground. One of the wraiths disappeared in a puff of smoke, leaving two others.

Eliza flung herself at the closest one, a leap that nearly crashed her into the wall as she snarled and bit and clawed at the wraith. Black lightning sparked in its center as it reached for the buff-colored wolf. Her teeth shredded it and she lunged one more time before the whole whirling mass seemed to freeze then suddenly fell into nothing.

Meanwhile, Tony had been worrying at the last wraith. I stayed near the head of the stairs and tried to breathe through the heavy exhaustion weighing down my bones. Tim rushed past me to Tony's assistance and the two of them tore apart the final wraith.

"You all look gray around the edges," said Sheila in a quiet voice. She still held the gun in her right hand, pointed conscientiously at the ground. "We've lost any element of surprise—we need to regroup. And we might need our Salamander."

We retreated downstairs, back toward the front room of Mindspring.

The world exploded.

The door flew outward and crashed into the hall. A blinding white light erupted all around us with a bang I felt in my chest. Someone yelled. Something crashed into me and I struggled to keep my feet. I blinked, but all I could see was the purple afterimage. A smell of char rose into the air.

What—? I was sinking. I scrambled with my paws, but it felt like I pushed against cotton.

"Julie!" Sheila yelled.

Someone—Tony—grabbed the nape of my neck and yanked. My feet found solid ground and I heaved myself up and away. I knocked against Tony and we both went sprawling, me lying half on top of him at the edge of the hallway. I shifted back into myself, my human form.

My vision started to clear. Tony: grim-faced and wide-eyed. Eliza stood in the doorway facing the waiting room, still in wolf form with her hackles raised and her muscles tense as if she might spring at any moment. Sheila leaned against the desk in the side alcove—she must have crashed into it, because the lamp had fallen and the desk was crooked. She panted and the sharp smell of pain spiraled from her. Tim had an arm on her shoulder.

Across the width of the hall—right where I'd stood—a circle of glyphs smoked, dark with char against the wooden floor. In the middle of the glyphs...

"Is that your shoe?" I said. "What happened?"

Sheila's shoe. Well, half of it, anyway. Half of her

shoe lay on top of the wooden boards within the glyph-circle as if something sliced it. Half a red Converse, one lace lying in sharply chopped bits.

Eliza growled, her nose questing the air.

"Not sure," said Tim. "Are you okay, sunshine?"

Sheila nodded, although I could see her shaking. "I'm fine. Just startled."

"Are you hurt?" I asked.

"I just wrenched my ankle trying to get free."

Free of... I pulled myself off Tony and knelt next to the glyphs, ready to jump away if I needed to. After looking at Sheila for a nod of permission—she was our resident magic-user—I reached over to pick up her sneaker.

The sneaker stuck to the floor. Actually. As I looked closer, the sneaker was somehow *in* the floor. Not sliced after all, but sunk into the floor. Like it was water or quicksand.

I remembered the feeling of sinking, of falling, and how Tony grabbed me, hauled me up. I'd been sinking through the floor? My hands started to shake and I clenched them into fists to hide my delayed fear.

"What the hell happened?" I said.

"I'm not sure, Jules. My best guess is the floor went incorporeal and then snapped back," said Sheila.

"Snapped back..." I echoed. It could have been me—half of me—stuck in that floor. I could have been killed. A flush spread across my face as my Were energy rose. "You're okay? Your foot? It didn't get you?"

"I'm okay." Sheila held out her sock-covered foot and wiggled her toes. The pain and shock emanating from her grew dimmer. Tim tightened his arm around her shoulders and held her.

"What now? Is the rest of the house safe?"

Eliza shifted form. "We won't be safe until we're on a plane to Greybull. We have no idea what else this guy can do."

Sheila knelt on the floor and carefully snapped pictures of the glyphs on her phone.

"Maybe we should get Newt," I said. "To help."

"The longer we delay, the longer the Pneumaphage has to plan his next attack," Tony said. He paced across the hall, energy nearly crackling off his skin. "We should go back upstairs and find him. Now."

"We know he's not on this floor," said Tim. "Those wraiths upstairs were guards. Let's go back upstairs now before he has the chance to prepare any other attacks. Newt will come find us as soon as he deals with the wraiths in the basement—he's needed there right now."

After a brief moment, I nodded in agreement.

Sheila said, "Watch out for traps. I'm not sure what activated these glyphs. If anyone starts to fall, we need to be ready to grab them and pull them up."

"The Penumaphage doesn't stand a chance," Tony said, "I'm already recovering from those wraiths. Aren't the rest of you?"

I felt nearly feverish as my Were healing kicked into overdrive and my body regained its vitality. My rush of adrenaline sped up the healing. Tony was right. I felt better than I had only moments before.

Tim stepped forward. "I'm in the lead. The rest of you had a hell of a lot more contact with the wraiths than I did. Tony, can you bring up the rear? Eliza, call darkness to obscure DeVossen's vision. Sheila, you can walk okay?"

"I'm fine," she said. "Everyone can stop asking me."

She didn't place her full weight on that right foot, but none of us called her on it.

"Will your light spell still be working?" Tim asked.

"Yes, for another twenty minutes or so," Sheila said.

"I didn't even know you knew a light spell," I said.

"I like to keep you all guessing," Sheila drawled with a wink. She made a show of checking her gun and clip.

Sheila and I stayed in the middle of our group. I tried not to feel like the others were guarding me. It made sense for Sheila to be in the center, though, and I would protect her. After I dropped back into my wolf form, I padded close by her side.

As we crept up the stairs, I took a minute to examine Sheila's light spell. A glowing orb hung near the ceiling. It looked almost like a moon from a child's mobile or something, with bluish-white light emanating from it. I made a mental note to ask Sheila how she did that once we were finished with this fight and on the way home.

As that thought slid through my head, I had a sudden twist of longing for home. Home and safety. But where would that be? I would never feel at home in Greybull, Wyoming with the pack. What did home mean, anyway?

Not now. No distractions.

As we crept up the stairs and into the lighted area, Eliza pulled on her Were ability to call darkness, obscuring sight and shifting the air around us to confuse vision. We were surrounded by layers upon layers of magic: Whatever force the Pneumaphage used to create darkness, countered by Sheila's hanging orb of light then hidden from DeVossen by Were powers. Hopefully at this point, we could see and he couldn't, if I'd figured out all the magic correctly.

We reached the landing. No wraiths visible in the hallway. I made a low wuffing sound and pointed with my nose to the library. We got five feet down the hall before the Pneumaphage attacked.

Lightning arced from the doorway of DeVossen's bedroom and struck Tim. The smell of singed hair and char flooded the air as Tim roared in pain then charged the remaining feet toward the Pneumaphage. DeVossen stood in the open doorway with his arms held out and an exalted look on his face. He wore faded jeans and a white, billowy shirt. A nimbus of power gleamed around him.

Tim barreled into him and the two of them disappeared into the bedroom as a blur of fur and bodies. Tony barked sharply in warning as he and Eliza darted down the hallway after them.

Sheila grabbed the fur of my shoulder. "Stay with me!" she yelled.

My entire body quivered with desire to join the fight, to attack the man who'd taken my baby.

"Stay, Julie. We need to guard the rear." A note of urgency in her voice cut through me and I paused, shook the beast from my brain, and looked at her.

She stood pale and resolute, pointing her gun down the hall with her finger on the safety. But she trembled and I felt panic pouring off her in waves. She favored her right foot, the one almost stuck in the floor. Her jaw clenched. The raised red burn scars stood out vividly on this side of her neck.

I would protect her. Always.

I bumped my shoulder into her leg to show her I was right here with her and not leaving. Her hand on my fur loosened.

"Okay," she said. "Okay. Let's sneak to the door and see if I can get off a shot."

In response, I pulled darkness around the two of us and we crept down the hall. Flashes of light erupted in the Pneumaphage's bedroom—hot white light and pale gray flickering. Crashes and growls. A manic laugh.

Suddenly, Tim careened toward us and the doorway erupted in a flash of white that splintered the frame and left gouts of flame. He skidded to a halt and shifted form, still on the floor.

He panted. "Sheila, he has some sort of personal force field. Can you break it?"

"Yes. Probably." She moved her gun into her left hand, fumbled into her pocket with her right, and came up with the same dinner knife she'd used to pop the shield around the house. She grabbed it overhand and moved forward, huffing breaths through her mouth like preparing for a sprint.

"Sunshine," Tim said, pushing up from the floor. He put a hand on her arm. Sheila stopped. "Let me."

She hesitated and they looked at each other for a moment, as if we had time to argue. Another crash came from the bedroom. I barked and thumped Sheila's side.

"Okay," she said. She looked at both of us and then handed Tim the spelled knife. "Be careful."

"Not just careful," he said. "Lucky." He touched

the collar of his shirt where he'd placed her charmed bobby pin.

"I love you," she said.

"I love you, too. Be safe, Sunshine."

Tim turned and crept down the hall in human form, holding the butter knife. I thrust my nose into Sheila's hand before loping after him and calling more darkness. Perhaps I could get him into the room without being seen. Behind me, I heard Sheila click the safety off her gun and follow us.

The doorframe still burned with licks of orange, sending smoke into the air. The sight evoked memories of my house, burned to the ground last year, but I pushed the thoughts from my head and focused on this fight, now. Half the door lay splintered in the hallway covered in a spray pattern of charred lines from the Pneumaphage's power. Tim crouched low and poked his head around the frame. I padded after him, pressed my belly against the floor, and looked inside.

Eliza and Tony held the Pneumaphage in the corner of the room. Their two bodies—the buff and the black—literally pressed him into the walls, but they obviously couldn't actually touch him. They swarmed against him, just an inch away, and held him immobile with their strength against his force field. Tony held his front foot off the ground and burned fur marred his right shoulder. Blood ran down his leg to drip onto the ground. Reddish-brown marks smeared the floor and the coppery tang hung heavy in my nose.

"He can't strike them without hurting himself," Tim said in my ear. "If I can get close enough to dispel his field without him seeing me, we'll have a few seconds before he attacks. Eliza can call madness. Or, well, Tony can just tear out his throat."

The sleeping potion! Did Tim still have his?

I whined and tilted my head.

"What?" Tim frowned down at me.

I made a show of closing my eyes and lowering my head, then glanced back up at Tim.

"Ah! Yes. The sleeping potion." Tim reached into his pocket and found his little shampoo bottle. He loosened the cap slightly and cupped the bottle in his hand.

I nodded and gestured him forward with my muzzle while I focused on holding the darkness around us. From the flick of their wolf ears, Tony and Eliza knew we were there and stood ready to pounce. Tim crept toward DeVossen, one slow, quiet step at a time. When he got within a couple of feet, all hell broke loose.

Eliza sidled over to make sure Tim could approach with the spelled knife. Just as he raised the knife to strike, DeVossen lunged wildly to the side, grabbed hold of a chest of drawers, and flung it to the floor. Glass shattered from somewhere inside. DeVossen yelled and wraiths streamed out from the toppled furniture into the room. Tim stabbed down and the air around the Pneumaphage popped with a flash of gray. Tony snarled. He leapt forward with teeth bared, but DeVossen met him with a thrust-out hand. Sparks flew from DeVossen's palm and Tony jolted backward and sprawled on the hardwood floors, his claws scrabbling for traction. Wraiths swarmed.

A soccer-ball-sized wraith spun at me and whipped a tentacle toward my head. I crouched to avoid it. Then, just as I was about to spring up and grapple with it, a shot rang out and pierced its seething cloud. It whirled like a vortex for a moment and then darted toward me again. I met it with my fangs. I tore into it, fighting through the gray spots in my vision as the wraith tried to pull my life force into itself. Instead, I shredded it with my teeth. I bit and pulled and snapped until the entire wraith dissolved against my tongue like cotton candy.

I braced myself and panted, shook my head to focus. I'd lost track of the rest of the fight. When I looked, I saw Eliza and the Pneumaphage battling by the window. Wraiths swirled around them so densely my eyes strained to see the fight. She leapt at him over and over as he flung sparks at her. Tony and Tim battled other wraiths while Sheila backed herself into a corner and waited for clear shots. Eliza's flanks heaved as she panted with exhaustion. I pounded across the room to her side, only to be pushed back by the force of several wraiths. I didn't know if I could handle touching them any longer—gray haze swirled in the corners of my vision—and I shifted forms to grab my knives, using the weapons to slash and provide distance.

The serum-treated metal sliced into the wraiths like butter and I realized I didn't need much fighting skill to hack at amorphous creatures who just wanted to touch me. I focused on dodging them and recovering some energy. Slash, hack, stab. I attacked whichever wraith came closest. I severed tentacles and gouged chunks out of their swirling bodies. Sweat ran into my eyes and I blinked to clear my vision. Slowly, surely, I cut my way through the room toward the Pneumaphage. I just needed to get to the vial of sleeping potion in my pocket.

Tony's body flew through the air and crashed into the closet doors with a thunderous crack. He got up on three legs, shook his head, and staggered.

"I've got him!" Eliza's voice rang out in triumph. She held the Pneumaphage pressed against the floor, and I felt power surging around her as she called on the moon to bring madness.

I ducked under a wraith and slid to a stop at her side.

"The jaws that bite, the jaws that bite," DeVossen said. His blue eyes looked nearly black, the irises swallowed by his pupils as he stared at Eliza. "Do we gyre and gimble now, my friend? Gyre. Gimble. My friend, my friend. My furry friend."

The skin on the back of my neck crawled with his eerie talk.

"Callooh! Callay," he said and broke into laughter.

"That's from 'Jabberwocky,' " said Sheila.

"Oh, good. We have a literate Pneumaphage trying to kill us. That makes it extra special," I said.

"Do something. I can't hold him forever," Eliza said. Her jaw was clenched so hard my own temples ached in sympathy, while sweat stood on her forehead. Meanwhile, the Pneumaphage's eyes rolled back and his body twitched as he tried to shake off her powers.

I reached into my pocket and grabbed the small bottle of sleeping potion. I sidled up to DeVossen, removed the cap, and splashed it all over him. His whole body went limp immediately, while his eyes rolled up into his head. He let out a deep sigh and then snorted in a long breath.

"Wow," I said. "That really worked."

"The note of surprise in your voice is a huge vote

of confidence. Thanks, Jules," said Sheila.

Eliza sprang up from her crouch on the floor. "Shall I do the honors? Or is one of you going to kill him?"

"Kill him?" I echoed.

Tony let out a growl and limped closer to the Pneumaphage.

"That is why we came, isn't it?" asked Tim. "To stop the Pneumaphage from preying on the people who live here?"

I looked at DeVossen, fast asleep on the floor, his chest rising and falling with deep, even breaths.

"It's just...I mean...He's asleep," I said.

"Jules?" Sheila said.

"Can we...imprison him?" I asked, before answering myself. "We don't have anywhere to put him and we can't just lock him up forever. Sheila, can you strip his powers? Like a Were would?"

She shook her head. "No. A ritual of that nature would take thirteen skilled Witches. Better skilled than me."

"Can we find somewhere to hold him until we can gather thirteen Witches?" I asked. I rubbed my forehead.

DeVossen mumbled on the floor.

Tony shifted into human form. He cradled his left arm in his right. "We kill him now and end this," he said. "We can do it quickly and humanely."

Eliza said, "I don't see any other option."

Tony strode toward the Pneumaphage and unsheathed a knife.

"No!" I said. "We can't murder him in cold blood. Maybe we can talk to him. Convince him he needs to work with only willing donors. Like normal Pneumaphages. Maybe we can take away his powers to access the wraiths. Let's…tie him up, wait until he wakes, and talk to him."

Tim fixed a steady gaze on me. "Julie, if you want to protect the community, you have to be willing to do what it takes."

"I…" I stopped, flummoxed. I hadn't thought this through. I hadn't thought any of this through. I wish we'd killed him in the heat of battle. Not while he lay helplessly asleep. "For now, let's just hold him."

I crossed to DeVossen's closet and yanked open the doors. "Here," I said, emerging with a purple paisley tie. I held it out toward Tim. After a moment, he took it from my hands and crossed to the Pneumaphage.

"You're letting your emotions outweigh your sense, Julie," said Tony. "We should kill him now while we can."

"No," I said. I looked at Sheila for support and she twisted her mouth, as if indicating she wasn't sure what came next, either.

Tim bound DeVossen's hands behind him and pulled tight on the knots. DeVossen snored and sighed on the floor. Tony stood at the ready with his knife held as if he still wanted to slit the man's throat. My stomach roiled with tension and I thought I might throw up. After securing the man, Tim pulled a pair of socks from the jumble spilled out of the overturned dresser, stuffed them in his mouth, and gagged him by tying another necktie around his face to hold the socks in place.

All the while, Eliza directed her stony stare at me.

"What, Eliza? Just say it," I said.

She sprang toward me and yelled, "What the hell,

Julie? It was your idea to come here in the first place. You said you wanted to protect the community. You said DeVossen couldn't be allowed to operate unchecked. You said it was our duty. And now you chicken out when we have a chance to put an end to the whole thing?"

Tony nodded in agreement. He opened his mouth as if to speak, but I shook my head violently at him and turned away from them both.

"Sheila? How long will he be asleep" I asked.

"About an hour," she said.

In almost the same moment, DeVossen gave a muffled yell from his place on the ground. His eyes narrowed over his gag. He was awake. Somehow. His shoulders strained as he tested the strength of his bonds. Tim stood next to him on high alert, his body tensed to react to any sudden movements.

"Shit," said Sheila.

Dual growls rose from Tony and Eliza.

"DeVossen," I said. "We don't want to kill you."

"Speak for yourself," muttered Eliza.

"We don't want to kill you," I said with a frown in her direction before turning back to DeVossen. "But we will, if we can't find some way to guarantee you won't feed on innocent people in this community."

I gestured to Eliza and Tony. "Some of us don't even think you deserve a chance. They'd kill you in an instant, if I let them. But I'm willing to see if we can come to an agreement, even though you kidnapped my son." I stopped for a moment as a wave of anger crashed over me and breathed twice to calm down. I would not be ruled by vengeance.

"If we remove your gag, do you promise not to try

anything? Will you discuss an agreement?" I asked.

"Julie, you're being an idiot." Eliza's voice rose and she spat the words out at me as she stepped closer.

"Stop it," I said.

"Stop what? Telling the truth? Trying to make you see reason?"

"Eliza, you're only here because Lily sent you as her spy."

"That's not true."

"It is true! You didn't want to be in this fight to begin with. You should have left. You should have gone back to Greybull, back to your precious pack. I don't need your help and I don't want you here. Just go away! I don't even want to look at you. Just go away, Eliza," I yelled and watched her expression move from anger to hurt and then back again.

Then everything happened at once.

The Pneumaphage twisted violently, spat out his gag, and shouted three words. The air around him glowed so bright I had to blink away tears.

Eliza leapt at him, shifting form mid-air. Lightning sprayed from the Pneumaphage's hands—his hands, suddenly free of their bonds and stabbing the air—and the room exploded with white flames. Someone screamed. Was it me? The room seethed with light and smoke and motion and noise. A violent splintering crash rose above everything else and I saw Eliza's body hit the window frame, smash through the glass, and fall, fall outside, fall onto the lawn. DeVossen stood, his hair raised with static, his mouth half open, light shining from his eerie blue eyes. A huge bolt of energy surged from his raised palms and arced out the window.

"No!" I shouted.

I jumped at DeVossen, but I couldn't get there in time. I couldn't get there.

I rushed toward the broken window and saw Eliza's body jerk as the bolt arced into her.

Blue-white lightning consumed the world. I flew across the room and hit the wall with a thud that stole my breath. An instant later, the pain surged. I'd been hit.

I shifted into my wolf.

Chapter Nineteen

I lay against the wall, my mind stupid with pain. The smell of burned hair and blood clogged my nose. I registered everything in slow motion, like frames of a photo strip that clicked past almost before I understood what I saw.

Light streaked from DeVossen's hands and the bolts snapped into runes mid-air. Runes. Familiar runes. Adrenaline sparked me to action and I barked in alarm. The runes flickered. The hardwood floors pulsed with them, then suddenly—

Sheila's gun went off as she lurched and sprawled on the floor. Partly on the floor. Her upper body clung to the leg of DeVossen's bed frame as her feet disappeared through the floor. She'd dropped her gun. It still spun idly on the floor next to her clenched hands.

Tony leapt at the Pneumaphage but couldn't reach him through the sparking jolts of lightning radiating off his hands. The black Were let out a sharp yip of pain. Tim raced to Tony's side and growled at DeVossen with teeth barred. Sheila screamed something—maybe Tim's name?—and tried to drag herself up, out of the incorporeal floorboards.

Sheila.

I dragged myself to my feet. I gritted my teeth and growled to shut out the pain throbbing from my burns. As soon as I could balance, I made my way to Sheila. I felt like I moved through pudding. The very air of the room felt thick with magic or my own pain and confusion, but I kept going, one paw in front of the other, my left paw stumbling every time it hit the ground. I kept my eyes on Sheila, my Sheila—Eliza, whispered my mind, and I saw again the bolt strike her, her plummet through the window—Sheila, here and now, needing me.

Finally, I reached her. She turned panicked eyes toward me.

"Jules!"

I grabbed the back of her jacket in my jaw and pulled, braced all four feet with claws digging into the wooden floor as I ignored the pain shooting through my left leg and yanked on Sheila until my vision blackened at the edges. I had to get her out of the floor, before…before…

Then she had a knee up and the other joined it and I tugged again and we both went rolling along the ground, the solid ground. Safe.

A loud crack and the smell of burned fur and flesh bloomed newly in the air. Sheila shouted. Tim and Tony still launched themselves at the Pneumaphage, who had fallen down on one knee. His face was frantic and he thrust at the wolves. Tony's teeth latched onto one of DeVossen's arms.

Eliza.

She'd fallen. She…

I stumbled around the edge of the room toward the window. I barely remembered to test the floor ahead of me with one paw to make sure it was solid. Eliza.

She lay on the ground. A buff wolf broken on the lawn. A ball of blue lightning still danced around her, as if…had all this happened in an instant? Her body convulsed once and then—oh, then—lay still. Horribly still. So still. My heart beat frantically in my ears.

No!

I jumped out the window. Nearly as smooth as Eliza could, except my leg collapsed and I fell to the ground upon landing. My side stabbed with pain. My chest ached so badly I could hardly breathe.

I crawled to her side and shifted back to myself, just as a dark haze hovered over her buff-color wolf self and cleared. Leaving Eliza behind. Her human shape.

Eliza.

No.

I shook her, felt her pulse, patted her cheeks. I called to her. I pleaded. I begged. All the while, tears streamed down my face because I knew the truth. I knew there was nothing I could do.

Eliza was dead.

I collapsed over her body, hugging her to me. I smoothed back her fawn-colored hair. Her body still felt warm, but horribly lax, horribly inert and wrong.

Eliza.

She hadn't wanted to be here. This wasn't her fight. If I'd agreed to leave—if we'd flown back to Greybull and left this horrible place—she would still be alive. She'd stayed because of me. If only I had killed the Pneumaphage. This was my fault.

"Julie."

I looked up through swollen eyes to see Sheila kneeling at my side. Tears ran down her face, too, but her voice held steady. She put her hand on my arm.

"She's dead," I said. "Dead."

"I know."

"How…Sheila? What do I do? She's dead. She's dead and the last thing I said…I told her to go away. Sheila?"

She winced and more tears leaked out. "I know."

"It's my fault. I killed her."

"You didn't kill her, Julie. She could have left. She chose."

"I didn't kill the Pneumaphage. And then he killed her."

"I know," said Sheila. "But you didn't mean this to happen. You tried to do what you thought was right."

"And Eliza paid the price. It's all my fault."

Sheila reached out and helped me lay Eliza down. We both stared at her until I turned toward Sheila and collapsed against her shoulder. Her arms held me tight and I knotted my fists in her shirt. If I weren't crying so hard, I thought I might scream.

Sheila murmured through her own tears and held me with arms more solid than anything else in the world. She didn't tell me it would be okay. We both knew it wasn't okay. It would never be okay. But she said Eliza knew I loved her. Our friendship was real. Eliza knew and, in the end, Eliza chose friendship. She chose to protect me. And she knew I loved her, even when I was mad, even when I didn't understand her. Sheila said the love was the real part, the part to hold onto.

"Tim? Tony?" I finally said.

"They're okay. The Pneumaphage's dead."

Dead. Like Eliza.

Good. DeVossen deserved to die. We should have killed him immediately. But even as the thought went through my mind, I knew I couldn't have killed him while he lay sleeping and unaware. That wouldn't have been right, either.

"How badly are you hurt?" asked Sheila.

I shrugged. Burns traced across my side and down my leg. My whole body ached and—I breathed in—yes, I thought I had a cracked rib. "I'll heal," I said.

I looked back at Eliza, past healing, and rubbed my eyes.

"What do we do now?" I asked.

"What do we do now?" Sheila echoed. "I guess we're done. I guess we go home."

Tim said, "Not quite that easy, I fear."

I looked up and he crouched next to us, one hand on Sheila's shoulder. She leaned into him as I leaned into her.

"What do we do about..." My voice trailed into silence as I looked at Eliza's body. I wanted to scream. I wanted to hurt someone. How could I hurt this much? I pressed my hands into the raw skin and burns on my hip, just so I could feel that pain instead.

"I'll call her Full," said Tim. "Then we need to make sure we've taken care of all the wraiths and eliminated the threat to this area."

"And we call the Council," I said.

Tim looked at me. "I'm not here as a representative of the Council, Julie," he said. "Traditionally, Eliza's pack would decide whether or not to involve the Council. At this point, we're not asking them for help. We give them information and they can choose to call the Council."

"The Council needs to know what happened. They do. Eliza's dead and it's all because Lily wouldn't involve the Council earlier and get help. And because of me, but if we'd had more help—if the Council... They need to know Carson was kidnapped and Lily didn't even report it. And then she sent Eliza here and Eliza's dead. All because the pack wanted to save face."

Sheila shook her head.

"Don't say it." I pointed at her. "I know it's my fault, too. I've risked all our lives. I get it. But if the Council had handled this right from the beginning, this wouldn't have happened. I want to call the Council."

Tim's expression was unreadable. "Julie, individual Werewolves don't call the Council."

"Why not?"

"They're not congressional representatives or something. They don't hear from each individual Were. You need to work within the pack structure if you want them to respect you."

"Maybe that needs to change."

"Julie," said Sheila.

I held up my hand to stop her.

"If the pack called the Council when Carson first disappeared, maybe Eliza would still be alive," I said.

"I know you want someone to blame, Julie. I get it. But why don't we call Lily, clean things up here, and then figure out what else to do? We don't have to decide everything today," said Sheila.

I shook my head.

"Where's Tony?" I asked, suddenly aware he wasn't around. "And Newt and Carson?"

Tim frowned. "I left Tony upstairs with the body. Newt hasn't come back yet. He must be still down in the basement incinerating the wraiths."

My heart lurched and I stood up, almost toppling over from the sudden movement as my muscles screamed. "I'm going to find Newt and my son. To make sure they're okay."

Please, God, let them be okay. Not like...I looked at Eliza then scrubbed my hands over my face and turned toward the house. My feet felt numb as I limped away, like nothing was real.

****

Inside, the house was very still. Over the heavy scent of smoke, I caught a whiff of blood. DeVossen's. Tony's. Tim's. The mingled blood scent made my stomach churn.

I walked through the corridors, my senses on high alert even though I felt wrapped in a fog. My whole body flushed with heat as my Were powers raced to heal me.

At the top of the basement stairs, I called out, "Newt?" Then I cursed myself because he wouldn't be able to hear me in the incorporeal realm. We really needed to work on some sort of a communication system, said the chattering part of my brain, but hopefully we weren't going to spend much more time around wraiths or incorporeal. But if we were, that was a clear place for improvement. Yes. My brain circled round and round, as if trying not to think about Eliza.

Eliza.

I made my way down the steps and my ears started to feel an increase in pressure, as if I were on an airplane. I yawned to pop them. I hurried halfway down the stairs, crouched, and peered into the basement with my breath held. Seeing nothing, I continued to the ground and into the side room where the wraiths had been trapped.

The room looked like a tornado had hit. Most

obvious—there was no whirling, stormy vortex field full of wraiths. Instead, the gray candles lay on their sides, one rolled almost to the wall, and the former lines of sand and chalk were now spread across the floor as if whipped by wind. The basement was silent. I opened my mouth wide again to clear my ears.

"Newt?"

Damn it, I really needed to stop acting like he could hear me. My palms started to sweat. Where was he? And Carson? Where was my baby? I swallowed down my nausea and forced myself to look closely around the room. My feet scuffed on the sand strewn over the cement. I saw no other signs of the paranormal conflict that must have taken place. I sniffed the air, but couldn't smell any fire or ash. That would stay on the incorporeal plane.

I stopped myself before calling for Newt again. I checked every area of the basement, just to make sure, but they weren't down here. That was a good sign, I told myself. If something had happened to them, they would still be there, like...I grabbed the sides of my head and squeezed. Focus.

Holding my side so my cracked rib didn't jostle, I ran up the stairs to the main floor and quickly opened each door in the hall: client rooms, office, kitchen, bathroom. Even the hall closet. No sign. I darted to the second floor and the scene of our fight. Char covered the walls and I coughed on the smoke still hanging in the air. I didn't want to see DeVossen's body. I didn't want to see any more bodies.

The door to the Pneumaphage's study stood ajar and I pushed in to see Newt holding Carson. As I moved into the room, Newt saw me out of the corner of his eye and turned. His face lit up in a smile and then dropped into a look of concern as he took in my burned clothes, my limp, my hand holding my side. He took half a step toward me then shrugged, probably remembering he wouldn't be able to touch me. Carson, on the other hand, held out his arms for me and strained away from Newt's side. He opened his mouth and cried, but I couldn't hear him.

Newt mouthed, "Are you okay?" and gestured to me.

I nodded then shrugged, then nodded again and made a brushing gesture with my fingers. I was fine. I would be fine. Not like...

Carson screamed—silently to me—and tears sprang from his eyes. I grimaced and walked closer to them. "It's okay, Carson. Mama's right here. I just...you can't touch me now, but I'm right here."

Carson thrust his hand right through my arm. He pulled back, surprised enough that he stopped crying and his eyes opened wide. Then I watched his face turn red as he screamed. He seemed more angry than afraid.

Newt bounced him and spoke some words then swooshed him around the room until he settled down. Carson nestled into Newt's side and grabbed his shirt with both his fists. The sight eased something in my throat. Carson trusted Newt. And Newt was one of the few people I trusted my son with. I studied him. His tall, fire fighter frame, his hair sticking up like living flame, freckles covering his face and glinting like copper in the sunlight that streamed into the room. Carson kicked his feet.

Newt turned in my direction and our eyes met. His crinkled up at the corners with his grin. He cocked his head at me and made a gesture toward DeVossen's bedroom. He must have seen the room, seen the body. I nodded. Yes, we took care of the Pneumaphage.

I paused, the grief and shock of Eliza's death crashing down on me again.

Newt's eyebrows rose and the smile dropped from his face as he read my expression. He shook his head and mouthed something. I thought he said, "What is it?"

I pulled out my cell phone and typed, "Eliza's dead."

I stared at the words, so cold and stark, before turning the phone to Newt.

He shook his head in disbelief.

Sudden tears ran down my face again—sorrow so close to the surface—and I nodded. It was true. Newt rubbed his forehead with one hand and I saw tears standing in his eyes. Carson squawked, probably upset by a change in Newt's temperature or the scent of his sudden grief and shock. Newt bounced him and did the baby-soothing two-step, all the while shaking his head and staring off above my head. God, I wanted to hold them both. After a moment, I watched his sorrow shift to something more like anger. His jaw set and his shoulders straightened. He pointed to the books shelved around the room.

I looked around at the bookshelves. Yes, these were probably books that we needed to investigate, maybe even confiscate so no one else learned those powers.

Mother moon, I was tired. I wanted to sit down. I wanted to rest. I wanted…I wanted to stop hurting. I wanted to stop. To go back in time.

Newt floated over to the desk where an open book

and notebook lay among other papers. I walked to stand next to him. He pointed to the book and mimed turning pages. Ah, yes. He couldn't touch anything.

I walked over to look at the front cover. *Ring of Brodgar: A New Understanding of Old Henges.* Newt and I shrugged at each other. On the corner of the desk lay a slim silver laptop, closed, and another thick volume: *The Ohio River in American History.* I rifled through the pages but saw nothing about wraiths, Pneumaphagy, or life magic. I opened the laptop to confirm it was password protected, then closed it again. Damn it. There must be something useful in this study.

I walked around the room to look at the rows and rows of book spines. Suddenly, I paused. My nose tingled, almost like the moment when a sneeze built up. The feeling cut through my numbness. I stopped. Was it just a sneeze? I moved my head up and down near the various shelves, locating the center of the sensation. There. The scent—or whatever it was—jabbed at my nose and sinuses. I'd not smelled anything like it. I looked carefully at each book on the shelf, second from the bottom. After a moment of hesitation, I reached toward the books. My fingers tingled as if they woke up from being asleep. I hovered over the spines of the books. They looked like literature. A volume of Shakespeare's collected works. Some poetry books.

One book stung as I ran my hand over it. Navy cloth binding, gold imprinted letters of the title: *Collected Poems of the Eighteenth Century.*

What?

I pointed at the book and gestured Newt over. He looked at the book and held up his hands in bewilderment. I shrugged. I reached out a finger, touched the spine and snatched my hand back with a curse as an electric shock arced into me. I shook my hand until the pain from the jolt subsided. I had to get Sheila. Maybe she could counter whatever spell surrounded this book.

I moved next to the section of the shelves that housed DeVossen's extensive library of self-help and motivational books. I pulled them out one by one, none of them magic, all of them full of pithy tips on how to become influential by using strategies like climbing the ladder of success, moving cheese, becoming a tiger, and #Winning. Next to those were celebrity autobiographies. Pneumaphage, new age hippy, celebrity-stalker, and wanna-be motivational speaker? I shook my head in puzzlement; Newt mimed equal confusion.

I gestured Newt to follow me and we returned outside to find the others. My feet felt heavier and heavier as we left the house. I found myself moving slowly, forcing my body inch by inch to face the reality of Eliza's death. Tony had rejoined the others while we were inside; he knelt by Eliza's body. As we approached, I saw him press his sleeve over his eyes. When he dropped his arm, the stark expression of grief and anger on his face made me falter.

Newt saw Eliza's body and he flew to her in a rush then hovered in absolute stillness, like a marble statue instead of the living flame he usually resembled. Carson struggled and dropped free of Newt's arms to float gently to the ground. He reached out a hand to pat Eliza but passed right through her instead. He moved closer to her head and peered down at her with a frown on his toddler face. I wasn't sure if he knew she was dead. Or if he even knew what death was, really. But he understood something was deeply wrong. He looked around for me with a wild look on his face then zoomed in my direction. I reached out for him, but we couldn't touch. The panic on Carson's face broke my heart. Newt moved over quickly and spoke to Carson, then enveloped him in his arms and rocked him, still speaking. Carson clung to Newt.

I passed a shaky hand over my eyes, wishing I could stop crying. Crying helped nothing. Grief was worthless. Only action mattered.

"Did you talk to Lily Rose?" I asked Tim. "Also, Sheila, there's at least one magical book in the Pneumaphage's study that maybe you could look at. Plus some other weird things and his laptop."

"We'll have to do a full sweep of the house," said Tim. "And, yes, I talked to Lily."

"And?" My throat hurt with the force of my voice.

Tim used his most non-threatening Council-investigator voice. "Lily is deeply sorrowed to hear about Eliza. She doesn't blame you, Julie."

"Blame me? Blame *me*?" Anger surged through me and evaporated the tears in a flash. Guilt shook my core, but I pushed it down, way down, to seize my fury instead. "Tell her *I* blame *her*. Tell her if she had informed the Council as she should have, Eliza might still be alive. But, no. Pack Full Lily Rose was too concerned about the image of the Greybull pack and not concerned enough about people. Her hubris and insecurity killed Eliza. This is her fault."

"Julie," Sheila started to speak, but I waved her silent.

"No, I'm done. I've had it with the pack. I'm not

going back. Ever," I said. "That is, I'm going back to get my things, but I won't live in Greybull anymore."

Tim said, "Julie, you don't have to decide now. Don't give some sort of ultimatum. You should wait until things aren't so fresh. Until you can think clearly."

"I'm thinking more clearly than I ever have."

"Where would you live?" asked Sheila. "Would you move back to Oregon?"

"I...Maybe. I'm not sure. Somewhere. Oregon." I paused. "Colorado."

"They'll label you a rogue," said Tim.

"I'm not a rogue. I just refuse to live within their strictures," I said.

"That's the definition of a rogue."

"But it's not. A rogue implies...I don't know what it implies. But I'm not a threat. I just want to live another way. Alongside Salamanders, Witches, humans. Treating them equally. I want to forge a new path, a new model."

"Do you mean you intend to reveal Were secrets to humans?" asked Tim. The faintest hint of growl came through in his voice and my anger swung toward him.

Focus, Julie. Tim wasn't the enemy. Actually, it wasn't about enemies. Lily, the Council, Eliza—damn it, I winced—were all as bound by their rules as I was. They were unable to see what needed to change.

"No," I said. "I won't reveal us to humans. But I do want to live in a society that recognizes the value of humanity and recognizes we're stronger when we work together."

Throughout all of this, Newt bounced Carson and looked from face to face. I wasn't sure how much he could understand by reading our lips, but I was sure he understood the tenor of our conversation.

"Tim," I said. "I need to talk to the Council."

"Not yet, Jules," Sheila said.

I turned on her in irritation.

"Let's take care of things here first, while you decide exactly what to say to the Council," Sheila said. "Let's go through the house and confiscate anything dangerous. We need to clean up and figure out how to cover all this damage."

Chapter Twenty

The damage to the house wasn't the only thing we needed to cover up. Sheila hadn't said the obvious, but I knew we were all thinking the same thing. We needed to figure out what to do with Eliza's body. And the Pneumaphage. The whole time we'd been outside in the yard, Tim had called darkness to cover us from sight, but we couldn't obscure the property forever. Tomorrow, patients would arrive. We couldn't let them find DeVossen's body.

"We should move inside and search the house," Tony said, his voice gruff. He cleared his throat—if he felt anything like I did, tears threatened to close it—and stooped over Eliza's body. "I will carry Eliza."

Just as I might gather Carson to me, Tony carefully lifted Eliza, cradled her with ease. Her ponytail hung down from his arms and swayed back and forth as he walked, just as it did when she was alive. I wanted to scream, but instead I followed them inside with Sheila by my side. She didn't touch me, I didn't think I could stand it if someone touched me right now, but having her close brought me some measure of comfort. Newt and my son floated to a stop near the front door. I hoped they would turn corporeal soon. When I glanced at Newt, he held my gaze and nodded. Then he pointed to the front step, to his own eyes, and out across the walkway and the yard. Ah, he would keep watch at the front of the house. I gave him a double thumbs up and the rest of us proceeded into the reception room.

"What..." I cleared my throat and started again. "What will we do with Eliza's body?"

"When Newt returns to this plane, he can cremate her," Tim said. "Along with the Pneumaphage."

"Is that what she would have wanted?" I asked.

Tony said, "Yes. We can bring her back and spread her ashes with the pack. She would want to go home."

Home. The word echoed in my skull and I felt its shape in my mouth. It tasted bitter as ashes. It burned my throat like bile.

"We're going to have to burn down the house," said Tim.

"But this house is beautiful!" said Sheila. "Historic. I bet it's been here since the early 1900s."

Tim reached for her hand and held it, running his thumb along the back of her knuckles. "I know, but I can't think of another way to cover our tracks. We search the house for magical items, take whatever we can use, destroy what we must, wait for Newt, and then arrange it to look like some type of electrical fire. How else would we explain the char marks?" He pointed to places where the Pneumaphage's lightning hit.

"Also," he said, "Newt can make sure it looks like DeVossen died in the fire."

Sheila nodded with some reluctance. "I guess you're right. I don't see another option."

We'd reached the second floor. Tony used his shoulder to push open the door to the guest bedroom, the one with white wicker furniture and a nautical theme. He laid Eliza gently on the bed. I stood and looked at her for a moment, then covered her with the blanket folded at the bed's foot. She almost looked like she could be asleep, except she was so still. As if by some unspoken agreement, we gathered around the bed in silence. I kept remembering moments Eliza and I had shared. The night in Greybull when she'd climbed into the bedroom window and we planned to avenge Mac's murder. The relief I felt when she arrived in Oregon right after rogue Salamanders burned down my house—like everything would be okay now that Eliza was by my side. The way she could eat half a pizza in about three seconds flat. Every time, I joked that she "wolfed" it down and, every time, she groaned and threw a pizza crust at my head. The mixture of patience and frustration she showed when teaching me how to be a Were. Then I remembered the shuttered look on her face when she took the side of the Council and wanted to take Carson into their custody. Even now, I was sure the Council might have stripped Carson's Were powers from him. I saw Eliza's straight spine, her fawn-colored ponytail. Her buff-colored wolf, with mouth hanging open in a smile, chasing me and Carson in the Wyoming woods.

Eliza.

I sighed, rubbed the back of my sleeve over my eyes to blot the tears that wouldn't stop falling, and turned away from her body. Sheila put her arms around me and I leaned into her for a quick, fierce hug. Sheila's blue eyes were swollen from her own tears. Her face looked pale and exhausted, red scars vivid where her neck met her shoulder.

"Let me show you what we found in DeVossen's study," I said, as my own level of fatigue suddenly crashed over me with such intensity I swayed on the spot. I shook my head to focus. Not time to rest yet.

With a nod, Sheila and Tim followed me down the hall. As we left the room, Tony dropped into his black wolf, turned around three times, and curled into a ball near the foot of the bed. He buried his nose in his tail. The sharp scent of sorrow and loneliness rising from him almost made me want to shift, just so I could howl into the void of the evening.

"Is he…?" I glanced at Tim and shrugged. I didn't even know how to finish my question.

"I think he'll be okay," Tim said.

"Tony's had to face a lot of emotions in the last few days," said Sheila. "He's not used to it. He's not used to needing people enough to grieve."

"I think all he does is grieve," I said. "His parents. His brother. Now Eliza." And maybe me, I thought, but didn't say out loud. Five years living as a wolf, five years denying himself any companionship. Then six months fleeing the relationships he couldn't fight.

Sheila sighed. "You might be right. But Julie? It's not your job to fix him. You can't make this easier. He has to find his way back to life with the rest of us."

"In here, yes?" Tim tapped on the door frame of DeVossen's study.

I nodded and we filed in. I led her immediately to the shelf where I'd noticed the book exuding magic. Sheila dropped to her knees, held her hands out in front of her as if warming by a radiator, and frowned at the books. She made an inquisitive humming sound while feeling the air with her hands. After a moment's study, she plucked the book from the shelf. I caught my breath, waiting for it to sting her fingers, but she showed no reaction. Still humming under her breath, she flipped open the cover and turned some pages.

I peered over her shoulder to look at the dense writing covering the pages. The script seemed to waver like I looked through a blurry window; I couldn't make out the words. Handwriting. Several different inks. I sneezed as the tingle of the book's magic rose from the script, making my eyes water.

"Can you read it?" I said. "I can't."

"It's spelled. I can read it, hold on a second." Sheila continued to page through the book. She stopped at several places to read a bit.

"That's a wraith," I said, pointing to a vivid drawing that captured the likeness so well it almost looked like it moved on the page.

"Brilliant deduction, dear Watson," she said. She frowned and flipped a few more pages. "Did you say something about motivational books?"

"Yes, he seems to have collected them," I said, gesturing to those shelves. "Why?"

"This guy wanted to use Pneumaphagy to set himself up as the next great thing. Look." Sheila flipped back to the beginning of the book. "This is full of spells for charming people, boosting charisma, and convincing others to follow you. I'm not sure if he wanted to be a motivational speaker, a psychic to the stars, or just a celebrity."

I moved to the desk, pulled open drawers, and started sifting through more papers. For a few minutes, the librarian in me took over and I focused on the research—forgot about Eliza, forgot about confronting the pack. I pulled out three laminated newspaper clippings. A feature article praising a workshop DeVossen ran. An interview with DeVossen explaining aura work he did with a second-string country artist in Nashville, Tennessee. A piece from the *Indianapolis Star* profiling Kenneth DeVossen as an up-and-coming Hoosier making a splash in the region. I pulled out a file folder with other clippings, slid the laminated articles inside. I paged through DeVossen's notebooks and suddenly stopped short as my eyes caught on several words.

"He found out about Carson from the mafia," I said.

"What?" Tim moved to look over my shoulder.

Taped into DeVossen's notebook were several small newspaper blurbs and obituaries from Las Vegas. The papers didn't mention the mafia or Werewolves, but we knew the names. We'd killed those people after they murdered and tortured Weres to try to create a group of Were-mafia.

"I wonder how they were connected," I said. "I wonder how he found out."

"Maybe the notebooks will tell us. Pack them up," said Tim.

"I'm bringing this with us, too," said Sheila, holding up the spellbook. "Part of me thinks we should destroy it, just to prevent anyone else from exploiting wraiths like DeVossen, but it may contain information we need. We have to make sure he acted alone."

Sheila identified several other books to bring and rounded up items and stacks of papers for Newt to burn thoroughly, just in case they contained anything dangerous. After that, we moved to the bedroom.

The heavy tang of blood hung over the smell of char. As I moved into the room, my gaze went unerringly toward the body lying in a crumpled heap near the window. I didn't really want to get closer, yet I found myself drawn across the room until I stood over his body. His throat had been torn out. Blood pooled on the floor. Tim's footsteps sounded behind me and I fought the urge to turn around, to look at his mouth. Did he kill DeVossen? Or had it been Tony? A shudder crept over me. I stared at DeVossen, memorized every bit of ripped flesh, each drop of blood. This was my responsibility. His death was on my hands, no matter who ripped out his throat. His death. And Eliza's.

"We had no options," said Sheila. "I know you wanted to neutralize him, to protect the local people. In the end, the only way we could do that was to kill him."

"I know."

I dragged a coverlet off the bed and hid DeVossen from sight while Sheila and Tim methodically searched the room. Sheila dumped items into a small pile on the end of the bed. She'd soon accumulated quite a number of things: three gray rocks, a magnifying glass, a flashlight, a fine-linked gold chain necklace, a bookmark, a pair of leather gloves with suspicious-looking stains on one hand, and a bunch of other similar items that looked like regular detritus from a busy life and a messy room.

"These are all magic?" I asked, poking at the pile.

"Yep," Sheila said.

"What do they do?" I picked up the bookmark and looked at both sides.

"I'm not sure. Might be better not to know."

Tim bundled the items in a pillowcase and Sheila made quick work of searching the rest of the house. In each therapy room, we found several sealed containers holding small wraiths, like the one I'd seen DeVossen use when he "treated" Sheila. I started to call for Newt, remembered he couldn't hear me, and collected the containers in a trash bin I confiscated from one of the rooms. After it was full, I brought the basket out to where Newt and Carson still floated.

Newt's eyebrows lifted and he grinned. With a flick of his fingers, he made the wraith inside each container burst into flames. I watched the wraiths writhe and settle into taffy-like goo. The last one was extra small, only the size of a peach pit, and I cursed my human tendency to think all tiny things were somehow cute. Wraiths were not cute, I reminded myself. Even small purplish ones in jelly jars. That thing would devour my life force whole, if given the chance, and then it would morph into an uglier, bigger version of itself.

A huge yawn brought tears to my eyes, as if I hadn't cried enough tonight. I looked at my watch and saw it was nearly ten p.m. Carson was asleep in Newt's incorporeal arms with a thumb stuck in his mouth to compensate for the lack of incorporeal pacifiers. I thought I might be able to sleep right there, right on the porch of Mindspring. Instead, I sat down on the top step. Newt hovered by my side. Gods, I was tired, but I knew this night would only get longer before any of us would get any rest.

"I wish I could talk to you," I said to Newt.

He cocked his head and looked at me with eyes as deep as the night sky.

"Hi," I said.

He smiled and mouthed, "Hi."

I blew him a kiss and he mimed trying to catch it then fumbling the kiss and nearly dropping it before bringing it to his lips. We were going to be okay, Newt and I.

I sat in the stillness of the night. Cars drove past from time to time, but no one looked askance at Mindspring. Below the scent of blood and char, the spring air smelled of wet greenness. Renewal. Trees beginning to flower. A bat looped above us, darted after an unseen bug, then flurried away toward the Ohio River. The low hoot of a barred owl sounded close by. Who-cooks-for-you, it sang.

The front door opened behind me and Tony's wolf-musk surrounded me. I looked at him. His great black body padded closer, his amber eyes glowing lambent in the night. He glanced at Newt, still hovering in the air with Carson in his arms, then walked over to me. With the utterly unconscious grace of a wild animal, he laid down at my side and let out a long sigh, a sigh of sorrow, of exhaustion, of pain. Tony leaned—almost collapsed—against me. His dark fur felt warm in the cool April air and I shifted closer. He placed his head down, his neck outstretched and vulnerable, and closed his eyes. I put my hand on his fur and we sat there together while something between us healed.

Chapter Twenty-One

Tim and Sheila found us on the front steps sometime after midnight.

"We searched the rest of the house," Sheila said.

"I think DeVossen was setting himself up for the national stage and accumulating power to magic his way to success." Tim yawned and stretched so widely I heard his spine crack. "And somehow he had mafia connections."

"Now what?" I asked.

"We burn the house. Sheila's going to bring his spellbooks and some other items to a coven for further examination."

"Then what?"

"We go home, I guess," said Tim.

"I meant what I said earlier. I'm not going back to Greybull and I'm not living with the pack," I said.

Sheila sat beside me on the steps. Tim assessed me with a level look then handed me his cell phone with a contact open: Mohamad Alanazi.

"Member of the inner Council, Full for the Western region," he said.

"Okay," I said.

My stomach churned with some combination of nerves and anger—anger I channeled hotly while punching the dial icon.

Two rings.

"Tim. Hello," said a voice on the other end.

From the name, I'd expected a Middle-Eastern accent and I blinked, momentarily distracted by the man's Southern drawl.

"Actually, it's not Tim. This is Julie Hall from…" I faltered for a moment, not wanting to say I was from the Greybull pack since that was, after all, the whole point of the conversation. "This is Julie Hall."

"Yes? Can I help you?" The man's voice sounded puzzled but not uninterested.

"I'm calling to report several things."

"Why are *you* calling? And why on Tim's phone? Is Tim okay? Is your Full there?"

"Tim's fine. Listen. My son Carson—you know about Carson?—was kidnapped a few days ago by a Pneumaphage who figured out how to use wraiths as supernatural batteries. The wraiths drained people's life force then the Pneumaphage harnessed the wraiths and used them as energy for his spell casting."

"What?"

"Lily Rose didn't want to report it to the Council because she didn't want you to think her pack couldn't protect their own. Especially after a member of her pack betrayed Were-kind last year."

"Where are you?"

"Don't worry, we got Carson back and we killed the Pneumaphage. I did. My friends and I. One Werewolf died. Eliza Minuet died all because Lily wouldn't call for reinforcements from the Council. Or because…" My voice faltered, and I paused for a second. "But that's not even the main reason I'm calling you."

I wasn't sure if I made any sense at this point but

forged on nonetheless.

"I'm calling to resign from the pack. I don't want to be part of the Greybull pack anymore. I don't want to be part of any pack, actually. Carson and I will live on our own. We have plenty of help and support from our friends—not just Weres, but Salamanders and Witches. Humans. We won't live in a pack structure."

After a long pause on the other end of the phone, Mohamad spoke. "Ms. Hall, Julie, let me make sure I've got this straight. You don't want to be part of a pack. You 'resign.' "

"Right."

"Pack isn't something you can resign from. Pack is like family. You're stuck with it."

"That's not true," I said. "I met a Were in Las Vegas who didn't live in a pack. Her name was Suzy something."

"Some Weres wish they were human and vow to refrain from using all their powers. They continue to live within the Council strictures, and they register as lone wolves. Is that what you want to do?" Mohamad sounded like he thought I was a kindergartener, as if explaining the sun rose in the east and set in the west.

"No," I said.

"Ms. Hall, there are only three options. You stay within a pack structure, you register as a lone wolf, or you're treated like a rogue wolf who needs to be contained for the safety of all Were-kind. We can't have random Werewolves running around doing God knows what with no supervision or control. That kind of mass chaos will lead to persecution."

"No."

" 'No?' These are simply facts, not something you

can argue. Even if we allowed you to leave the pack—even if we stripped your powers and returned you to being human—you have no right to make this decision for Carson. Your son will grow up to be the strongest Werewolf in our recorded history. He will be a pack Full. He may lead all the Weres in North America. You cannot deny him training and guidance."

"You Weres only want to train and guide my son's power. You don't care about him as a person."

"Julie."

I sensed exasperation in Mohamad's voice with the lapse of formality.

He said, "Carson's power is part of him as a person. He needs to be taught or he could cause immense destruction."

"What would the pack teach him?"

"To control himself. To use his powers for the good of all Werewolves. To protect our kind and our way of life."

"I want him to use his powers for the good of *all*. Not just Werewolves. We need to protect humans from things they don't even know about. Did you know that most babies who die from SIDS are actually drained by wraiths?"

"What? So?"

"So, if Werewolves and Salamanders and Witches and…others…" I faltered for a moment and then continued. "If we all work together, we can hunt and kill wraiths. We can protect those babies. We can watch for people using black magic, trying to harness paranormal powers for evil purposes. We can fight other things."

"Do you know how many Werewolves there are in

the United States, Ms. Hall?"

"No."

"Twelve thousand one hundred and eighty-two. That's all. A hundred years ago, we had nearly twice that many."

"What happened?"

"Young Weres who care more about 'true love' than preserving the pack. Mating with humans." His voice rose. "Our very existence depends on putting pack first."

"We don't deserve to exist if all we care about is ourselves," I spat the words.

He sighed. "You're young and idealistic, Julie. And you haven't been a Were long enough to understand."

"You're old and cynical and you've been so indoctrinated by Werewolves you can't think for yourself."

Next to me, Tim shook his head and looked up at the sky as if he knew nothing else Mohamad Alanazi said could have angered me quite so much.

"So, what, you're founding some paranormal vigilante group?"

"Actually. Yes."

"Put Tim on the phone."

I looked at Tim, who grimaced, but held his hand out for the phone. I passed it over with some feeling of foreboding. Tim walked several steps away, seeming to know exactly how far he needed to travel so my Were senses couldn't pick up the other side of the conversation. I smelled his anxious perspiration break out, though he looked utterly calm.

"Yes," he said. He frowned and turned his back to the rest of us. "Yes." Long pause. "I understand."

After a few more moments of similar conversation, Tim ended the phone call.

"Well?" I asked the next second. "Are you supposed to capture me or something?"

Tim shot a glance at Sheila, who took a step closer to stand next to me.

"Tim?" she said.

"I'm supposed to convince you of the error of your ways, monitor you, and inform the Council of your movements. If I consider you a threat, I'm supposed to neutralize you. At all costs, I'm supposed to keep Carson under our control and bring him back to the pack."

I swallowed hard as a spike of panic raced through my gut.

" 'Supposed to'?" asked Sheila.

Tim ran a hand over his close-shorn curls. "You know I don't want to do any of those things."

"Yes, but will you?" I asked. I glanced at Newt, holding Carson in the incorporeal plane, and wondered how much of this interchange he understood. He could get Carson away. How long could I keep Carson incorporeal if I needed to?

Tim let out a huge breath. "I'm not going to take Carson."

"Thank God," said Sheila, so quietly I wouldn't have heard her without Were senses.

"But?" I said.

"Julie, I'm going to do my best to negotiate a truce between you and the Council. But you need to promise me you'll be reasonable."

"I'll be reasonable if they're reasonable!"

"Right. We're going to negotiate. Reasonably.

Which means you may not get exactly what you want, but neither will they. We need to decide what your non-negotiables are, then find a way to get the Council to agree."

"So...you're on our side?" I asked.

Tim looked at Sheila, whose body language softened at the shared gaze as if tension ran out of her.

"I'm on your side," said Tim. "But I don't want to break with the Council. Like I said, I want to find a middle ground."

"I can live with that," I said.

Newt waved his hands to attract my attention and I hurried to type on my cell phone and update him. He nodded at several points then gave me a big thumbs up when he read my words: "Need to find middle ground."

****

I startled awake in confusion before realizing I'd somehow fallen asleep on the front steps of the DeVossen mansion.

"Jules? Sorry to wake you, but I'm back now," said Newt. He knelt by my side and held Carson out to me.

My son was deep asleep, his mouth moving slightly as if he dreamed. I reached out and gathered him close. Burying my nose in his hair, I breathed in deeply and closed my eyes to better feel the warm weight of him. I looked up at Newt and, my arms full, leaned toward him while hoping he'd take the hint.

He did. He wrapped his arms around me.

My skin tingled at his touch; my breath caught in my throat.

"Newt? I'm sure," I said. "I'm absolutely sure of what I want."

"Oh, you are, are you?" His voice held a note of

teasing.

"I am. So kiss me, Newt Sanders," I said.

He kissed me lightly, as much a promise as a kiss, as if we sealed something.

When we pulled away, I asked, "What are the others doing?"

"Waiting for us and readying the funeral pyre."

My stomach fell and I swallowed hard against the sudden urge to vomit. Newt raised his eyebrows at me; I nodded to indicate I was fine then gathered my feet under me and stood. With Newt close behind, I walked inside and up to the guest bedroom where we'd laid Eliza's body.

As they heard us—or smelled us—approach, the others gathered. Tim and Sheila, Tony in wolf form with amber eyes blazing. The scent of grief hung thick in the air. We stood around the bed, looking at Eliza lying so still, so horribly still on the white and navy coverlet.

"Does anyone want to say a few words?" asked Tim.

I forced my voice out through tears. "I'm sorry, Eliza. I'm so sorry." My throat closed off before I could add anything else. Too much lingered unsaid in the air. I'd have to hope Eliza's spirit could somehow sort through the love, the anger, the sorrow, and the guilt that swelled in me.

"Rest in peace, dear Eliza. Your memory is a blessing," said Sheila.

"I'll miss you, crazy dog," said Newt.

Tony's voice raised in a howl that tore through the pre-dawn silence. As his keen hung in the air, Newt called fire, the white-hot flames that burned only human flesh. The fire sprang up like a corona with a dry, hot wind circling the body and forcing the heat higher.

Moments later, the flames snuffed out and left only ash behind.

I turned and walked out of the house. Newt would burn the Pneumaphage's body. Tim and Sheila would make sure he destroyed any evidence at MindSpring.

We'd won. It was over.

Chapter Twenty-Two

Later that afternoon, Tim set down his coffee on the diner table and said, "I have a plan."

After we all turned to look at him, he continued. "Hear me out. Julie, we need to petition the Council for you to form your own pack as the Full."

"What?" I said. I blinked at him, bleary from lack of sleep and not sure I'd understood.

"I know. You want to get away from pack hierarchy completely. But in your new pack, you can live the way you want. You can even include Salamanders or Witches in your pack."

"In the pack?"

Sheila asked. "Tim, isn't there some Council rule that everyone in a pack needs to be a Were?"

"There are rules against revealing our existence to humans or involving them in our affairs, but no one's ever thought about a ruling against other paranormal creatures joining a pack. Probably an oversight—no one thought of it as a possibility—but one we can exploit."

"Tim, that's all well and good," I said, "But I'm not a full moon Were. I'm definitely not strong or skilled enough to be a pack Full."

"Here's the beauty of it. You hold the Full position in trust for Carson."

I looked down at Carson, who'd fallen asleep on my lap and spawned a small trail of drool on my sleeve.

"Carson's a baby, Tim. He's a pup."

"True. You have to realize, Julie, asking the Council to form your own pack is mostly a way for everyone to save face. The Council gets to pretend they have control and influence over you, thus, over Carson. You get to mostly live as you want, as long as you abide by some basic regulations and report to the Council every once in a while. Everyone can walk away from the negotiation feeling like they've won what's most important to them. You could even let the Council assign Weres to come and train Carson, to teach him skills."

"Sheila? What do you think?" I asked.

"I think it's so crazy it's brilliant. And I'm in, at least in spirit. Maybe not physically because I'm not moving away from southern Oregon—that's where my job is. Hunting rogue paranormals and protecting humans doesn't pay the bills."

"Plus, you love teaching and research."

"That, too."

"Newt?"

"If you're okay with me training with the hotshots and chasing fires half the year, I'd love to be an honorary member of your pack, Jules. Maybe we can even come up with a catchy name for ourselves," said Newt.

I rolled my eyes at him and he responded with a grin that sent a flush to my cheeks.

Tim said, "You know I don't report to a regular pack. I report to the Council and work for them. But I'll be your liaison."

"So…basically, I would have a pack of two. Me and Carson. With a Salamander and a Witch as close allies. That doesn't seem...Do you really think the Council will go for this?"

Tim shrugged. "Best idea I have. We should try."

I cleared my throat and looked at the last member of our group. "Tony?"

"I want to continue my work bringing back Weres who've turned wolf."

"Okay, understood."

"But," Tony paused for quite a moment, looked around at each of us. "When I come home to a pack, I'd like to come home to you."

I wasn't sure if his "you" was plural or singular and that phrase sounded awfully significant, but I'd been clear with him about my boundaries. I'd leave further discussion for another day. "Tony, you're a much stronger Were than I am. Won't it be weird for you not to be the pack Full?"

"I've been in a regular pack. I lived five years as a wolf. I've spent the last months as my own boss nominally tied to Greybull. Might as well give this a try, too."

Too many thoughts crowded my brain and I wasn't sure how to sort them. My own pack? As Full? Acting as a placeholder for my toddler son? I didn't want to order anyone around. But, well, with a pack of three Weres, me, Tony, and Carson, I doubted I'd order anyone around. Sheila, Newt, and Tim would be honorary pack. That wasn't any different than how things were now.

"You may end up collecting more Weres," said Tim. "Not everyone's happy with the status quo. Especially the younger Weres. Over the long run, others may find us."

" 'Collecting more Weres,' " I said, my mind running over the Weres I knew. Ian, maybe. Some of his friends. There must be other Weres who felt like I did. "Collecting. That's what I'd want this to be. A collective. Everyone with a voice and everyone contributing."

I looked around and saw general agreement.

"Okay. If we can convince the Council, I'm in. Let's do this."

A word about the author...

Sarah's love of reading, writing, and all things fantasy started with her explorations of Narnia, Middle Earth, and Pern. She is a huge enthusiast of all fantasy, paranormal, and science fiction. Flying her geek flag early, she started D&D with the good old boxed sets (and still plays today). Her stories focus on strong women, strong friendships, magic, and love.

She lives with her husband Gary, their three kids, and three cats. She's also an artist and a board game geek.

http://sarahestevens.com

Thank you for purchasing
this publication of The Wild Rose Press, Inc.

For questions or more information
contact us at
info@thewildrosepress.com.

The Wild Rose Press, Inc.
www.thewildrosepress.com

To visit with authors of
The Wild Rose Press, Inc.
join our yahoo loop at
http://groups.yahoo.com/group/thewildrosepress/